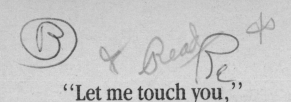

"Let me touch you,"

Rochella pleaded, her voice husky, all modesty vanquished under the powerful effect of the tea.

"I said go back to your bed. This is no place for you." Gareth struggled with the desire raging through him. If she did not obey soon, he would not be responsible for what happened.

Rochella raised a knee to the mattress and began to crawl into the bed beside Gareth. "I am your wife and should share your bed."

"You have no idea of what you are saying, Rochella. You do not even like me," Gareth pointed out, the war being waged within him making his voice harsh.

Rochella raised a hand and caressed the side of his cheek. She smiled down at him. "I know exactly what I am saying."

He swallowed hard and sought to quell the desire searing every inch of his body, reminding himself of his vow never to consummate his marriage.

Dear Reader,

For your summer reading pleasure, we present our Harlequin Historicals titles for August, four adventuresome tales that bring the past to life.

In Mary Daheim's *Improbable Eden,* an unsophisticated young woman discovers love when she is swept up into the dangerous world of intrigue at the English court of William and Mary.

With *Golden Prospect,* her second Harlequin historical, Shirley Parenteau takes the reader to the Yukon and Alaska as she weaves a delightful story of fame and fortune during the Klondike gold rush.

Surrounded by madness and deceit, the lovers in Catherine Blair's *Devil Wind,* must put to rest the past before they can build their future, while the characters in award-winning author Elisabeth Macdonald's *Estero Bay,* are swept into the age-old fight between the old ways and the new, set against the backdrop of California's wild central coast.

We hope you will join us for some summer reading fun.

Yours,

Tracy Farrell
Senior Editor

Devil Wind

Catherine Blair

Harlequin Books

TORONTO • NEW YORK • LONDON
AMSTERDAM • PARIS • SYDNEY • HAMBURG
STOCKHOLM • ATHENS • TOKYO • MILAN

Harlequin Historicals first edition August 1991

ISBN 0-373-28689-9

DEVIL WIND

CATHERINE BLAIR

began her writing career when the end of a book she'd read left her unsatisfied. Catherine, once a painter, found writing to be a more fulfilling career, and now channels her creative talents to that profession. Catherine makes her home in Georgia with her very own romantic hero—her husband.

A cry in the night,
two Devlins born.
One be cursed, the
other scorned.

Prologue

Gareth's deepening frown marred his handsome features as he stared past the manicured lawns to the outcrop of black granite marking the line of cliffs on which Devil Wind had been built by his ancestors more than three hundred years ago. Generations of Devlins had stood exactly where he now stood and looked out at the stunted trees and bushes that grew bowed to the west from the constant force of the sea wind.

Glancing up toward the round stone towers, Gareth listened to the ever-present sound that filled his home. Even on a clear day such as this, with the sun relieving the gloomy atmosphere that surrounded the castle in bad weather, the siren's song never ceased. It was as constant as the change of seasons, varying only in degree. At times it was as gentle as a spring morn, filling the days with its laughter. Then at other times it was as cruel as a winter storm, beating the land and its inhabitants until they thought they would be destroyed by the gale's ferocity. And from that devil wind, Gareth's home had gained its name.

"How do you plan to respond to the marquis's request?" Robert Sinclair asked.

The question jerked Gareth's thoughts back to the present and the letter he still held crumpled in his hand. He desperately wanted to deny the marquis's request, but knew he was bound by family honor to agree to it. Slowly Gareth turned to look at his blond-haired, blue-eyed cousin, who took after his mother's side of the family. Robert was a prime example of the fair-haired Charmonts, while Gareth had inherited none of their golden good looks. He was pure Devlin, as dark as the devil himself.

Gareth shook his head as he ran a long-fingered hand through his ebony curls. "I never intended to marry at all but what choice do I have in the matter? I can't refuse to honor my father's promise, even if it was made years before I was born."

"Surely you could explain your feelings to the Marquis de Beauvais and he would understand your decision?"

"I doubt he would understand my reasons any better than I understand his wanting to marry his only child to someone he's never met."

"Then you will marry the girl?"

Gareth gave a snort of disgust and his dark eyes glittered with annoyance. "As I've said, I have no alternative. The marquis saved my father's life, and now I must do the same for his daughter. My protection will be because of the upheaval in France."

"Try to look at the bright side. The girl might make you a wonderful wife, and it's time you started a family. Devil Wind needs an heir," Robert said in an effort to ease his cousin's feelings about the situation in which he now found himself.

If that were possible, Robert's statement made Gareth's mood blacken even further. "Robert, you of all people should know why that can never happen. I will not bring children into the world and have them suffer because of the blood that flows in their veins."

"I had hoped you'd put such foolishness from your mind. You're an intelligent man. Look around you, cousin." Robert encompassed the Devlin estate with a sweep of one graceful hand. "This is your heritage. You cannot let everything be lost because you choose to live your life in the shadows of superstition."

A cynical smile curled Gareth's lips up at the corners. "I wouldn't call the Devlin curse a mere superstition, Robert, nor would you had you lived in its shadows as I have all my life. It has tainted every aspect of my being since my birth, and I refuse to allow it to continue beyond me. I will end the curse by never allowing another child to be born into this world with Devlin blood in its veins."

Robert rolled his eyes toward the ceiling of Gareth's study. "May I ask one small question?"

"One," Gareth said, unable to stay annoyed with his cousin. Robert's easygoing manner was his most charming trait. There had been few times he could remain angry with him for very long no matter what he did or said.

"How do you propose to marry the marquis's daughter and then keep from having children? You are wealthy and powerful, Gareth, but you cannot as yet control nature, as far as I know."

"But I can control how I choose to live with my wife."

Robert arched a curious brow but refrained from asking the question on the tip of his tongue. He suspected Gareth did not plan to consummate his marriage. However, he would not probe any further into his cousin's personal affairs. What Gareth did in his bed-chamber was his concern.

"So, when do you leave for France?"

"That is another question," Gareth said. He chuckled under his breath as he crossed to the side table that held a crystal decanter of brandy. Pouring two glasses, he offered Robert one and took a long sip from his own before he finally said, "I am not able to travel at this time."

Robert shot Gareth a questioning look but refused to say a word.

Again Gareth chuckled. His cousin's curiosity was devouring him but he was putting up a valiant fight. Downing the last of the amber liquid in the brandy snifter, Gareth continued, "But as the marquis says it is of the utmost importance that the marriage take place as soon as possible, I thought you might do me the honor of standing in as my proxy."

Robert's blue eyes widened in surprise. "You want me to go to France in your stead?"

"Yes, Robert. I need your assistance. The king has requested the use of my ships, and I must go to London to see that they are ready to sail."

Robert frowned. "Why would George want your ships when he has the entire British navy at his disposal?"

"There are things I'm not allowed to divulge to even you, cousin," Gareth said. The king had sworn him to secrecy about the cargo his ships would carry to Turkey to help in the fight against the Russians.

A haunted light entered Gareth's dark eyes as he glanced toward the stairs. He hoped the king would be understanding because of his own family history. He, more than anyone, should realize Gareth's responsibilities now lay at Devil Wind.

"I didn't mean to pry," Robert said, drawing Gareth's thoughts away from his problems. "And I don't honestly know how to answer your request."

"Say you'll act as my proxy. That will be sufficient."

"I'd be honored," Robert said, smiling.

Gareth clasped Robert's hand affectionately and shook it. "You have always been a good friend as well as a cousin."

"As you have been to me," Robert answered. He loved his cousin even when he was in one of his black moods. The world might view Lord Gareth Devlin as the dark, sinister master of Devil Wind; yet Robert knew the true man beneath the cool, aloof exterior Gareth presented to the world.

Chapter One

"No, Papa! You can send Monsieur Sinclair away. I will not go through with this marriage you have planned." Rochella flashed a searing emerald stare at the Englishman standing quietly beside the French doors, looking decidedly uncomfortable.

"Rochella, since the day of your birth, there have been few times that I have not let you have your own way, but in this you will do as I bid," the Marquis de Beauvais calmly answered to his daughter's outburst. He would not allow her stubbornness to jeopardize his plans.

Rochella glowered once more at the Englishman. He was to blame for all of her troubles. Had he not come to France to do his cousin's dirty work she would not have been placed in the untenable position of having to defy her father's wishes.

Already disturbed by having to witness the confrontation between the marquis and his firebrand of a daughter, Robert Sinclair shifted uneasily under her fierce look. Seeking to separate himself from the situation, he concentrated his attention on the beautiful flowers in the garden beyond the beveled glass doors. A rueful grin tugged at the corners of his mouth at the irony of the situation. It would almost be amusing if the happiness of two people didn't stand in the balance.

"Monsieur Sinclair," the marquis said, once more drawing Robert's attention. "I apologize for my daughter's petulance, but I can assure you the marriage will take place as agreed."

Robert glanced again at the marquis's daughter and felt envy for his cousin well within him. Undeterred by her father's threats, she stood proudly, her back stiff and her chin thrust forward. Her full breasts peeped enticingly above the square neckline of her sprigged muslin gown. The morning sun streamed through the tall windows, haloing her beauty in its golden light and turning her dark chestnut hair to fire with auburn highlights. Her emerald eyes sparkled with defiance.

Observing the strength of character exhibited by the young beauty, Robert knew that she was a match for any man, even the brooding master of Devil Wind; his envy began to fade. Rochella was still a young and untried girl, but Robert predicted that in a few years she would become a woman whom only a man like his cousin could equal. For himself he wanted a simple and uncomplicated wife. A woman who would look at him with awe in her eyes instead of rebellion. A convent-bred miss who thought only of raising children and seeing to his comfort.

Robert jerked his eyes away from the gaze that had pinned him to the spot, and cleared his throat as he nodded his understanding. "There is no apology needed, sir. I'm only sorry that your daughter has misgivings about the match you have arranged for her. I'm sure once she's settled at Devil Wind, she will see the wisdom of your decision."

"Wisdom!" Rochella exploded, furious that they were talking about her as if she were no more than a piece of the château's furnishings. "I am to be sent away to be the wife of a man who does not even have the courtesy to come to his own wedding."

"Child, I have explained all of that to you. Lord Devlin had urgent business to attend to and was unable to come for you in person."

"Then I suggest we postpone the wedding until Lord Devlin does have the time," Rochella shot back.

The marquis abruptly shook his head. "No. The wedding will take place in the morning as planned. Everything has been prepared and the priest will arrive this evening."

Rochella felt like screaming in vexation. Tears of frustration brimmed in her eyes and she struggled with the temptation to stamp her feet and jump up and down as she'd done when she didn't get her way as a child. She knew, however, a tantrum would gain her nothing. Her father was a stubborn man, and unless she could reason with him, she would be married in the family chapel before noon the following day.

"Papa, can you not understand my feelings? I am not objecting to the fact that you have arranged a marriage for me. I know it is the way of things. But what I cannot tolerate is that the man is English. Why am I to be sent so far away from my home and family? I should marry a son of France." Rochella's hopes rose at the look of anguish that momentarily flickered across her father's lined features before he again shook his head.

"I have made my decision and you will abide by it, Rochella. There is nothing more to be said on the matter."

No longer able to contain her tears, Rochella ran from the study and fled up the winding staircase to her chamber. The sound of her door slamming echoed angrily throughout the château.

The marquis gave another sad shake of his head and slowly sank into a delicately wrought Louis XIV armchair. He raised haggard eyes to his guest. "I have done what I had to do to keep her safe, but she will never forgive me when she learns the true reason for my sending her to England."

"You've only done what you thought best," Robert said sympathetically. "While in London I heard rumors of the riots but until I reached Paris and saw with my own eyes the mob-filled streets, I had no idea things had progressed to such a state in your country. I would suggest that you and your wife also consider coming to England with me."

The marquis looked out the windows toward the vineyards, which had supplied wine to the kings of France for the past two hundred years, and he knew he could never leave. He would die here as his father had and his father before him.

"I must stay," he replied, glancing back to the young Englishman. "In time, this madness will leave France, and then my daughter and her children will claim what is rightfully theirs."

"But what if it doesn't end? Louis has been imprisoned and the Jacobins have taken power in the provinces. Under the new constitution the regime as you know it no longer exists," Robert said in an effort to make the older man realize the seriousness of the situation.

"We have had problems before and the monarchy has always survived. My grandchildren will once again see a king on the throne of France."

Robert didn't answer. After what he had seen and heard on his way to Beauvais, he feared the marquis's dreams were doomed. The summer heat had added fuel to the fires of dissension. Rats, flies and the lack of food had turned the poor of the Paris slums into blood-thirsty mobs led by men like Robespierre and Marat, men determined to see the upper classes crushed into the soil they had laid claim to for generations. Robert doubted that France would ever be the same again. It was in the grip of a revolution whose aim was to destroy everything the marquis represented.

"Now, *monsieur,* if you will excuse me, I shall go to my daughter."

"Would it not be simpler if you just explained to her the reasons behind your decision? She is young, but I suspect she would understand the situation."

"No. If she should learn the truth, I fear no man alive could make her leave France. You have seen only a small sample of her stubbornness this morning. She would fight to her death to defend what she loves. And my daughter loves Beauvais."

"Then I shall say nothing. Your secret is safe with me."

"Thank you, Monsieur Sinclair. I love my child and would see her safe, but she is also the future of the Beauvais bloodline and that must survive at all costs."

"Then I will leave you to speak with your daughter. I hope you will be able to convince her that marriage to my cousin is not the horrid thing she has come to believe. Gareth is a handsome man and wealthy in his own right. They should do well together."

"I pray you are right," the marquis said.

A sultry summer breeze cooled the warm afternoon, rippling the tall meadow grass. White daisies on delicate stems raised their showy heads toward the cloudless azure sky and swayed to the gentle urging of the breeze. Butterflies and honeybees flitted from blossom to blossom, seeking out the sweet nectar that sustained them. It was a beautiful tranquil day, yet for Rochella, who sat glumly staring at the vineyards and absently tearing the white petals from a flower, the world seemed dark.

She had come to the meadow to try to reconcile herself to the fate that awaited her on the morrow. Yet the longer she looked at the land she loved, the harder it became for her to accept her father's dictate. It was nearly inconceivable to Rochella that her father would heartlessly send her away from everything she knew and loved.

Agonizing over her bleak future, she turned to view the château and felt a new lump of despair rise in her throat. Resting on a small knoll overlooking the vineyards, the three-story mansion resembled a jeweled crown with the leaded panes of its windows reflecting the afternoon sun like diamonds. Its stone walls, worn smooth and white by time, stood in testament to the power and wealth of the generations of de Beauvaises who had lived beneath its slate roof.

"And I will be the last de Beauvais to live here," Rochella mused aloud, her vision blurring with a fresh wave of tears.

Disgusted with herself, she tossed away the daisy and wiped at her eyes. It seemed as if all she had done during the past week was cry like some spoiled child. In truth tears were unusual for her. She had always prided herself on the fact that she was not like the young girls of her acquaintance who would swoon at the least thing and weep buckets of tears at the bat of an eye.

Rochella swallowed back another lump rising in her throat. After all the years of telling her how proud he was of her, boasting she possessed the lion's courage of the Beauvais line, her father had now decided her future without even consulting her.

Rochella drew in a steadying breath and sought once more to come to grips with the future awaiting her. Her soft muslin gown billowed about her as she stood. Her eyes deepened to emerald green as she dug her nails into the palms of her hands and surveyed the land of her birth. As far as the eye could see, the grapevines grew, draping the softly rolling plains like necklaces of jade. The white grapes that had made the region famous were as valuable as the Oriental gems the vineyards resembled.

Rochella bent, scooped up a handful of dirt and sifted it through her fingers, scattering the rich loam into the gentle breeze. This was her heritage, the fertile soil of France. It had sustained her family for generations, and if she was forced to leave it, she vowed that someday she would return and claim what was rightfully hers. She wanted her children to feel the same pride that she felt when looking at the land of her ancestors. She wanted them to feel their heritage beneath their feet and to know they carried the blood of the generations who had labored to make the land prosper.

"I cannot leave," Rochella said, unable to sustain her show of bravado when her heart was breaking from grief over her lost dreams. All she had ever wanted was to live at Beauvais with a husband who loved her. Even that small dream was now going to be denied her. Her marriage to the Englishman was one of convenience. Her large dowry had been far too enticing to be rejected. Her father had deeded half of his estate outright to her future husband as well as a fortune in gold to persuade him to take her to wife. She suspected that their union was as distasteful to him as it was to her, but that his greed had made him accept her father's offer.

The thought crushed Rochella's grief and made her temper simmer anew. He could use any excuse he wanted but she saw through him. Without even meeting Lord Devlin, she knew him for what he was—an unkind, selfish man who thought of no one but himself.

Rochella stiffened her back and her nostrils flared as she drew in an angry breath. She might be powerless to prevent her marriage, but in the future she would allow no one to treat her like a puppet on a string. If her husband thought he was getting a wife who would meekly do his bidding without question, then he had made a grievous error. She was a human being with a mind of her own, not a lapdog. She would have the respect of her station if nothing else, and as Lady Devlin she would tolerate no one—and that included her husband—trying to rule her again.

As he watched his beloved child from the distance, the marquis's frown deepened. Rochella had been blessed with the fortitude of her ancestors, and he prayed it would be enough to see her through this time when she felt as if he had betrayed her.

Knowing not to expect her forgiveness for his decision yet needing his daughter's understanding, the marquis made his way through the tall meadow grass to her side. She did not turn to look up at him when he placed a gentle hand on her shoulder, but continued to stare at the vineyards in the distance. Her voice was only a soft whisper when she finally spoke. "Papa, I beg you not to force me to marry. I want to stay here with the people I love."

"My lovely child," the marquis said, his voice husky with suppressed emotion, "there is no other way. You must marry. It is time."

Rochella turned to her father and wrapped her arms about him.

The marquis gently brushed a shining copper curl away from her temple and smiled. "I understand your feelings. But the man I have chosen for you will provide for you. He has a large estate as well as his own shipping business. Few marriages are made on love, but if given the chance, love will come as it did to your mother and me. Our union was also arranged by our parents, yet we have been happy as you will be in time."

"How can I live with a stranger, Papa, and hope he will come to love me?"

The marquis cupped Rochella's cheek in the palm of his hand. "Rochella, you are still so young. You do not understand that love is not something that comes instantly into our lives, no matter what the minstrels say. It must grow."

Turning Rochella to face the vineyards, the marquis motioned toward them with a sweep of his hand. "Love is like the grape. It begins with the tiny roots that are planted in your heart. Then it twines upward as the vine thickens to bear first the fruit of friendship and then in time what we call love. Love grows and is nurtured by sharing the joys as well as the sadness life brings to all of us."

"But—" Rochella began.

The marquis placed a silencing finger against her lips. "Someday, you will understand what I am trying to tell you. And you will realize that what I am asking of you now is for the best. I want only your happiness."

Tears glistened on the tips of Rochella's thick, dark lashes and spilled down her softly tinted cheeks as she looked up at her father. In the eyes so much like her own she saw the reflection of her own agony, and in that moment she knew his decision to marry her to the Englishman had been a painful one. Her father loved her and was acting in what he believed was her best interest. And she must not make it harder on him by showing her own feelings.

"Papa, I love you so much," Rochella said, hugging him about the waist. "I shall try to understand and do as you ask."

"I only want your happiness," the marquis said, wrapping his arms tightly about her. He looked over her head at the vineyards and sent a silent prayer to God, asking Him to protect the precious gift He had given him eighteen years before on the day Rochella was born.

Chapter Two

Her cheeks ashen from the harrowing ride along the narrow cliff road, Rochella sat white lipped in the plush coach, firmly gripping the hand strap. Through the mist-shrouded window she could see her new home in the distance. High on the granite cliff overlooking the angry sea, Devil Wind castle loomed ominously up out of the eerie swirling caul of fog. Three storied, it dominated the area. Huge gargoyles sat perched on its black granite towers as if to warn those of weak heart to beware of entering its portals. Their snarling grins seemed to taunt Rochella as the coach rolled to a halt in the cobbled courtyard.

All the sinister stories about ghosts and goblins she had heard as a child came rushing back as she gazed up at what was to be her new home. A shiver passed down her back and she felt gooseflesh rise on her arms. She glanced uneasily at her quiet companion and swallowed back the uncertainty that filled her with apprehension. This place of shadows and darkness was a perfect setting for the devil.

The roar of the surf against the cliffs blocked out all sound as the coachman opened the door and adjusted the steps for Robert. He gave her a reassuring smile before he swung down and turned to assist her. Rochella cast another wary glance over the rain-drenched exterior of the castle and took Robert's proffered arm, fighting to control the shudder that her thoughts created as she stepped down.

Robert felt the slight tremble of her hand and urged her toward the entrance. "I must get you out of this weather. Gareth would never forgive me if you became ill because of my lack of forethought."

Rochella flashed him a look that fully proclaimed her exact views on his cousin's interest in her well-being as the wide, iron-bound double doors swung open before them and they entered the vaulted foyer. Italian marble tiled the floor, and dark raised paneling gleamed richly upon the walls. Overhead, intricate carved beams rose in an arch above a magnificent gold and crystal chandelier. It cast a warm glow over the household staff, who stood in a neat line from the doors to the massive wooden staircase that wound upward toward the second and third floors.

Having no time to consider the contrast between the sinister exterior of the castle and its opulent interior, Rochella turned to the servants with a gracious nod and warm smile. A woman she judged to be in her midthirties stepped forward. Dressed in a severe black gown with a white lace collar, she wore her hair pulled tightly back from her face and wound into a bun at the nape of her neck. Her appearance was as plain as her gown and her smile was friendly, yet Rochella found no warmth within the woman's eyes. Rochella felt the hair at the nape of her neck rise in warning, her instincts sensing the woman's animosity toward her new mistress.

"We welcome you to Devil Wind, my lady. I am Hilda Bronson, Lord Devlin's housekeeper."

"Thank you and your staff, Hilda," Rochella answered, her voice betraying none of her feelings.

"I've had the servants prepare your chamber. When your baggage arrives, I shall have Alice unpack your things and see to your needs until you choose a girl suitable to be your maid," Hilda continued, her voice reflecting her authority.

"Thank you for your forethought, Hilda, but that won't be necessary. My maid came with me from France. She will arrive in the second coach with my luggage and will see to my needs."

"Very well, my lady," Hilda said, drawing herself up and unconsciously pursing her thin lips. "Should there be anything else that you require, please do not hesitate to ask. Lord Devlin has instructed me to make you as comfortable as possible."

"I'm sure Lady Devlin will need your assistance getting settled in, Hilda. But I think for now all she needs is a cup of good hot tea to chase away the chill of this wretched day. Do you think you might be able to arrange that?" Robert asked, giving the housekeeper one of his most charming smiles.

The stiffness seemed to leave Hilda as she turned to shoo the rest of the ogling staff back to their duties. "I shall see to it immediately, sir."

Robert cocked an eyebrow at Rochella and gave her a knowing look as he offered her his arm. "My lady, I know you must be exhausted from our journey, but a cup of Hilda's special tea will help you relax until the carriage arrives with your maid."

"Special tea?" Rochella asked, taking his arm once more and allowing him to escort her into the drawing room.

"Aye. Hilda has a way with herbs. She makes all the ointments and elixirs the servants use and her tea has a way of making the worst situation seem better." Robert laughed as he seated her in a wing-backed chair in front of the black marble fireplace.

"I doubt even Hilda's tea can work that miracle for me," Rochella said, taking in her surroundings and again noting the luxury of her new home. The walls of the drawing room, also, were paneled in rich gleaming wood, making the large room seem warm and friendly. Carved wooden spirals formed an arch over the fireplace, which was inset with a glass mirror. Six-foot-tall, elaborately crafted candelabras graced each side of the fireplace and each corner of the room, shedding their warm light over the graceful furnishings, made of cherry and fine mahogany.

Watching Rochella, Robert suspected his cousin's home was already working a tiny miracle. It had that effect upon people. After their first glimpse of its forbidding exterior, few could suppress their appreciation for the work that had gone into making Devil Wind one of the grandest homes in Britain.

"I hope you're not disappointed," Robert commented.

"No," Rochella replied, distracted by the portrait gracing the wall to the right of the entrance.

Seeing her interest, Robert smiled. "That portrait was done by Sir Joshua Reynolds when Gareth was twenty-one."

Absorbed in the intense features staring back at her from the portrait, Rochella found her interest piqued by the arresting high-cheekboned face. The expression in the twilight depths of his thickly fringed eyes seemed to hold a hint of mockery, and his shapely lips formed a devilish smile that made her belly quiver in the strangest way.

Seeking safety from the odd sensations, Rochella jerked her thoughts back to the present. She couldn't allow the first sight of a handsome face to make her forget she'd been married against her will to a man who wanted only her large dowry.

"At least now I shall recognize my own husband when we meet," Rochella said, her tone laced with sarcasm. "Since he failed to send a miniature of himself with you to France, I had begun to wonder if he possessed two heads or some other oddity. I suspect that my husband wants this marriage no more than I do."

Robert swallowed nervously and looked away, unable to disavow Rochella's assumption. Fortunately, a moment later Alice entered the drawing room with a heavy silver tea service. Robert breathed a sigh of relief as he took the proffered cup of the herbed brew. One cup of Hilda's relaxing tea, a good night's sleep in the guest wing, and then he'd be free to return to London. He had brought Lady Devlin to Devil Wind and had successfully managed on their journey across France to keep her unaware of the crisis tearing her country apart. Now he was anxious to wash his hands of the entire affair and leave the fiery Lady Devlin to her husband.

"Oh, *mamselle*," Babette said, pulling the brush through Rochella's coppery mane of hair. "This place gives me the shivers. I hear all kinds of things going bump in the night."

Rochella looked at the maid's reflection in the dressing table mirror and couldn't suppress a smile at the young woman's fearful wide-eyed expression. Babette glanced nervously around the room as if expecting to see a ghost pop out of the armoire or from under the bed at any moment. And it was all of ten o'clock in the morning.

"Babette, do not be so silly, it is just the wind in the towers," Rochella said, in an effort to soothe the maid. She herself had heard nothing at night. Since arriving at Devil Wind, her head no more than hit the pillow and she was sound asleep until Babette awoke her in the morning.

"*Non, mamselle.* It is more than the wind. In the week since our arrival, I have seen and heard all manner of things in this great heap of stones."

Fully knowing Babette's tendency to believe her own fantasies, Rochella sought to put an immediate halt to the maid's wild imaginings.

Rochella released a long breath. She could not afford the luxury of allowing her own imagination free rein. A message had arrived the previous day from her husband, stating that he would return to Devil Wind within the week, and the thought of finally meeting the man she had married was enough to fear without adding the maid's ghost and goblins.

"This is ridiculous," Rochella said. Taking the brush from Babette, she placed it on the dressing table and turned to face her. "Babette, I have heard enough of this nonsense. There are no ghosts prowling Devil Wind's halls."

"You are wrong, *mamselle.* I have seen them with my own eyes. They creep about in flowing black robes when they think all are abed."

"You have allowed your imagination to run away with you because of your new surroundings. There are no such things as ghosts and I will not hear any more of this, do you understand?" Rochella said. "If you keep this up I shall send you back to France." Rochella knew full well that was the last thing she would ever do. She could not imagine living at Devil Wind without at least one friend of her own. Babette might at times be a scatterbrain but she was the only family Rochella had on this cold, wet island.

Coming to her feet, Rochella crossed to the bed and picked up her silk shawl, edged in finely worked alençon lace. Draping it lightly about her shoulders, she turned back to Babette. "I am going down to breakfast and then I am going to take a walk. This is the first clear day we have had since our arrival and I am tired of being cooped up inside."

"Do you want me to accompany you?" Babette asked hopefully and cast an anxious glance about the room.

"No. You may have the morning to yourself."

"But *mamselle*. You should not go out alone. It might be dangerous."

Rochella gave the maid a reassuring smile. "I seriously doubt any harm will befall me walking in the gardens. Now enjoy your morning." Before Babette could find another excuse to accompany her, Rochella quickly left the room.

Pausing at the stair landing, she let her gaze wander over the tapestried walls and upward to the vaulted ceiling. Her husband had done his best to make Devil Wind a luxurious home, but all his renovations had not succeeded in hiding the fact that Devil Wind had once been a fortress.

A shiver passed over her and she pulled the shawl closer about her shoulders. "Stop it right now," she scolded. "You are as bad as Babette." But gooseflesh rose on her arms and the hair at the nape of her neck stood on end as the sudden sensation of being watched passed over her. Rochella quickly turned, hoping to catch anyone attempting to spy on her. Her breath stilled in her throat and her heart thudded uncomfortably against her ribs as she searched the shadows of the corridor that ran the length of the east wing. She saw no one.

Resolutely, she turned to the stairs again and forced herself not to look back as she descended to the sun-drenched dining room. She would not allow the maid's wild imaginings to cast a shadow over the first beautiful day she had seen since her arrival.

Rochella filled her lungs with a deep breath of sea air and lifted her face into the wind. Coppery curls webbed her features and with an unconsciously graceful sweep of her hand, she brushed them away from her face as she turned to view Devil Wind.

Robert had been right when he spoke of its beauty. The sunny day had vanquished the gloomy atmosphere that had shrouded the castle during the past week. Now it stood in all its glory like a proud queen upon her granite throne.

Rochella allowed her gaze to linger on her new home as she considered the contradictions that only a matter of days had wrought in her feelings about the "great heap of stones," as Babette had chosen to call Devil Wind.

A movement in a window on the third floor suddenly caught her attention. Shielding her eyes from the glare of the late-morning sun, she stared back at the man whose dark gaze held her pinned to the spot. A sinking sensation settled in the pit of her stomach when she realized her time of reckoning had come much sooner than expected. The man staring back at her possessed the same features as the portrait of her husband.

Rochella squeezed her eyes closed against the unwanted sight and drew in a steadying breath. She knew she had to face Lord Devlin. She had no choice. She was his wife. However, she had hoped for a few more days to prepare herself. Opening her eyes, she looked once more toward the window. It was empty. There was no sign of the master of Devil Wind.

Rochella blinked several times and breathed a sigh of relief, laughing softly at her own foolishness. She had let her thoughts conjure up the image of the man she had married in the reflection of the glass.

Encouraged by her reprieve, Rochella strolled back toward the castle, intent upon exploring the ballroom as well as the portrait gallery she had studiously avoided during the past days. It was time to face the future. She had accepted living at Devil Wind, now she must also accept the fact of her marriage.

The moment Rochella crossed the threshold into the ballroom, she again experienced the eerie sensation of being watched. Sensing a presence behind her, she spun about only to catch a fleeting glimpse of a man as he ducked behind the damask drapes of the minstrels' gallery. Her eyes had not been playing tricks on her earlier. Her husband had returned to Devil Wind.

Standing with arms folded over her breasts and foot tapping against the polished oak flooring, Rochella fumed aloud, "How dare he spy upon me!"

What kind of man crept about his own home to watch his wife without letting her know of his presence? Rochella wondered, frowning up at the spot where she had just seen her husband. And what kind of sinister game was he playing? He had returned home yet he did not want her to know of his presence. Or had he ever been away? Rochella wondered, her frown deepening at the thought. Perhaps that was the explanation for Babette's midnight specters. There were no ghosts and goblins roaming Devil Wind's corridors: only her husband, Gareth Devlin.

"But why would he keep himself hidden? What purpose would it serve?" Rochella mused aloud. Sooner or later he had to face her, even if he detested her.

The breath stilled in Rochella's throat as a frightening answer took root. Her heart thumped against her rib cage. Was it his intention to try to make her believe she was only seeing things? Did he plan on driving her mad in order to have her locked away, so he could enjoy her dowry without the encumbrance of her person? It would not be the first time in history a man had rid himself of an unwanted wife.

A moment later a far more terrifying thought made Rochella feel as if an icy hand had touched the back of her neck. Could her husband be contemplating a more devious method of dealing with her? She already knew that Lord Devlin was a greedy man, but would that greed make him stoop to murder?

"Stop it this instant," Rochella said, stamping a foot against her unruly thoughts. She had no idea what her husband's plans for her were but she would not drive herself mad by trying to figure them out. When the time came, she would be ready for him. She would not cower and succumb to bouts of the vapors. She would face Gareth Devlin on his own ground.

Rochella glanced once more toward the gallery. "I am not like one of your weak-kneed English misses. I am a Beauvais and I come from a line of warriors that dates

back to the reign of Charlemagne. We did not acquire
the title of Lion for our lack of courage, as you will
soon learn when you deal with me, dear husband.''

"My lady, will you take your luncheon in the dining
room or in the small salon?"

Startled, Rochella jumped and spun about to face the
housekeeper.

"I didn't mean to startle you, Lady Devlin. I heard
you speak and thought you knew of my presence."

"I am sorry, Hilda. My mind was on other things.
What did you want?"

"I asked if you'd prefer to take your luncheon in the
dining room or the small salon?"

"Where will my husband be dining?" Rochella
asked, watching Hilda's expression intently. It cooled
visibly.

"I'm sorry, Lady Devlin. I don't know where Lord
Devlin will dine in London today."

"Hilda, you can stop pretending. I saw him with my
own eyes less than five minutes ago. I would appreciate
it if you would inform him I would like to meet with
him as soon as possible."

"My lady," Hilda said, looking decidedly uncomfortable, "I assure you, Lord Devlin has not returned
from London."

"Then whom did I see in the minstrels' gallery a few
moments ago and earlier on the third floor?" Rochella
asked, eyeing the housekeeper skeptically.

"It must have been one of the servants. They are
forever sneaking about trying to avoid their duties."

The housekeeper's lame excuse only served to infu-
riate Rochella further. "I seriously doubt the man I saw
was a servant. I demand that you go and tell my husband I want to see him."

"Lady Devlin, I've been instructed to do as you bid of me but I cannot do the impossible. Lord Devlin is not in residence at this time, no matter what you believe you saw," Hilda said, drawing herself up. Her expression reminded Rochella of that of a cat whose tail had been caught under a rocker.

"*Madame,* you wished to see me?" a deep male voice asked from the doorway. Startled, both women spun about to face the master of Devil Wind.

"Lord Devlin," Hilda said, regaining her composure first. "We didn't hear you arrive."

Gareth glanced from the housekeeper to the young woman staring at him through narrowed, emerald eyes, and one corner of his shapely mouth curved upward. "I doubt much could be heard over the conversation you two were having."

Hilda glanced uneasily at Rochella. "I apologize, my lord. I was just trying to explain to Lady Devlin that you had not returned from London."

"I understand," Gareth said, his voice slightly hoarse from the burst of sensation spreading through him. He could not take his eyes off the young woman who stood glaring at him. She was a vision of loveliness, her eyes sparkling with anger, her small chin raised haughtily in the air and her folded arms emphasizing her full breasts against the soft muslin bodice of her gown. He found himself wanting to forget the vows he'd made to keep himself aloof from his new bride. All good intentions seemed to have deserted him at the sight of the enchantress he'd married.

After a long uncomfortable moment, Gareth managed to collect his wits enough to turn his attention back to the housekeeper. "That will be all for now, Hilda," he said. "Will you see that luncheon is served immediately. I've been on the road since before dawn and I'm famished."

"As you wish, my lord." Hilda cast one last hostile look at Rochella before lifting her skirt and quickly leaving the room.

Rochella felt her blood begin to simmer at Gareth's rude inspection. He was eyeing her as if she were a prize mare. She fumed as she returned his audacious stare. To make matters worse, he acted as if he had never seen her before, when he had been spying on her all morning.

Shaken by the strange turn of events, Gareth forced himself to relax. If he had any chance of ever keeping his vows, he had to keep some distance between them, and it was best to start off their relationship on the right path. Resigned to what he had to instigate, he arched a dark brow, folded his arms across his massive chest and leaned one wide, velvet-covered shoulder against the door frame, waiting for Rochella to speak. When she did not, he asked, "Well, *madame?* You seemed to have an urgent need to see me when I arrived. Have you now lost your tongue?"

"Oh!" Rochella spluttered, fuming. "You are exactly as I imagined you would be." Another quizzical look from twilight eyes snapped the last thread holding her temper intact. She had had enough of this man's games for one day. "You are an arrogant, unfeeling— blackguard. How dare you act as if you don't know the reason I wanted to see you?"

"My lady, I assume you are my wife, since Hilda called you Lady Devlin, but I assure you I do not know any more than what I overheard between you and Hilda."

"Do not toy with me, Lord Devlin."

"Toy with you, *madame?*" Gareth asked, his expression hardening as he shrugged out of his casual stance.

"Yes, toy with me. I shall not play your games and I do not appreciate being spied upon," Rochella shot back.

"If you will recall, we have only just met. I have hardly had the chance to play games with you." Gareth's tone reflected his own annoyance.

"There is no need to lie. I saw you with my own eyes," Rochella accused.

Gareth felt a cold chill ripple down his back, and every muscle in his body tensed. His wife's words confirmed that all had not gone as he'd ordered in his absence. "*Madame,* I assure you I have no need to lie. Now if you will excuse me, I'll leave you to regain your composure. If you care to join me for luncheon, you are welcome." He turned to leave the ballroom.

"Where are you going?" Rochella asked, catching him by the sleeve. "You cannot walk away from me as if I have only imagined you spying on me."

Slowly Gareth turned once more to his wife. He was not angry with her but with Hilda, yet his expression darkened as he looked down at Rochella. "*Madame,* I don't know what you are talking about. I never laid eyes on you until a few minutes ago."

"You can deny it all you want, my lord. But I saw you watching me from the balcony. You tried to hide behind the curtain to keep me from seeing your face, but you were not quick enough."

"If you do not believe me then I suggest you ask the coachman who drove me from London. He is in the kitchen enjoying his luncheon, much as I would like to be doing at this moment," Gareth said, lifting Rochella's hand from his sleeve.

Rochella hesitated only a fraction of a moment. "I doubt it would prove anything, my lord. Since the man is in your employ, he would say what was expected of him."

"For your information, *madame,* the coach is rented. My coachman remained behind with my own coach when it broke a wheel and could not be repaired until today. However, I shall make no further excuses. You may be my wife, but I shall not have you or anyone questioning my word. If you do not believe what I tell you, then believe what you will. I am going to partake of my luncheon. Excuse me." Gareth turned and strode from the ballroom, leaving Rochella staring after him, feeling suddenly as if she had erred.

"I am not wrong," she muttered in one last burst of temper. "I know what I saw and I intend to prove it. And when I do, I shall make you admit your lies." That thought in mind, she marched toward the kitchen to find the coachman.

A short time later the chagrined Rochella entered the dining room. Her husband was seated at the head of the long mahogany table, devouring his meal of cold venison and beef with an assortment of fresh vegetables and fruit. A half full goblet of ruby wine sat to his right.

"*Madame?*" Gareth said, carefully placing his linen napkin on the table and coming to his feet. He made no further comment but stood regarding Rochella coolly.

Rochella felt her skin heat with a blush of mortification. She swallowed hard and cleared her throat before moistening her dry lips nervously. After all she had said to Gareth Devlin, it was not going to be an easy task to apologize. She had made a fool of herself.

"My lord," she began and then hesitated. Drawing in a steadying breath, she forced herself to continue. "I know neither of us wanted this marriage, but I had hoped we could live together amicably. I fear my actions earlier have set us on a path that will make it impossible for us to achieve tranquility between us. I have come to apologize for not accepting your word and for accusing you of lying."

Gareth felt a stab of guilt as he regarded his new wife with admiration. He had been too hard on her, yet he could not apologize for his action without telling her everything. Instead, he merely nodded graciously. "*Madame*, I, too, am sorry for what transpired earlier. Let us put it behind us and begin anew."

Still embarrassed by her behavior, Rochella smiled sheepishly up at Gareth and found herself caught within the ebony depths of his eyes. For a long moment, they seemed to caress her like soft black velvet against her naked skin. A strange new sensation quivered to life within her, and she glanced away from Gareth's disturbing gaze. He had graciously accepted her apology and she would not add another insult by crumpling to her knees at his feet.

"Shall we dine?" Gareth asked, sliding back her chair. As she took the proffered seat, he couldn't stop himself from admiring the sweet curve of her neck beneath the tumble of riotous chestnut curls that fell down her back nearly to her waist. From that interesting perspective, he allowed his gaze to wander to the soft skin of her shoulder before gliding down to the smooth expanse exposed above the square-cut neckline and then to the ripe curves of her breasts. For a dangerous moment he allowed his gaze to linger in the shadowy cleft between the ivory mounds and felt his pulse quicken.

Moving back to his own chair, Gareth turned his attention once more to his food, firmly reminding himself that Rochella Beauvais was his wife in name only and he would treat her as such. No matter how hard it became to be constantly in her company and not be able to quench his desires.

Chapter Three

Gareth watched Rochella ascend the stairs until she passed from view. His luncheon with his wife had been less than satisfactory but far better than their first encounter. She had eaten little and had spoken even less, but at least they hadn't gone at each other's throats.

Running a long-fingered hand through his dark curls, Gareth turned and made his way to his study. He poured himself a glass of wine, then pulled the bell cord to summon a servant. A few moments later Alice peeped around the door and smiled timidly up at the master of Devil Wind. "Is there something you wish, Lord Devlin?"

"Aye, Alice. Tell Hilda I want to see her immediately."

Alice bobbed her head with its curly mop and disappeared as quietly as she'd come.

A thoughtful expression played over Gareth's handsome features as he downed the deep red liquid in his glass. It slid smoothly into his stomach, warming him as he turned and refilled the crystal with more of the fine French wine, which had been smuggled into the country by the locals. Holding the glass up to the light he eyed the clarity of the ruby wine. England's embargo against French goods had reestablished the old illegal trade that had sustained the coastal residents for generations. Many were growing rich from their excursions across the channel to bring back wine, lace and other highly valued commodities. King George's revenuers patrolled the coastline with dogged persistence, but their efforts did little to hinder the smugglers. The wine in Gareth's hand was evidence of their failings.

"George would not be pleased with me if he ever suspected I deal in contraband," Gareth mused aloud, a smile breaking his sober expression as his deep chuckle filled the room. Relaxing somewhat under the spell of the burgundy, he settled himself behind the large mahogany desk that dominated the room filled with well-read, leather-bound volumes.

"You wished to see me?" Hilda asked from the doorway.

"Close the door behind you, Hilda," Gareth said, his mood darkening once more. Setting his glass aside and bracing his elbows against the shining surface of the desk, he leaned forward, regarding the housekeeper solemnly. "I believe we need to have a long talk."

Unnerved by the look on Gareth's face, Hilda quickly obeyed. Her sweaty palms belied the air of composure that surrounded her as she crossed the thick Turkish carpet to stand quietly before Gareth's desk.

"If what I have gleaned from my wife is true, then you have failed to do as I bade you. I gave you strict orders before I left for London, Hilda. Why weren't they obeyed?"

"I did my best, sir. But things have been awkward since the arrival of Lady Devlin. She's been an unsettling presence. I tried to warn you before you left."

"You are Devil Wind's housekeeper and you have full authority in my absence, Hilda. It was your responsibility to see that things went as we planned. If you value your position, you will see that a repeat of today never takes place."

Hilda nodded, her face flooding with color under his censure. "My lord, will you go to the north wing now? It might help."

Gareth released a long breath. Dread coiled about his insides like a serpent bent upon strangling its victim. After a long moment he finally nodded. "Yes, I'll go up now. I shouldn't have stayed away so long." As he came to his feet, Gareth's haggard expression reflected his weariness. "See that no one follows me."

He paused at the door and looked back at his housekeeper. "Did you carry out the rest of my instructions?"

"Aye, Lord Devlin. Nary a word has been said that you wouldn't approve. And Lady Devlin has slept like a babe since coming to Devil Wind. My only worry has been that nosy maid of hers. She swears she sees ghosts roaming the halls at midnight."

Gareth smiled. "Perhaps she also needs a dose of your tea before bedtime. That would solve all of our problems."

Hilda nodded. Yes, it would solve at least one problem for her. And if she was patient, in time all the rest would also be solved.

Gareth slowly made his way up the winding stairs and unlocked the thick iron-bound door that kept Devil Wind's north wing separate from the rest of the castle. The newer wing held little resemblance to the older section of the fortress. Dark paneling gleamed upon the walls and thick Turkish carpets absorbed the sound of his footsteps as he made his way along the corridor to the locked chamber.

Gareth paused and drew in a deep breath, preparing himself to face what he would find. Turning the key he pushed open the door and took in the room with a glance. As usual it was in a shambles. Tables had been overturned. Books were strewn everywhere, their pages in shreds. Pillows had been disemboweled and the sheets had been torn from the four-poster bed and stamped upon. Gareth briefly closed his eyes against the sight before searching out the person who had wrought such havoc.

"It's about time you decided to return and let me out of this prison, dear brother."

Gareth turned toward the sound of the deep masculine voice and came face-to-face with the image of himself. Only the eyes were different—not in color or shape but in the expression within their twilight depths. They held the look that had claimed one Devlin twin out of every pair since the curse had been placed upon his family. It was the look of madness.

"How are you, Adam?" Gareth asked, ignoring the destruction.

"How do you think I am? How would you feel if you were cooped up in this room day in and day out without a break?"

"From what I gleaned from my wife this morning, you've managed to enjoy some freedom."

Adam chuckled and gave Gareth a wide, charming smile. "You are a fortunate man, brother. She is a beautiful woman. It's too bad you plan to deny yourself the pleasures of her luscious body." Adam cupped one hand in front of him. "Her breast would fill a man's hand nicely."

A flash of fury flickered over Gareth. His swarthy complexion deepened in hue. "Enough, Adam. You know as well as I that my marriage is in name only, and you also know the reason."

Adam threw back his dark head and howled with laughter. "I know well your reason because I am responsible for it."

"You have nothing to do with my decision, Adam. You've been ill for a long time but you are not mad. If you keep improving the way you have in the past few months, soon you'll be able to come out of the north wing and join the rest of the family again."

Adam shook his head and feigned a shudder. "You know I don't like to have people staring at me."

"They won't stare at you," Gareth said in an effort to reassure his brother.

"Yes, they will. They always do. That's why I come out at night when everyone is asleep," Adam said, forcing a quaver into his voice.

"You did venture out of the north wing this morning," Gareth pointed out.

Adam turned away to hide the glint of ire sparkling in his cold, dark eyes. He stared out the window, past the manicured landscape. The roar of the turbulent sea beating against the black granite cliffs reflected the feelings he kept well hidden within him. Over the years he had become an expert at hiding his true self behind the mask of madness decreed by the family curse. Narrowing his eyes, he pursed his shapely lips. He had missed being the master of Devil Wind by two minutes, but someday it would all change. He knew how to use the fate thrust upon him to his own advantage.

Steeling his features, Adam turned to look at Gareth. "I only wanted to see your wife, brother. I know

I'll never be able to marry because of my nervous condition, but that does not stop me from wanting the same things as every other healthy man.''

Gareth felt a hand grip his heart and twist. He crossed to his brother and hugged him. The lie slipped easily from his lips, for he would have done or said anything to ease the pain he saw in his brother's eyes. "Someday, Adam, you'll be well enough to marry."

"I pray you are right," Adam replied. His mood swiftly changing, he danced out of Gareth's embrace. Cocking his head to one side and tapping his chin with the tip of one finger, he arched a dark brow at his brother. "Do you think, since I'm crazy like old George, he would let me marry one of his ugly daughters?"

"I'm sure he'd be honored," Gareth said, unable to stop himself from laughing at his brother's antics. Adam changed moods and personalities as swiftly as the breeze changed direction.

"Then I shall venture to London with all haste," Adam said, laughing. "Have Hilda pack my bags at once. We mustn't waste time."

"I fear George would not be too pleased to see any Devlin at present. He is already thoroughly annoyed with me, without you going there to steal the hearts of his daughters."

"What did you do to annoy our good king?" Adam asked, his curiosity overcoming him.

"I refused to sail to Turkey because of my marriage."

"What is so important about Turkey?"

"At the moment the king is worried that without England's help the Turks will fall to the czarina of

Russia. Should that take place, it would make Russia a power in the Mediterranean."

"But how do you fit into the plan, Gareth?" Adam asked, wanting to learn all he could about his brother's life.

"My ships carry weapons for the Turks, and since France has withdrawn its support, Turkey has only England to come to its aid."

"Oh," Adam said, storing the information away. His questions had been answered and it was time to slip back into his role of the mad Devlin. He turned on Gareth, his eyes blazing. He stamped his foot and thrust out his lower lip peevishly. "You did it on purpose, didn't you? You refused the mission so King George would not allow me to come to London and marry his daughter. You never want me to be happy."

"Adam, calm yourself. You're becoming too excited," Gareth said in an effort to forestall the fit of temper he knew to be brewing.

"Get out of my sight. You are just jealous because the king wanted me to marry his daughter. Get out, I tell you, get out!" Adam began to kick the furniture lying in his path.

"All right, I'll leave. Now calm yourself and I'll have Hilda bring up your tea."

"Get out." Adam seemed close to tears. "I don't want you here."

Gareth's shoulders sagged as he picked his way through the mess on the floor. He cast one last agonized look at his twin, then he closed and locked the door behind him.

He found Hilda waiting by the entrance to the north wing. "Go to him, Hilda. Perhaps your tea will soothe him."

Gareth didn't wait for her reply but turned in the direction of the master bedchamber.

Entering his room a short while later, he wearily removed his velvet jacket and laid it aside. Rubbing the back of his neck he crossed to the tall leaded windows overlooking the cliffs. His gaze turned toward the horizon and he longed to be far away from Devil Wind where he had only the elements to battle.

A movement in the garden below drew Gareth's attention. The glint of coppery hair caught his eye and he immediately recognized his wife. She strolled slowly along the graveled path toward the cliffs, a basket of flowers over one arm. The sea breeze molded her light muslin gown to her lithe body, giving him a view of her youthful curves. Again he felt his pulse quicken at the sight. Adam was right about one thing. His wife was a beautiful woman. "Far too beautiful for my peace of mind," Gareth murmured aloud.

Abruptly he turned from the sight below and crossed the room. Settling himself in a high-backed chair in front of the cold fireplace, he propped his booted feet on a small damask-covered footstool and laced his fingers across his hard, flat abdomen. Moodily he stared into the gray ash and wondered if this was how his life would be in the future: hiding away in his own chamber to avoid facing the young woman in the garden.

A grin tugged up one corner of his mouth. "Perhaps both Adam and I need to be locked away. I have vowed to keep my distance from my wife and here I sit brooding over her like a moonstruck boy."

Gareth chuckled and laid his head back. Should he fail to have the strength to keep his vow, he had but to tell his young bride of the family curse and of his mad brother in the north wing. "That would soon solve everything," he said, giving voice to his rancor. He released a long breath and nodded. Yes, if he could not resist the temptation of his beautiful wife, he would tell her the truth about the family she had married into.

But Gareth knew he could not tell Rochella about Adam. If she found out the truth, she would want to return to France, and that he could not allow. Especially not now, after everything he had learned in London. The situation in France was growing more precarious each day, and it was fortunate that the marquis had had the foresight to get his daughter to safety while he was still able.

Gareth closed his eyes. He was back at the beginning. There would be no easy resolutions to his problems. In all of his thirty-two years, there never had been.

Adam stood watching the woman in the garden. A devious smile curled up the corners of his shapely lips and his eyes glinted with malice. Gareth's wife was by far the loveliest creature he had ever seen. He felt himself swell with desire at the thought of taking the lovely Rochella to his bed. It would be interesting to teach her the arts of love. For once in their lives Gareth would have to take his leavings. Adam chuckled at the thought.

"Soon, dear brother, she will be mine," he murmured softly.

"Must you destroy everything in your path just to impress upon Gareth that you are mad?" Hilda questioned as she bent to retrieve the bed sheets from the floor.

Startled from the thoughts of his brother's wife, Adam turned and gave Hilda a dazzling smile. "Yes, I must, Hilda, or all our work will be for naught." He held out his arms. "Come here, sweetings."

The sheets fell once more to the floor as Hilda forgot them and went into Adam's arms. Girlishly, she snuggled against his lean frame, cuddling her head beneath his chin and wrapping her arms tightly about his lean waist. "I am so tired of these games. Today he threatened to dismiss me if I did not keep you under closer supervision."

"His time is coming, Hilda. We do not have much longer to wait."

"Let it be soon. I cannot take much more of his highhanded manner."

"Don't worry, sweetings. Once we have Rochella convinced, then our plan will be set. Have you begun to weaken her tea?"

Hilda shook her head. "I thought it best to leave that until your brother returned."

Adam smiled confidently as he caressed Hilda's back. "A wise move. Now that Gareth has returned, you can begin tonight. Just add enough herbs to keep her groggy and I shall do the rest."

The eagerness in his voice pricked Hilda's jealousy, and she leaned back to look into Adam's twilight eyes. "You don't want her, do you?"

Adam cocked one brow. "Want her, when I have you? Don't be ridiculous. I have only one use for my brother's wife."

Hilda pressed herself against him and clung to him as if he were her lifeline. "I believe I would go mad if you ever looked at another woman."

Adam stroked her hair, the curve of her cheek and the swell of her breasts. "Dear sweet Hilda. You know you are the only woman for me. What I do with my brother's wife is only to make sure our plan to have Devil Wind succeeds. And you mustn't forget that. I love you, Hilda. Now show me how you love me."

Hilda wrapped her arms around Adam's neck and drew his head down to hers. As he lifted her into his arms, they fell together onto the unmade bed, moans of pure animal pleasure escaping them as they rode the fierce current of their lust.

Adam rolled away from Hilda and straightened his clothing. As if as an afterthought, he tossed down her skirts and then stood, feigning a tender smile.

Hilda sat up and raised a trembling hand to straighten her hair. Lank strands had escaped the tight bun in the heat of passion, and now they hung in wisps about her face and neck.

"Now, it's time for you to get back to your duties. And I need some time to think before I venture out tonight."

Dismissed by her lover, Hilda hurried from the chamber. As instructed by Lord Devlin, she locked the door behind her, knowing full well that Adam possessed a key of his own. Leaving the north wing, she made her way to her own chamber off the servant's wing. There she collapsed onto her narrow bed and, as in the past, gave way to tears of frustration.

The dream began with a gentle caress. Rochella smiled and snuggled closer to the warmth at her side. Again came the caress against her cheek, rousing her to awareness. She slowly opened her eyes to a room filled with shadows cast by the dying embers in the fireplace. She turned her face toward the caress and found the dark image of a man sitting on the edge of her bed. Though the light left his features in shadow, she immediately recognized her husband. Oddly, she was not alarmed to find him in her bedchamber, and she stretched as a lazy yawn slipped from her.

"What are you doing here?" she murmured, and like a pampered kitten rubbed her cheek against the knuckles slowly moving along the curve of her jaw.

"You are my wife, Rochella. Where else should a husband be?" His voice was husky with desire.

Groggily, Rochella accepted his explanation without question and smiled up at him. "But earlier, you seemed not to like me."

"Not like you? *Non, petite.* You are far too beautiful for any man to not like." He stroked her throat, gentling her as if she were a young filly.

At the caress a sigh of pleasure escaped Rochella's lips and she smiled again. She had desperately needed to be reassured that her husband did not hate her, for despite her objection to her marriage, somewhere within her mind a small hope had taken root that she could possibly make her marriage work.

"You are by far the most beautiful woman I have ever seen."

Rochella suddenly found her voice had vanished. A strange current of excitement rushed through her, making her feel breathless and giddy. His tender words had again roused the curious feelings she had experienced that afternoon when she had looked into the velvet softness of his eyes. Her stomach quivered and she felt her nipples harden. Her pulse began to race and her lips parted.

"You are mine, Rochella, and soon you will come to know the true master of Devil Wind."

Caught in the spiral of new feeling, Rochella could only nod.

"Now, my lovely bride, close your eyes," he demanded softly. She obeyed and felt one last gentle caress as her lashes came to rest on her cheeks. She found herself slipping back into the black void of sleep, and fought to remain awake. For the first time since coming to Devil Wind she felt as if she belonged, and her heart cried out for him to stay with her. She heard the squeak of a floorboard, felt a cool draft of air against her flushed skin.

Struggling to come out of her stupor, Rochella opened her eyes to find she was sitting upright in the middle of her bed, staring into the darkened empty room.

Bereft, she searched the ebony shadows for the man who had just left her side. Her spirits once more sinking into the mire of loneliness, she lay back and curled into a ball, staring at the red coals in the fireplace and wondering why Gareth had come to her room. Suddenly another thought struck her with agonizing clarity. Had she dreamed Gareth's nocturnal visit? It had seemed so real, but with her mind still dazed with sleep, she could not be sure. There was only one way she would know, and it was to ask Gareth when she saw him at dinner the following evening. Still groggy, Rochella once more succumbed to the effects of Hilda's tea.

Chapter Four

A loud crack of thunder shook Devil Wind, startling Rochella out of the light doze she had fallen into. Disoriented, she came out of her chair in a flash, dropping the thick volume of Walpole's *Historic Doubts on Richard III* onto her foot. The pain brought her fully awake. Reaching down to the sore spot, she cast a disgruntled look toward the windows, where the relentless rain continued to batter the leaded panes.

"Does it never do anything here but rain?" she muttered, retrieving the book. She hadn't meant to fall asleep, but the dreary day combined with the dreary book had worked like a sedative.

"As if I needed anything to make me sleep," Rochella grumbled, settling herself back into the overstuffed leather chair. Her life of late was more than enough to put an insomniac soundly to sleep. Each day reflected the previous one. She would awaken, take her breakfast alone in her room and then try to find something to occupy her time for the rest of the day.

In the past weeks she had come to depend heavily upon the books in Gareth's study. She had read so many she was becoming an expert on English literature, yet she found the knowledge hadn't changed the boring pattern of her life.

Fortunately, she rarely saw her husband except in the evenings at dinner. Each night was the same. After a few polite questions and equally polite answers about her day, they would eat in silence. When the meal was finished, he would graciously bid her good-night and retreat to his study.

Her life-style was beginning to play havoc with her nerves, as was the distance between her and her husband. Even for the short time they spent together it wasn't easy to pretend her life at Devil Wind was satisfactory. Since the day she apologized for doubting his word, an unspoken truce had developed between them, and she was loath to disrupt it with complaints about her inactivity. Instead she continued to spend her days reading.

Rochella's restlessness had also begun to affect her in other ways. She was irritable and found herself snapping at Babette for the slightest infraction. Her appetite was nearly nonexistent and she had lost weight. Her greatest worry, however, was something she could not control. It was the strange dreams about her husband. They came nightly and each was so real that when he took her into his arms and brushed his cheek against hers, she was able to feel the raspy stubble of his beard.

After the first night, she had thought to confront Gareth about his visit, but she had changed her mind. His attitude at dinner the following evening had made her realize how foolish she was to have even considered that the dream was real and that he possessed such a gentle side to his nature. No man made of flesh and blood could act one way at night—so loving and tender—and then return to the cold aloofness she faced across the dinner table each evening.

"I'm becoming more like Babette every day," Rochella grumbled to herself. "I have to stop this." Laying the book aside, she came to her feet. "There must be something more to do with my time than to sit daydreaming about the man I was forced to marry." If her husband thought to relegate her to such a status then he was sorely mistaken, she decided. She was Lady Devlin and she would take her rightful place within her husband's household, no matter what Gareth or his shrewish housekeeper thought.

Determination stiffening her spine, Rochella resolved to find her husband and tell him of her decision. She turned toward the door, but before her hand touched the shining brass latch, a shrill scream echoed down the corridor. Her heart lodged in her throat, she threw open the door and bolted into the hallway. Spying Babette lying at the landing of the stair with a tall cloaked man standing over her, she felt a foreboding chill race down her spine—until she recognized her husband.

"My God, what did you do to her?" she accused, hurrying forward to assist the prone woman.

"*Madame,* I did nothing but come down the stairs. When she saw me, she screamed and fainted at my feet. But for the scream of fright, it's a charming scenario, don't you think?" Gareth said, one side of his mouth quirking upward in a wry grin.

Finding nothing to smile about in her husband's unusual display of humor, Rochella flashed him a look that would have withered a weaker man, and knelt at Babette's side. Gently she patted the maid's cheek in an effort to revive her. "Wake up, Babette. There is nothing here to harm you."

Slowly Babette's eyes flickered open and she blinked up at Rochella. Momentarily disoriented, she lay still until she managed to collect her wits enough to recall the ghostly specter on the stairs. Her eyes widening with fright, she abruptly sat up and glanced in all direc-. tions. "It was the ghost, *mamselle*. He came at me with his great black wings swirling in the air."

Rochella heard Gareth chuckle behind her. "Babette, I fear it was only I whom you saw."

Slowly Babette turned to look at Gareth, shaking her head. "No, it was the ghost who haunts these halls each night."

"Babette, you have let your imagination mistake Lord Devlin for one of your fantasies. Now let me help you up to your room so you can rest," Rochella said, making an effort to assist Babette to her feet.

The maid resisted, stubbornly shaking her head. "I know what I saw."

"Babette, we have already explained what you saw. Now I suggest you do as your mistress bids you and quell your wild ravings," Gareth said, his smile fading.

Babette came to her feet, bristling with insult. Her voice was edged with hysteria as she looked from Rochella to Gareth and said, "No matter what you say, I shall not stay another night in this great heap of stones. I am leaving."

"Babette, you cannot mean what you say," Rochella said, feeling her stomach twist at the thought of Babette leaving Devil Wind.

"I mean every word, *mamselle*. I love you, but I shall go mad if I stay another night here." Great tears slipped down Babette's pale cheeks and she trembled from head to toe.

Rochella cast an anxious, beseeching glance at her husband and saw him nod his understanding.

Gareth could not ignore the plea he saw in her eyes. "Babette, my wife would have you stay with her here. She needs you."

"I am going home," Babette answered vehemently as she stubbornly faced him. "The marquis promised I should be allowed to return to Beauvais should I not like it here."

"Babette, you cannot leave me here all alone" was Rochella's anguished plea. If Babette returned to France, then she would be left with not even one friend at Devil Wind.

"Oh, *mamselle*." Torn between her love for Rochella and the fear that had been eating away at her soul, Babette choked on her tears. She gulped several times, unable to explain her feelings further. Surrendering to her need to put Devil Wind and its ghosts behind her, she turned and fled to her quarters. It would take her only a few minutes to pack what few belongings she possessed, and then she would set out for the village. Nothing could make her spend another hour in this great heap of stones.

Rochella covered her mouth with a trembling hand and watched Babette scurry out of sight. This could not be happening. Babette could not leave her here all alone. It had to be some cruel jest.

Gareth followed Rochella's gaze until the shadows on the third floor hid the maid from view. He realized that in his effort to avoid Rochella and escape the physical attraction he had felt for her since their first meeting, he had failed to give her the companionship she needed.

"I'm sorry," Gareth said, placing a comforting hand on Rochella's slender shoulder as if she were a child. "I know you will miss her."

Rochella turned her misty gaze up to meet Gareth's twilight eyes. A shudder shook her and her lower lip trembled slightly. "She is all I have left of home. When Babette leaves I shall have no one."

Taking Rochella into his arms, Gareth hugged her close. "Your home is here now, Rochella, as is your family."

Desperately needing solace, Rochella burrowed into Gareth's embrace beneath the folds of his cape. She pressed her face against the white silk shirt covering the wide expanse of his chest.

Gently Gareth stroked Rochella's chestnut curls and murmured soothing words of comfort. Her hair was silken beneath his fingers, and the sweet fragrance of her perfume filled his nostrils.

"All will be well. You will see. Alice will make you a perfect lady's maid."

Rochella drew in a shaky breath. "You do not understand. Nothing has been right since my father decided I should marry, and now, even Babette is deserting me."

"Rochella, I know things have not been easy for you," Gareth continued, "nor have they been for me, but we must accept the fact that we are married. You are now Lady Devlin and the mistress of Devil Wind."

"Married?" Rochella said, her voice tinged with sarcasm. She leaned back and gazed up at Gareth. "A priest read the vows and our names were signed on the marriage contract, yet you and I are not husband and wife. We are little more than strangers. We live under the same roof but we share nothing, not even a civil conversation when we dine together.''

Gareth could not deny her words. Some things were going to have to change in their relationship, even if others could not. "I agree, things have been awkward between us. Perhaps it is time we try to act as if we are man and wife.''

Misunderstanding the direction of his thoughts, Rochella shook her head vehemently. She had no intention of sharing this man's bed, no matter how attracted she was to him. "I did not mean we should act, ah, as man and wife in every way. I only meant we know nothing about each other.''

Gareth smiled his understanding. "I only meant perhaps we could become friends.''

"Friends?'' Rochella asked, relieved and slightly bemused by the prospect of befriending her own husband.

"Yes. It would make our lives together much easier. We might even find we enjoy each other's company if we give ourselves a chance. We were both opposed to this marriage, but since it is now a fait accompli, we should try to make the best of it, don't you think?''

"Do you mean I may act as the true mistress of Devil Wind?''

"It is your right,'' Gareth said, surprised by her question.

Rochella's face lit with a smile. "Then I have your permission to manage your household as I see fit?''

"Within reason,'' Gareth said, unable to hide his own smile at the look of excitement glowing in her emerald eyes. "Should you decide to renovate, or rid yourself of my staff, I should expect to be advised of your decision.''

"My lord, I do not know how to thank you," Rochella murmured, feeling a glow of happiness warm her insides. It was the first time since coming to England that she had experienced even a momentary glimmer of the emotion.

"There is no reason to thank me, *madame*. You are the mistress here and should have the authority to handle things as you see fit. Should you have any problems, please feel free to come to me."

"But I do have reason to thank you. You cannot imagine what this means to me. I have nearly gone mad from inactivity. You can only read so many books and take so many walks. At least now I shall feel I have some purpose to my days."

Gareth gave Rochella a tender smile and involuntarily raised a hand to cup her smooth cheek. He absently brushed his thumb against her lightly tinted skin as he gazed down into the mesmerizing depths of her eyes.

"I have been remiss for not thinking of it sooner. I should have realized how you would feel being cooped up here without anything to occupy your time."

An ahem behind them on the stair landing jerked Gareth's attention from his wife and halted further conversation between them. He let his hand fall to his side and quickly stepped away from Rochella. "I see Hilda has brought your evening tea so I shall bid you good-night."

Glancing at Hilda, Gareth continued. "Hilda, my wife and I have been discussing her duties at Devil Wind, and I feel it is time she took on the responsibilities of chatelaine. I am sure you will help her in every way possible."

Hilda nodded, her expression closed. "I shall do my best to be of service to Lady Devlin, my lord."

"Good. Then I will bid you both good-night." Gareth descended several steps before he turned and looked back up at his housekeeper. "My wife's maid is returning to France immediately. See that Alice is given her duties." Gareth turned once more to the stairs, anxious to escape his wife's unsettling presence before he succumbed to the urge to take her once more into his arms. A long walk along the parapet would cool such thoughts.

Smiling smugly at her success in ridding Devil Wind of the nosy French maid, Hilda followed Rochella to her chamber. When the door closed behind them she asked, "Since your maid will not be here this evening, shall I help you undress, my lady?"

"Thank you, Hilda, but I shall manage tonight by myself," Rochella said, crossing to the rain-splattered window. It was a harsh night out and she could not stop herself from wondering what reason her husband could have for venturing out in such weather.

"Very well, *madame,*" Hilda said. Setting the small tea tray on the bedside table, she proceeded to pour the steaming, golden liquid into the gold-trimmed cup. "Your tea, my lady."

Rochella shook her head. "Just leave it on the table, Hilda. I am in no mood for tea at the moment."

"But you must have the tea, my lady," Hilda said, offering the cup to Rochella.

Rochella frowned down at the brew in the elegantly patterned cup.

"My lady, it will help you rest after all the excitement."

"Hilda, I do not want the tea tonight. Now please take it away."

Hilda pressed her thin lips together resolutely and set the cup down on the night table by Rochella's bed. "It is Lord Devlin's order that you drink the tea, *madame*. I am only doing as bidden."

"My husband ordered the tea for me?" Rochella asked, puzzled.

"Aye. You are to have the tea each night. It will help you sleep."

After Gareth's earlier generosity and the warm feeling it had created within her, Rochella did not question the reason behind her husband's need to ensure she slept well. She took the cup and sipped the steaming brew. At the odd flavor, she frowned and handed the cup to Hilda. "I think I have had enough tonight."

Hilda shook her head. "You must drink it all. Lord Devlin insists."

Afraid that the housekeeper would stay all night if necessary to ensure Lord Devlin's orders were carried out, Rochella once more took the cup and lifted it to her lips.

A look of satisfaction crossed Hilda's face as she watched Rochella drink the tea. It was time to see that Lord and Lady Devlin became man and wife in every sense of the word. The herbs she had added to Rochella's tea would accomplish that. She knew that Lady Devlin was far from indifferent about her husband, and when the tea took effect, the woman would not be able to deny her feelings any longer.

Hilda smiled her triumph. Once the marriage was consummated, her worries would be at an end. Adam would want nothing more to do with the fair Rochella when he learned she had slept with his brother. He would never take his brother's leavings. Since birth he had always been second in line for everything, and he had vowed never to be second again.

Hilda had furtively watched Adam each night from the doorway of Lady Devlin's chamber and knew that he was becoming obsessed with his brother's wife. The tea would ensure the consummation of Lord Devlin's marriage as well as save the housekeeper's relationship with the only man she had ever loved.

"You may go now, Hilda. I shall finish my tea and then go to bed," Rochella said, hoping the housekeeper would leave so she could pour the terrible-tasting mixture in the chamber pot where it belonged.

"My lady, I have been instructed to see you drink all of your tea," Hilda urged, determined to see every drop of the herbed brew down Rochella's throat. She wanted no mistakes tonight.

For one brief moment Rochella thought of refusing to drink the brew, but quickly decided she did not want to cause any dissension with Gareth. They had begun something this evening, and she did not want to see it end before it had a chance to mature. Their lives were now inexorably linked and would be much easier if they could live peacefully together.

Before she could change her mind, Rochella downed the tea and handed the cup to Hilda. "Now, you may go and tell your master I have had my tea and gone to bed."

Hilda nodded and smiled. "Good night, my lady. Sleep well."

"Good night, Hilda," Rochella said, relieved to be rid of the housekeeper at last.

Rochella undressed with some difficulty and slipped on a shimmering blue silk nightrail. Its deep V neckline was edged in fine hand-worked lace, as were the long flowing sleeves and hem. The clinging fabric molded to her body, revealing the firm mounds of her breasts and the soft flare of her rounded hips.

Gazing at her reflection in the cheval glass, Rochella felt an odd stirring start deep in the pit of her belly. Heat seemed to radiate outward from it, curling through her body, warming her until her skin tingled. Her eyes seemed to glow with new life as she watched, mesmerized by her own reflection.

"What is wrong with me?" she murmured to her reflection, trying to rid herself of her strange mood.

The dreams of her husband's visits to her bedchamber involuntarily came to her mind. She raised her fingers to her lips, lightly tracing their shape with her fingertips. Even in her dreams Gareth had never kissed her, and she could not stop herself from wondering what it would feel like to have his mouth upon hers. The thought made her heart lurch crazily against her rib cage and again affected her breathing. Her mind would not let go of her nightly fantasies. They came rushing back to torment her body. Vividly she recalled the tender caress Gareth had given her before Hilda had interrupted them on the stairs, and she wanted to feel his hands upon her again.

Unable to stop herself, Rochella crossed to the door and slid open the latch. Without a backward glance, she left her bedchamber and moved along the corridor to her husband's. She didn't knock but opened the door and entered.

No candles burned to illuminate the room, yet the meager firelight broke the darkness enough to reveal the man sleeping in the large four-poster bed. He lay on his side, one muscular arm cushioning his head, his upper body bare and a sheet draping his narrow hips. Rochella thought him magnificent. Unable to take her eyes from him, she stood devouring him with her gaze. Greedily her eyes moved over him, exploring the unfamiliar male body from his wide shoulders down to the expanse of his crisply matted chest. From there her gaze followed the trail of dark hair that narrowed just below his ribs and wove a path downward to disappear beneath the sheet.

Rochella's hands tingled with the need to touch his smooth, satiny flesh. She moved closer to the bed, unaware that the squeak of a floorboard had roused Gareth from sleep and that he now watched her from beneath thick black lashes.

Unable to believe his eyes, Gareth watched his wife approach his bed. Every muscle in his body tensed with expectation and his mouth went dry. His nostrils flared as he drew in a sharp breath, and his heart pumped furiously against his rib cage as his gaze came to rest upon the form illuminated beneath the translucent silk by the firelight. Mesmerized by the sight, he lay unable to make his body obey the commands of his mind.

The breath caught in his throat when Rochella paused and reached out to touch him. As if savoring the feel of his skin, she stroked the curve of his shoulder, fondling him. His teeth clenched, Gareth squeezed his eyes tightly closed as her fingers crept along his collarbone and began to explore his chest. He felt his body throb with the need to reach out and drag her down into the bed and put an end to his torment. Yet he forced himself to remain still. Rochella lightly traced the areola of one nipple with her fingertip, teasing it into a hard bud before allowing one lone finger to travel down the dark path of hair toward the sheet.

As he realized her intentions, Gareth's eyes opened wide. He swiftly reached out and clamped a hand on hers to stay it. "The game is up, Rochella. Go back to your chamber."

"Let me touch you," Rochella pleaded, her voice husky, all modesty vanquished by the powerful effect of the tea.

"I said go back to your bed. This is no place for you." Gareth struggled with the desire raging through him. If she did not obey soon, he would not be responsible for what happened.

Rochella raised a knee to the mattress and began to crawl into the bed beside Gareth. "I am your wife and should share your bed."

"You have no idea of what you are saying, Rochella. You do not even like me," Gareth pointed out, the war being waged within him making his voice harsh.

Rochella raised a hand and caressed the side of his cheek. She smiled down at him. "I know exactly what I am saying. Your skin feels like satin."

"Are you drunk?" Gareth inquired, unable to understand her strange mood. Throwing her hand away from him, he scrambled to the other side of the bed, pulling the sheet with him to cover his nakedness.

He swallowed hard and sought to quell the desire searing every inch of his body, reminding himself of his vow never to consummate his marriage. However, it was growing more difficult by the moment to recall anything except his throbbing need for the beautiful creature before him.

"Rochella, please," Gareth pleaded, struggling to his feet as he wrapped the sheet about him. "Stop this foolishness. I am not sure what you expect to accomplish by coming here uninvited, but I suggest you return to your own chambers.'' His voice was fraught with tension.

Suddenly Gareth stumbled over the sheet and fell backward onto the thick Turkish carpet. The sheet fell away, leaving him naked. Rochella paused and then reached for the hem of her own nightrail, pulling it over her head. As she stood before him, unashamed, Gareth released a long breath. The battle was over. He could not run from her any longer. His heart would not let him.

When he lifted his arms to her, Rochella came into them, capturing his mouth in a fiery, devastating kiss that rocked them both to their very souls. Gareth rolled her onto her back, and she moaned her pleasure at the feel of his flesh touching hers. His tongue plunged between her lips and inside her mouth to stroke hers, sending liquid fire raging through her. Her breathing became rapid and she caressed him, running her hands through his hair, down his neck, along his shoulders and down his back to the curves of his firm buttocks.

Rochella trembled at the sensations racing through her. Never in her life would she have believed she could find such pleasure in touching a man. Gareth looked down at her, a look of pleasure and pain on his face, and she sensed only he could quench the fire searing every inch of her flesh. Instinctively, she raised her hips, rubbing them against him.

Indecision flickered over Gareth's handsome face and he murmured, ''God forgive me,'' before he succumbed to her heady invitation.

The first thrust tore away her maidenhead and she flinched in surprise. Then she moved with him, bringing her legs up about his waist to take him deeper inside her moist warmth.

Gareth savored the exquisite feel of her as he took her toward the edge of passion, dipping and rising until their sweaty bodies exploded into rapture. Gasping for breath and quivering with release, they lay together, limbs entwined.

Savoring the feel of his wife in his arms, Gareth felt reality descend upon him with the force of a blow. He pulled Rochella close, cuddling her. His heart still pounded against his ribs but not out of unfulfilled passion. He squeezed his eyes closed. He had broken his vow and now all he could do was pray that God would not see fit to punish him by allowing Rochella to conceive their child.

Rochella relaxed, and Gareth knew from the sound of her steady breathing that she had fallen asleep. Easing from her, he picked up his dressing robe and slipped it on. He retrieved her nightrail, pulled the sheet about her and lifted her into his arms. For a long anguish-filled moment, he stood looking down into her now peaceful face.

"You are a woman of fire, my Rochella. And were it not for the agony I would put you through, as well as the children we would bear, nothing on this earth could stop me from loving you as my heart demands."

Gareth turned toward the door and quietly carried his wife back to her own bedchamber. He put her to bed and sat for a long moment savoring her beauty. On the morrow, he would make her realize that what had transpired between them this evening could never happen again.

Releasing a remorseful sigh, Gareth brushed his lips against Rochella's brow and caressed the gentle curve of her cheek. He recognized his own weaknesses where his fiery wife was concerned, and knew if he allowed himself to touch her again, he would not be able to stop himself from making love to her.

Pulling the sheet up and tucking it about Rochella as if she were a small child, he released another long, weary breath. His shoulders sagged from the burdens of his life as he turned and walked toward the door. He left the room without looking back at the wife he had come to love in such a short time.

Adam's dark eyes narrowed as he watched Gareth quietly close the door to his wife's chamber and make his way down the corridor to the master bedroom. A muscle twitched in his craggy jaw and he balled his fists at his sides.

"Damn him," he swore, his hatred for his brother rising with each breath. Gareth had always been first in everything, and now he had taken the one woman Adam had decided to claim as his own. His handsome features contorted with rage as he turned to the woman standing in the shadows at his side. Needing to vent his frustrations, he snaked out a hand and grasped her painfully by the arm. "How could you have allowed this to happen?"

Hilda did not cringe from the fingers biting into her flesh but stood her ground. "You cannot hold me responsible for what has happened, Adam. I only followed your orders by weakening the tea. I had nothing to do with her decision to go to Gareth's bed."

"You realize this changes everything," Adam said through clenched teeth.

Yes, it changes things. Now I won't have to worry that you will leave my bed for hers, Hilda thought smugly. "Adam, I would not have told you what I saw if I had known that you would be so upset."

"Stupid woman," Adam said, stepping out of the shadows, "of course I am upset. All our plans could be ruined if the two of them become too close. We must keep them separated if we are to succeed."

Hilda shrugged. "That can easily be taken care of," Hilda replied calmly. "A few choice herbs in her tea and she will be in no condition to visit her husband again." Her thoughts turned to the herbs she would prefer to put in Rochella's tea. They would make her sleep forever.

Adam smiled down at Hilda. "I can always depend on you and your herbs, sweetings." Adam draped an arm about Hilda's shoulders and gave her a squeeze.

"I have only done what I feel is best for you. You are my life," Hilda said, wrapping her arms about Adam's lean waist and leaning her head against his chest. He would never know that she felt it best that his brother consummate his marriage.

"I know, but I fear we are going to have to move swiftly. Gareth is a normal man and he will not be able to stay away from his wife very long. She is far too tempting."

At the yearning she heard in Adam's voice, Hilda leaned back and looked up at him. "Are there other reasons why you want to keep your brother away from his wife?"

Adam's features hardened and lightning glimmered in his icy eyes. He set her away from him and turned toward the north wing. "Do not question me further. My reasons are my own."

"You cannot still want her after she has slept with your brother?" Hilda said, unable to control her wayward tongue.

Adam managed to suppress the urge to tell Hilda exactly what he did want; until his plans were complete, he needed her too much to antagonize her. "You should know by now that I would never take my brother's leavings."

Hilda relaxed. "Forgive me, Adam," she beseeched, hurrying to catch up with him. "I did not mean to anger you."

Adam raised a hand and stroked her cheek. A cunning smile touched his lips as he gazed down into her pale blue eyes. "My feelings for you have not changed, nor will they ever."

Wanting to believe that Adam loved her more than anyone else on earth, Hilda let his words soothe her worries. She would question him no more. He loved her and that was all that mattered.

Chapter Five

During the night the weather had cleared. The sun streaming through the windows and across her bed awoke Rochella. She blinked against the golden light filling her bedchamber with its warmth and dreamily stretched her arms over her head. A drowsy yawn escaped her as she curled on her side and snuggled lazily against her pillow. Groggily she took in the beauty of the day as her mind wandered to the dream she had had the previous night. Her cheeks warmed with a blush.

A mischievous little smile tugged up the corners of her mouth as she allowed her thoughts to linger on the man she had married. She doubted if Gareth would appreciate the dreams she had been having about him, and she wondered what he would think of her if he knew of them. From her observations, he was not the type of man who would care one way or the other about what she thought or dreamed. The previous evening on the stairs had been the first time he had even treated her as anything more than a tedious burden.

A small sigh escaped her lips. There was no need to dwell upon things that could not be changed. It could be much worse. Fortunately, Gareth had made no demands upon her person and she was grateful. She did

not know how she would have reacted had he expected
to share her bed.

Throwing back the covers, Rochella sat up, determined not to think of Babette's desertion or of her
husband's aloofness. It was a beautiful day and she
would not let anyone or anything ruin it for her. She was
going to enjoy every minute of it exploring the beach
below the cliffs. She had wanted to do so for some time
but had not been able to persuade Babette to go with
her. She hoped Alice would not be a frightened rabbit
as Babette had been.

She stood, paying no heed to the slight tenderness
between her legs, and cast a quick glance at her image
in the full-length mirror across the room. Her eyes
widened as she slowly allowed her gaze to pass down her
body. A puzzled frown knit her brow while she tried to
imagine how she could have gone to bed wearing her
nightrail, and awakened without it. Abruptly, she recalled her thoughts of a few moments earlier. The
memory of her dream created a blush that began at the
soles of her feet and moved slowly upward until she felt
as if her skin were on fire. Had what she thought a
dream actually taken place?

Rochella slapped a hand over her mouth to stifle her
groan and searched her reflection for any physical sign
of what had transpired. Visibly nothing had changed,
but within herself, she knew everything was different.

"My God! What have I done?" she agonized. Unable to look at herself a moment longer, she squeezed
her eyes closed. She had gone to her husband's bed,
uninvited. She would never be able to look Gareth in the
eye again.

A knock at the door jerked Rochella's thoughts away
from her unexplainable behavior. Wild-eyed, she

grabbed her robe and put it on before jumping back into bed and pulling the sheet up to her chin. She had to clear her throat several times before she could utter a strangled "You may come in."

Alice peeped around the door, her mop of curls framing her pixie face. Looking shyly at Rochella, she stammered, "My lady, Miss Bronson said I was to serve you."

"Yes." Rochella nodded briskly. "The first thing I want you to do is to prepare my bath."

A smile of pure happiness split Alice's freckled face. "Right away, my lady." She was gone before Rochella could blink an eye.

Before Rochella had time to sort things out, Alice was back with the hot water. "Do you need my assistance in bathing, my lady?" she asked, turning to Rochella when the last bucket had been poured into the large brass tub.

"No, Alice. I shall see to my own bath. But I should like you to take out my green riding habit. It will do well enough for a walk on the beach. I thought if you were not busy, you might like to accompany me. I do not know the area well enough to venture there alone."

"I'd be honored to go with you, Lady Devlin," Alice said, her blue eyes dancing with excitement. In all her days, she had never dreamed she would be allowed to serve the mistress of Devil Wind. Her family would be so proud of her when she told them. They had hoped that she would be able to better herself by coming to Devil Wind instead of staying to work in the tavern like the rest of her brothers and sisters. Her pa's tavern, Arthur's Dram, did a fair business with the locals, but there were just too many mouths to feed for what little it earned to go around.

Relieved that she would be able to escape Devil Wind for a little while, Rochella climbed from the bed and crossed to the steaming tub. Letting the robe slip to the floor, she gingerly tested the steaming water with the tip of her toes. Finding it hot but not unbearably so, she stepped into the tub. Ever so slowly she lowered herself until the water enveloped her to her neck, its heat turning her skin to a bright rose.

A good, hot bath would help ease her mind, as well as the tenderness between her legs. Rochella lay back and closed her eyes. Her expression grew taut as she sought an answer for her behavior of the previous night. It seemed all common sense had deserted her. Why else would she have gone to Gareth's room and seduced him when she had actually feared the thought of consummating their marriage? Until last eve, she had not even known what happened between a man and a woman in the wedding bed.

Questions raced through Rochella's mind, yet she found no answers. In truth, it all seemed like a dream. She would have continued to believe it a fantasy had she not awakened without her clothes and with a tender ache between her thighs. The last thing she remembered clearly was making an effort to avoid drinking Hilda's tea.

Suddenly her eyes flew open. There had to have been something in the tea. Recalling that Hilda had claimed she was only following orders, Rochella's eyes narrowed. What a fool I have been, she thought. My dear husband planned all of this from the beginning.

Rochella stood so rapidly that water splashed over the edge of the tub and onto the polished floorboards. She paid no heed to the mess, but wrapped the linen towel about her and stalked to the armoire. Ignoring Alice's startled expression as the girl scampered out of her path, she jerked down the first gown at hand and rapidly dressed herself.

Fuming, she ran her fingers through her tousled auburn mane and left the bedchamber without a thought for the bare toes peeping from beneath the hem of her gown. Her back straight, she marched down the corridor to Gareth's bedchamber. As she had the previous night, she entered without knocking, only to find a serving maid making the bed. "Where is Lord Devlin?" she demanded.

"Lord Devlin rode out early this morning, my lady," the maid explained, taking a step back. The angry light in Lady Devlin's eyes reminded her of the sea on a stormy day.

"Do you know where he has gone?" Rochella asked, her tone short.

The maid shook her head nervously. "No, my lady. I just saw him leave. He rode in the direction of the village."

Rochella released a long breath in disgust and returned to her chamber. Now she would have to wait until Gareth's return to give him a good set-down. If he thought she would stand meekly by and be drugged into doing his bidding, then he had better think again. His every whim might be granted by his servants but not by his wife.

"I won't wait," Rochella resolved, closing the door behind her, "I'll go to the village to find him. Alice, I have changed my mind. We shall go to the village today instead of the beach."

Alice quickly forgot her fear when Lady Devlin had stormed from the room, and her face now lit up with excitement. Maybe she could persuade Lady Devlin to stop at Arthur's Dram and have a cup of tea. If all went well, she would be able to show off her newfound glory to her family.

"Yes, my lady," Alice said, smiling. "Do you still want to wear your green riding habit?"

Rochella nodded, her mind already on what she would say to her husband when she found him.

Haggard-eyed from lack of sleep, Gareth reined his lathered mount to a halt and slid to the ground. Without a glance at the animal, he began to walk, hoping the exercise would do for him what his wild ride across the moors had not. Since carrying Rochella back to her bed, he had suffered the torments of hell.

He paused and looked out at the horizon. Before his eyes the sun-dappled waters of the Atlantic shimmered like diamond-studded silk, and his insides twisted with longing. He felt a deep yearning to turn his back on his name and all the burdens that went with it. His expression hardened and he clenched his jaw against the raw emotion ripping through him. Would he always have to remain a shadow, viewing life from the distance while others experienced it to the full?

Gareth sobered and shook his head. No. He would not be given a chance to find happiness. His ancestor had ensured Gareth's future when he had turned his back on his own flesh and blood and his bastard twins had starved to death from his neglect. How wise their mother the witch had been when she had placed her curse upon the Devlin family. She had known that dying would have been far easier than living under the shadow of madness as generations of Devlins had done. Her children had suffered for a short time, but she had ensured that her lover's family would suffer forever.

Releasing a long breath Gareth turned his back to the sea. No matter what he felt for his beautiful wife, no matter how much passion she stirred to life within him, he could not allow himself to succumb to his needs again. The wind whipped his hair free of the ribbon holding the curly strands in a queue at the nape of his neck and it webbed his features as he turned his haunted eyes toward the moors. At that moment the tract of rolling wasteland reminded him of his own barren soul.

Her temper rapidly fading under the noonday sun, Rochella rode silently along the cliff road toward the village. She was beginning to suspect that she was being unreasonable in not waiting for her husband to return to Devil Wind before she told him what she thought. She might be making a bigger fool of herself than she had done upon their first meeting, when she had accused him of lying and had had to apologize for her rash behavior. Now, as her ire cooled, she wondered if she had not misjudged him again. She frowned as her thoughts wandered back over the time she had spent in her husband's company. She had never once felt he had designs upon her virtue. She had no proof the tea had been drugged or that she had been the one to go to his bedchamber. Once again remembering the previous night, she muttered to herself, "What have I done? I have only made things worse between us."

"Did you say something, my lady?" Alice asked, her voice squeaky from the fear of falling off the horse and breaking her neck. White-faced, she clutched the saddle pommel with such force her fingers tingled from lack of circulation.

"I said I've changed my mind about visiting the village today," Rochella replied. "If we turn back now, we should still have time to explore the beach."

"But my lady, I thought we would take tea at Arthur's Dram. My ma and pa would be so proud to know I have been allowed to become your personal maid."

"Oh, all right," Rochella said, watching Alice's face spread into a wide grin. At least going to Arthur's Dram would make Alice happy.

In less than an hour, Rochella found herself ensconced at a hurriedly wiped table with a cup of steaming tea and a plate of sweet biscuits before her. Alice jabbered excitedly, introducing Rochella to her entire family before leaving her to drink her tea in peace.

Amused by Alice's exuberance, Rochella allowed her gaze to wander over what had once been the girl's home. She could well understand Alice's pride in having achieved her position at Devil Wind. The tavern was little more than a hovel filled with rough-hewn tables, and the evening sun spilled into the smoky room through cracks in the walls.

The tavern's only customers seemed too involved in their own conversation to notice Rochella, but her attention was drawn to one of the men at the corner table when he raised his voice and shouted at his companion.

"Damn it, Harry. I said I heard all hell's breaking loose over there. They be killing folks east and west. I heard tell King Louis hisself will shortly be led down the path to Madame Guillotine."

"Ye don't have to shout at me, Ben," the man called Harry shouted back. "I can hear all right."

"You're as deaf as a bat," Ben muttered, his voice still loud enough for Rochella to hear.

"What did you say?" Harry asked, raising a hand to cup his ear.

The first man shook his head. "Harry, I wish ye'd bring along yer horn. Everybody gets tired of hearing me holler at you."

"Yer right, Ben. Any of them with a bit of aristocratic blood in their veins are the ones paying the price. Ol' George himself is taking a closer look at what's going on. Him and all the nobs are worried the same thing could happen here."

The man called Ben ran a hand through his thinning gray hair in exasperation. It was much easier just to carry on the conversation and hope his friend caught most of it. "They're sending 'em to the guillotine quicker than a fishwife can gut a mackerel."

Rochella paled as she realized the two men were talking about France. She attempted to drink her tea, but her hand trembled so violently the steaming liquid spilled over the rim of her cup onto the table. White-lipped, she clutched the cup between both hands and tried to understand everything she had just heard. From what the two men had said, France was in a state of revolution.

Rochella squeezed her eyes tightly closed and sent a silent prayer heavenward asking that she be mistaken in her assessment of the men's conversation.

"Rochella," a familiar voice said at her side. "What are you doing here?"

Rochella jumped with a start, her eyes flying open to stare up at her husband. She had been so caught up in her reveries that she had not heard his approach.

"Did you know of the troubles in France when you agreed to marry me?" she asked, ignoring Gareth's question.

His expression grew guarded. "What are you talking about?"

"Do not play any more games with me! I am not a child to be protected."

Gareth drew in a deep breath and took Rochella by the arm. "Come. It is time we returned to Devil Wind."

Rochella jerked her arm free of his hand. "I am not going anywhere until I know the truth. My father knew there was danger for me if I remained at Beauvais, and that is why he chose you to wed me. He wanted to ensure my safety. Is not that right?"

Gareth glanced around the smoky room. "This is no place to discuss this matter. Now come back to Devil Wind and we shall talk."

"Do you expect me to believe you will now tell me the truth, when all you have done since we met is lie? How could you be so cruel? My parents may now be in danger if what I have heard is true," Rochella said, feeling suddenly betrayed by this man to whom she had given far more than her body. Until this moment she had not realized that he had touched her more deeply than she would ever have imagined. Forcing the thought away she eyed Gareth hostilely, and sought to ignore the gentle ache forming about her heart.

Gareth reached out and grasped Rochella's arm once more. Forcing her ahead of him, he maneuvered her out of Arthur's Dram to where her mount was tethered. He made no excuses for his overbearing manner, but merely lifted her into the saddle and handed her the reins. Mounting his horse, he urged the beast alongside of

Rochella's and waited until she turned the filly in the direction of home.

A hostile silence remained between them until they were behind the closed doors of Gareth's study. Then Rochella's fury burst free.

"How dare you treat me as if I were a child? Neither of us wanted this marriage, but since it has come to pass, I will have your respect in public."

"You will have my hand against your backside if you do not stop acting the child and sit down so that we can discuss what you overheard this afternoon," Gareth growled, his ire rising at her demands. He pointed to the chair in front of his desk. "Now sit!"

Everything within her rebelled at his order, but common sense reigned. Rochella sank into the seat, her expression mutinous.

Satisfied, Gareth settled his lean frame into the chair behind his desk. "I know you are upset over learning what has been taking place in France, but there is nothing you or anyone can do about it."

Unappeased, Rochella glowered at her husband. "Everyone has conspired to keep me ignorant of the trouble in my homeland, have they not?"

Gareth nodded. There was no reason now to lie. The marquis had known this time would come eventually. "It was your father's wish that you be kept unaware of the madness that has seized France."

"But I had a right to know," Rochella ground out between clenched teeth. How dared anyone make the decision for her?

"I agree, but it was not my decision, it was your father's," Gareth said.

The hard edge to Rochella's voice faded. "I understand his reasoning but it does not make it right."

"No. It does not make it right, but it is too late to change anything. You are now Lady Devlin, and your home is here."

Rochella came to her feet. "I must return to France immediately."

"It is out of the question," Gareth said, his voice firm.

"But my parents may be in danger." Tears of worry glistened in Rochella's eyes.

"As I have said, there is nothing you or anyone else can do now in France."

"But I must try. I cannot remain here and let them be killed. The men said no aristocrat was safe from the guillotine."

"You would only endanger yourself if you returned to France, and for that reason you will remain here. Your father wanted you protected and I have given him my word that no harm will come to you."

Rochella moved around the desk to stand before her husband. Her eyes pleaded with him as she slowly sank to the floor at his feet. Taking his hand, she looked up into his twilight eyes and begged, "Please, Gareth, take me to France."

His proud Rochella humbling herself before him twisted Gareth's insides. His heart urged him to give way to her request, but reason managed to supersede his emotions. For her sake, he could not give in. It would mean her life. Gareth cleared his throat and determinedly shook his head. "I am sorry, Rochella. But you must remain at Devil Wind."

Rochella's shoulders slumped and she bowed her head. Her chestnut curls fell about her face, obscuring it from Gareth's view. When she spoke, he had to lean close to hear her strained whisper. "I hate you, Gareth

Devlin, and you will not stop me from returning to France.''

Her words were like a blade rending his heart asunder, but Gareth forced himself to laugh. ''I do not doubt your word, my lady. Now, I suggest you retire to your chamber and reconsider such a rash move. You have had a trying day and I am sure that your exhaustion is coloring your reason.''

Slowly Rochella got to her feet. The look she flashed at Gareth before she turned away was icy with contempt. She left the study without a word for there was nothing left to say.

Gareth watched his young wife go, unable to say or do anything to ease her feelings. He understood her reaction to his denial to help her. Had a member of his family been in the same kind of danger as Rochella's parents, he would have moved heaven and hell in an effort to save them.

Running his fingers through his dark curls, Gareth sank back into the heavily cushioned chair. His expression was grim as he reached for the quill pen and dipped it into the inkwell. He would write to the king's chamberlain and ask for assistance in helping the marquis and his wife to flee France before it was too late. According to the reports filtering out of France, the unrest had now spread to the provinces and no one was safe from the tribunal.

Rochella paced her chamber like a caged animal, silently damning the man who had refused to take her to France. She would not allow herself to consider that he was only trying to protect her. Pursing her lips and narrowing her eyes, she turned and stared at her reflection in the dressing table mirror.

"You will not stop me from helping my parents, Gareth Devlin," she vowed. "With or without your help I shall return to Beauvais."

Her resolve glowing in her eyes, Rochella seated herself at the dressing table and picked up the tortoiseshell brush. As she raised it to her thick hair, a knock sounded at the door. A moment later Alice peeped into the room, her face pale with worry.

"Oh, my lady, can you ever forgive me? I should not have left you unattended so Lord Devlin would have to escort you home. Lord Devlin has every right to dismiss me for such behavior."

Rochella blinked up at the girl, her mind still filled with thoughts of her family and Gareth. "You will not be dismissed, Alice. Should Lord Devlin inquire about the reason I was alone when he arrived at the tavern, I shall explain that you were visiting your sisters and brothers."

"Oh, my lady, I'd be ever so grateful. I'd hate to lose my position here. Even with Pa making a profit from the wine the men bring over from France, there's little enough to go round as it is."

Her interest sparked at the mention of her homeland, Rochella asked, "What do you mean, Alice? Are you saying your family is involved with smugglers?"

The girl slapped a hand over her mouth and swallowed with difficulty. She had said far too much for her own safety.

"Alice, I asked you a question. Is your family involved with smugglers?" Rochella said again, swinging around to face the frightened maid.

Alice gulped and sank to her knees before Rochella. Her voice trembled as she begged, "My lady, please don't ever let on I said anything."

Rochella stood and pulled Alice to her feet. "You do not have to worry. It will be our secret."

Alice breathed a sigh of relief and gave her mistress a wobbly smile. "I be ever so grateful, my lady."

Rochella gently patted Alice's work-roughened hand. "Now, run along. I need to rest."

As the maid scampered from the room, Rochella turned back to the mirror and gazed at her reflection, smiling triumphantly. "Thanks to Alice, I may have found a way to return to France without my husband's help."

Chapter Six

Unable to sleep, Rochella stood watching the full moon creep over the horizon. The porcelain clock on the mantel ticked off the minutes as the moon inched its way across the indigo sky and shimmered upon the waves beyond the cliffs. Her thoughts, however, were not upon the beauty of the night, but upon her life at Devil Wind.

Two weeks had passed since her confrontation with her husband and there had been no further incidents between them. They lived as strangers, rarely speaking or taking meals together; when they were forced to endure each other's company, the strained silence between them was as icy as a winter's morn.

Though Hilda had made her disapproval quite clear, Rochella had assumed the role of mistress of Devil Wind. Ignoring the housekeeper, she went on about her duties as if nothing were out of the ordinary. Acting as chatelaine of Devil Wind occupied her days and satisfied her husband that she had accepted his feelings about her wanting to return to Beauvais.

A sigh escaped her lips now as she leaned her head against the cool stone of the window facing. She had never actually caught her husband watching her, but she sensed his eyes upon her as she went about her duties. She also suspected he had instructed the servants to watch her when she ventured from the castle, because there was always someone close at hand should she need anything.

Frowning, she drew her light robe closer about her shoulders. Spring had slipped quietly into summer and it seemed as if the right moment to flee her black granite prison would never arrive. She lived each day with the same hope but nothing ever changed. She had found no opportunity to seek out the smugglers and ask for their aid in returning to France, and she was beginning to believe she never would, without involving Alice. Rochella's frown deepened. She was hesitant to put the girl in such an untenable situation, but if something did not happen soon she would have no choice. She could not think only of Alice when her parents' lives might be in jeopardy.

Rochella's pensive expression reflected the turmoil of her thoughts as she glanced toward the tall four-poster bed. Her days were uneventful, but she wished she could say the same for the nights. Since the night she had brazenly seduced her husband, she had refused to drink the tea that Hilda brought her, afraid of its effects on her. She was not sleeping well, and when Morpheus finally did claim her after hours of tossing and turning, her dreams were filled with the man she had sworn to hate.

Her dreams had also begun to affect her during her waking hours. She had found herself watching Gareth at times when he didn't realize he was being observed. Each evening when he took a stroll outside, she would make some excuse to be in the small salon overlooking the gardens. There she would sit in the window seat and watch him as he walked among the roses and then along the path to the cliffs, where he turned his handsome face into the wind, staring at the distant horizon. At those times she couldn't take her eyes off his features. Standing alone on the weather-beaten cliffs, unaware she was observing him, he would lower the barriers that shielded him from the world, allowing her a glimpse of a man who carried a heavy burden. A man whom she could love if things had been different between them.

She could not stop herself from recalling the one night she had spent in his arms. Yet, since Gareth's refusal to help her, she had avoided his company as if he had contracted plague. Now Alice was her only companion, and she found herself fretting over her need to return to France.

"I can wait no longer to set my plan into action," she said aloud to the darkened room. "Tomorrow I shall ask Alice to help me."

Her resolution made, Rochella relaxed. Soon this ordeal would be behind her and she would be with her parents at Beauvais. Turning away from the window, she crossed the chamber to her bed. She let her robe slip off her shoulders and draped it across the back of the delicately wrought Louis XIV chair before climbing into the high four-poster. Hiding a yawn behind her hand, she drew up the sheet and snuggled down into the soft mattress.

She closed her eyes and within moments she slept.

A howl of rage echoed through the north wing and down the corridors. A table crashed against the wall and another howl reverberated throughout the chamber.

"Adam, calm yourself," Gareth ordered, every muscle in his powerful body taut with tension. "You're disturbing the household." His brother's fit was worse than any he had ever witnessed, and he feared if he didn't manage to calm Adam down, he would hurt himself with his violence.

"That is all you care about, isn't it? You don't want anyone to know about your mad brother, do you, Gareth?"

"It is past midnight, Adam, and there are those of us who prefer to sleep at night," Gareth said, his annoyance mounting. After the previous two weeks spent denying himself the pleasures of his beautiful wife, his nerves were on edge and he was in no mood to placate his brother.

"Yes, I know you, Gareth. You would prefer to walk the halls of Devil Wind as the great master who was not touched by the taint of Devlin madness. You don't want to shock your new wife when she learns about us, do you? Nor do you want to see her scorn. You prefer things as they are—keeping me locked away up here out of sight and out of mind."

"That's enough, Adam," Gareth said, his tone reflecting his exasperation. "You know why your chambers are in the north wing. It's quieter here so that you may get the rest you require to calm your nerves."

"True, brother. It is so quiet here that only the servants you have bribed to keep silent about me know you have your own twin locked away. Are you afraid I might claim something you consider yours? Isn't that why you keep me locked away, Gareth? But you know as well as I, you have nothing to fear from me. I've known since we were mere babes that I was second."

"God, Adam. Why do you do this to us? We are brothers but you make us seem like enemies," Gareth said, his voice mirroring the anguish inflicted by his brother's remarks.

"Are we not enemies, Gareth? Are you not the arch-angel who can do no wrong, and I his opposite—Satan? You hold the grand title of Lord Devlin, while I am cast aside in the north wing."

"Surely you cannot believe what you say," Gareth replied.

"And why shouldn't I believe it? I am the one cursed. I am the one who has nothing, not you," Adam said through clenched teeth.

Gareth released a weary breath, once more feeling beaten. "Adam, you are my brother and I love you."

"And I love you," Adam said, his sharp tone as well as his dark gaze holding no warmth for his brother.

"Then that is all that matters between us."

"Yes, it is all that matters," Adam said coldly, turning his back to his brother. "Now I wish to be alone."

"Then I shall bid you good-night, brother," Gareth said, defeated once more by Adam's madness.

When the door closed behind Gareth, a contemptuous smile curled the corners of Adam's lips. He threw back his head and let out a howl of delight. The sound echoed eerily through Devil Wind's night-shadowed corridors and joined the howl of the wind in the turrets.

Rochella bolted upright in her bed. Cold sweat beading her brow and upper lip, she searched the shadows of her room, wondering what had jolted her awake. A moment later she knew, as an eerie, haunting sound like a human scream rose above the moaning wind. Gooseflesh pricked her arms and she shivered as she gripped the sheet to her breasts. Fear rippled through her as

Babette's stories of seeing ghoulish specters came rushing back.

"You are being silly," she chided herself after a long, tense moment of listening to her heartbeat pound in her ears. Resolutely, she lifted her chin, tossed back the sheet and slid her feet to the floor. Reaching for the flint on the bedside table, she lit the candle. Its mellow light illuminated her bed as she stood and slipped on her robe. She would prove to herself there were no ghostly specters walking the halls of Devil Wind. She closed her hand over the latch and swung open the door.

A croak of fright escaped Rochella's lips and she took a step backward. The room swayed before her eyes, and she reached for support as she slowly sank toward the floor. The figure standing in the shadows reached for her, catching her and drawing her into his arms before she fell.

"Rochella, are you all right?" Gareth asked, carrying her the short distance to her bed. He laid her down, her head against the pillow, and bent anxiously over her. Tiny lines of concern etched his face.

Ensconced safely on her bed, Rochella nodded and felt a blush warm her cheeks. Looking up at Gareth, she wondered why it was always her misfortune to make a fool out of herself in front of him.

"Thank you, I am fine," she murmured at last. "You just startled me. I was not expecting to find anyone at my door." Rochella brushed a stray curl from her brow with a shaky hand and pushed herself upright against the pillows.

Unable to stop himself, Gareth gently stroked the curve of her cheek. "Are you sure?"

"Yes, of course," Rochella said, gazing up into his eyes. She felt her pulse quicken at the heat she saw flare in their depths.

"I did not mean to frighten you. I thought I heard you moving about and was concerned," Gareth lied. He had come to her chamber to make sure she had not been awakened by Adam's screams. "Would you like me to have Hilda bring you another cup of tea?"

Lost in the trance of his penetrating gaze, Rochella slowly shook her head.

All thoughts of Adam vanished under the spell of her allure, and Gareth sank down on the side of the bed. He had not meant to enter her bedchamber but all his good intentions had evaporated the moment he had taken her into his arms to prevent her fall. Now he could not resist curling a long copper strand of her hair about one finger and using it like a rein to draw her toward him as he quietly murmured, "Rochella, you are the most beautiful woman I have ever seen."

His husky voice, combined with the look in his eyes made excitement throb through Rochella. Her blood turned to wildfire in her veins, making it impossible for her to deny the lips descending toward hers. When they claimed her mouth in a fiery kiss, she gave herself up to the sensations it created within her. Though inexperienced in the ways of love, she felt a tender urgency in his kiss, a sense of desperation she did not truly understand, and she knew instinctively it was in her power to give him comfort. She wrapped her arms about his neck and drew him down to her. She had seen his agony in the twilight of the day, and she knew he was still tormented in the dark hours of the night.

A shudder passed through Gareth as his heart cried out for succor from his painful daily existence. A moan of something akin to despair escaped him as he surrendered to his need to feel himself buried deep within Rochella's resilient warmth. Tonight he needed to pretend there was a future that was not as bleak as the barren cliffs overlooking the angry sea. He needed to feel alive and he needed the illusion of a normal life with the beautiful woman in his arms loving him as he craved to be loved.

"My darling Rochella. Let me love you," Gareth murmured against the softness of her throat, lightly placing tantalizing kisses along its slender column down to the curve of her shoulder. His lips followed his fingers as he eased down her robe and nightrail to expose the firm mounds of her breasts. A moan of pure pleasure escaped him as he buried his face between them and drew in her heady fragrance. For a long moment he lay savoring the sound of her heartbeat before his need to taste the small rose-tipped crests grew too strong to resist. Claiming the sweet bounty, he suckled the taut nipple, circling it with his tongue, lavishing it with attention until he felt Rochella arch against him.

Craving to know and feel all of her, he moved to the next tantalizing peak as he glided a long-fingered hand down her flat abdomen to the apex of her thighs. He stroked her there, enticing her with his caresses until he felt her muscles quiver in response and she opened her legs to allow him access to the passion-honeyed glen he sought.

Rochella arched back against the pillows and allowed him to work his magic upon her. All thoughts of leaving Devil Wind vanished under his assault. At that moment, all that mattered were the intoxicating waves of passion created by his caresses. They washed over her, engulfed her, flowing through her body with a current that made her senses reel. Tearing away his dressing gown, she stroked Gareth's resilient flesh, savoring the satiny feel of his bare skin beneath her hands. Her breaths shortened as her pleasure mounted, and she clung to him, calling his name, begging him to quench the burning need he had created.

Unable to deny himself or her any longer, Gareth covered her with his sinewy body. Capturing her mouth once more, he plunged into her warmth, driving deep as she wrapped her legs about his waist, taking him into the depths that had known no other man.

Spiraling on a whirlwind of passion, they traversed the boundaries of the universe. Shivers of ecstasy passed over them as they touched distant stars before gently floating back to earth, their bodies dewed in liquid diamonds that shimmered in the pale moonlight. Unwilling to break the enchantment, they lay for a long while with limbs entwined.

As the glow of their lovemaking began to dissipate, however, they could not keep their thoughts at bay.

Gareth eased himself from Rochella's embrace and sat up on the side of the bed. Without looking at her he jerked on his dressing gown, releasing a weary, resigned breath.

"I am sorry, Rochella. I did not mean to allow this to happen again."

"You need not apologize, Gareth," Rochella said, her voice a hoarse whisper of pent-up emotion. His apology stung her to the quick and left her uncertain that he had shared the same pleasure she had received from their joining. She quickly drew the sheet up to cover herself.

Guilt-stricken by his lack of self-control, Gareth turned haunted eyes upon her. "Yes, there is a need to apologize. I am responsible for allowing things to come to this pass, and I accept the fact. I promise it will never happen again.''

Rochella blinked rapidly to stay the sudden rush of tears that burned her eyes. Her pride would not allow her to let him see the devastation his words created. Twice she had given herself to this man, and twice she had been shamed. Struggling for composure, she drew in a steadying breath and raised her chin belligerently. ''I agree. It will never happen again. Now if you will be so kind as to leave, I shall try to get some sleep. It is nearing dawn.''

Gareth pushed himself to his feet and stood for a long moment regarding the pain in his wife's eyes. He knew he could not leave things as they were at that moment, or they would never be able to live amicably under the same roof.

Turning, he strode to the window and gazed out into the moon-silvered night. For seemingly the millionth time, he wished it were in his power to change things. Drawing in a long breath of the cool night air, he turned back to her. ''Rochella,'' he said quietly, ''we need to talk.''

''I think everything has been said,'' Rochella answered stiffly.

''No. It has not. There is much more we need to clear up between us. Though neither of us wanted this marriage, we are man and wife and we must come to terms with that fact, as well as with each other and with our actions.''

Rochella blushed and looked away from his penetrating gaze. ''I have done my best to come to terms with our marriage. I have accepted my role as the mistress of Devil Wind.''

"And from what I have seen you have done a splendid job, but you know as well as I that is not what I am talking about."

"Then what are you talking about, Gareth?"

Gareth ran a hand through his tousled hair. What could he say? He could not tell her the truth. The thought of seeing her lovely face fill with disgust when she learned of the family curse and Adam was agony in itself.

"Since we are in agreement that I should not share your bed again, you must understand some things. I am a man with a man's desires, Rochella. There will be times in the future when I shall need to appease those desires. And to do so, I shall seek out another's company," Gareth said without emotion. He knew of no other way to give Rochella a chance to reject him and save her own pride.

Rochella winced as if struck, and the color drained from her face. In no uncertain terms Gareth had made it clear how he felt about her. Tonight he had needed a vessel in which to release his lust and nothing more. Struggling to control the painful emotions tearing at her insides, she looked at her husband, her eyes glistening with unshed tears. "If you are seeking my permission to take a mistress, then you have it, sir."

"Then the matter is settled," Gareth said coolly. Her quick acceptance stung. "However, there is one more thing. I want peace between us, Rochella. It does neither of us any good to be enemies. Can we not end the hostility and live amicably together?"

"I see no reason why not," Rochella said, nearly choking on the words. At the moment, she wanted nothing more than to tear out his eyes. However, she would not give him the satisfaction of misconstruing such a gesture as jealousy.

"I am glad we have managed to come to terms. Now I shall leave you to your rest," Gareth said.

Rochella watched the door close behind her husband and wondered why she had ever imagined she could love a man like Gareth Devlin.

"But I will never make that mistake again," she vowed bravely, her throat clogging with emotion. Swinging her feet to the floor, she stood and picked up her nightrail. She tugged it on over her head and then turned and strode to the window.

A haunted look crossed her lovely face as she stared out into the moon-drenched night. She would not cry. Gareth Devlin meant nothing to her. But even as the thought came, great crystal droplets brimmed on her dark lashes and trickled slowly down her cheeks.

"I want to go home," Rochella whispered brokenly. She longed to feel the comforting arms of her parents. They would know how to soothe her hurt and ease the turmoil tearing at her heart.

At the thought, Rochella raised her head and drew in a steadying breath. Tonight had made it even more imperative for her to leave Devil Wind. Even if her parents had not been in danger, she could not now remain as Gareth's wife. She would never be able to act as if she did not care that he preferred another woman's bed to hers.

The hesitation she had felt about involving Alice in her plans was gone. Tomorrow, they would take a picnic lunch to the beach, and while there she would make the girl tell her everything she knew about the smugglers.

* * *

Rochella awoke feeling refreshed. Stretching languidly, she lay back against the satin pillows and mulled over her plans for the day. If all went well, before night she would have the information she needed to find someone to help her return to France.

A light rap at the door pulled her from her reveries, and she looked up. The door opened to reveal Alice, precariously balancing her breakfast tray.

"Good morning, my lady. I hope you slept well," the maid said. Approaching the bed, she placed the tray containing pastry and tea across Rochella's lap.

Rochella smiled. "It's a beautiful morning, Alice. Far too fine to be cooped up inside. Shall we have Cook prepare us a basket of food, and lunch down on the beach?"

Alice's freckled face lit with excitement. "Oh, my lady, it sounds wonderful. I love the beach, but I seldom have the time to go there."

"Well, today we shall make the time. Now hurry and prepare my bath so we can be on our way," Rochella said, breaking the flaky fruit-filled pasty into small bites.

Without hesitation Alice sprinted out the door, eager to finish her chores. Before Rochella managed to consume half her breakfast, she was back with the bathwater. "Will my lady wear her blue riding habit today or should I lay out the green?"

"Lay out the blue today, Alice," Rochella said, unable to eat any more. Setting the tray on the bedside table, she slid her feet to the floor. She was just as eager as the maid to be away from Devil Wind. She hoped that after their outing today she would soon be away from it forever.

* * *

Rochella met Alice in the garden, and from there they made their way to the cliffs. They paused at the top of the narrow path that had been cut out of the black granite by time and the elements, and Rochella shivered as she gazed down at the golden beach below. Bracing herself, and watching where she placed each foot, she followed Alice along the path.

When they were safely down, Rochella glanced up at the high, black granite cliffs overhead. Peering up in the same direction, Alice sensed her mistress's train of thought. "It's a ways to fall, my lady."

As she brushed away the loose curls the sea breeze had whipped into her face, Rochella glanced at her companion. "Yes, Alice. I should hate to lose my footing and plunge onto the jagged rocks."

"There are many who have done it, if the stories are to be believed," Alice said, and turned to walk down the sandy beach.

After choosing a place in the shade to spread their blanket, the two young women spent the remainder of the morning enjoying the small wondrous gifts washed ashore by the sea. They collected beautiful colored seashells and pieces of twisted driftwood that had been bleached white by the saltwater and sun, and marveled at the tiny sea creatures that abounded in the tide pools between the jagged granite slabs.

At noon, tired and hungry, they decided it was time to lunch. Their exercise had made them ravenous, and they dipped eagerly into the basket to see what delicious morsels the cook had prepared for them to eat. Settling back on the blanket, they devoured the golden-brown capon legs, hard cheese and meat pasties and washed it all down with a sweet French burgundy from

Gareth's cellars. Finally, relaxed and replete, they watched the gentle waves lapping at the beach.

Braced on one elbow, Rochella squinted up at the bright blue sky, watching the free flight of a gull. The time for play was over. Glancing at her companion, she asked, "Is this where your smugglers land with their goods, Alice?"

Alice paled and nervously glanced about. "Oh, my lady, we mustn't talk about them. It's too dangerous."

"There is no one here to hear us," Rochella assured her with a wave of her hand that encompassed the vacant beach. "And I find the thought of smugglers intriguing. Do you know them, Alice?"

Sitting up, Alice folded her hands in her lap. She liked Lady Devlin but was afraid to answer her questions. The smugglers weren't naturally bad men—most were just common, everyday fishermen who had hit upon hard times—but they could become dangerous if anyone threatened their livelihood. They had to make sure that no one reported them to the revenuers, and if silencing someone to prevent it was their only choice, they would do it. Lowering her eyes to her hands, she said, "My lady, it's best you do not know."

Realizing it was not going to be easy to get Alice to confide in her, Rochella knew she had to make the girl understand she meant her friends no harm. "Alice, you do not have to be afraid. I shall keep your secret."

Alice looked at Rochella, her eyes filled with uncertainty. "I don't mean to be disrespectful, but my lady, if I told you, they might harm you."

"You may trust me, Alice. You are the only friend I have left now at Devil Wind, and I would not place you in jeopardy by speaking of it."

A timid smile touched Alice's lips. Lady Devlin considered her a friend. She could ask for no greater reward for her service. Casting a furtive glance about the beach, she slid across the blanket to Rochella's side. Her head bent close, she whispered anxiously, "Then it's a secret between us?"

Rochella raised a hand and placed it over her heart. "Our secret, Alice. On my word of honor."

"Then I'll tell you" was Alice's conspiratorial reply.

She glanced once more about them to ensure their privacy before she said in a low voice that Rochella had to strain to hear, "I know the smugglers. My sister Bets is courtin' one of them. They come to my father's tavern to drink and make their plans. Pa helps them by keeping his ears open about the revenuers. The extra money helps to feed the family."

Rochella's face glowed with excitement. "Are they evil men?"

Alice shook her head. "Nay, most be just ordinary fishermen, but if they're crossed they can get mean. It's a hanging offense if yer caught smuggling, my lady."

Rochella momentarily found herself assailed with guilt at her duplicity in using Alice's knowledge of the smugglers to gain her own ends. The girl had placed her trust as well as her life in Rochella's hands by revealing such secrets about her own people. Yet if she wanted to return to France, Alice was her only means to achieve her goal.

"How often do they go to France, Alice?" Rochella asked.

"'Twill be soon now," Alice replied, glancing out at the blue waters. "The weather has cleared enough for them to make a run. They go on moonless nights to avoid the revenuers."

"Will you introduce me to your friends, Alice?"

The maid grew pale, her freckles standing out like tiny drops of cinnamon against the whiteness of her skin. She shook her head adamantly. "Nay, my lady. It would be too dangerous for all concerned."

Rochella clasped Alice's trembling hand and patted it reassuringly. "Alice, don't be afraid. I shall never betray your confidence. You have trusted me with your secrets and now I shall do the same. But you must never repeat what I am about to tell you. Do I have your word that no matter what happens after today, you will never tell anyone of what I tell you here?"

Alice nodded. "My lady, I give you my promise I'll never utter a word of what you say."

"I thought as much," Rochella said, smiling. "Now I am going to tell you the story of how I came to Devil Wind and the reason I now must meet your friends."

Rochella began her tale in France and brought it up to the previous night, leaving out only her involvement with her husband. How could she explain what had transpired between them when she did not completely understand it herself? As she finished her story, she drew in a ragged breath and looked at Alice through glistening eyes. "Now do you see why I must meet your friends?"

Alice nodded solemnly. "Aye, my lady. But it would seem to me Lord Devlin should be the one to take you to France."

Rochella let out a loud sigh of exasperation. "Alice, you have not heard a word I have said. He will not take me. He believes it is for the best for me to remain at Devil Wind safe and sound while my parents' lives are in danger. If you were in my place, could you stay away?'' Seeing Alice's cheeks flush with guilty color, Rochella continued. ''I did not think so.''

Alice lowered her lashes over her blue eyes and nodded. ''I understand, my lady. And I'll help you. I have a day free tomorrow. I usually go home to help my ma and pa at the inn. I will talk with Bets and see if her beau will meet you.'' Alice raised troubled eyes to Rochella. ''But if he refuses, I can do no more.''

''Thank you, Alice, for being my friend,'' Rochella said, her voice filling with emotion, her eyes bright with tears. ''I shall never be able to repay you.''

Alice's face brightened and she grinned sheepishly at her mistress. ''You've already given me the honor of your friendship, my lady. I need nothing else.''

Pushing herself to her feet, Alice glanced toward the sea and began to repack the picnic basket. ''My lady, it's getting late. We must start back or be caught down here by the incoming tide.''

''Then let us hurry. I cannot swim,'' Rochella said, bending to help Alice fold the sandy blanket.

By the time the two young women made their way back up the steep path to the cliff's summit, the beach was already narrowing. For a long thoughtful moment Rochella stood gazing down at the golden strand.

Chapter Seven

Rising from her chair for what seemed like the hundredth time, Rochella crossed to the windows and looked out for any sign of Alice's return. She wondered again how things were going at Arthur's Dram. She prayed Alice would be successful in convincing the smugglers to meet with her. If the girl failed, there would be little chance of finding another way to France in the near future. Gareth had made his feelings clear on the matter, and she would receive no help from those who served him.

Seeing no sign of the maid, Rochella retraced her steps and slumped into the chair. Resting her chin on her fist, she stared moodily into the fire and listened to the clock ticking off the minutes.

Finally, the knock she had come to recognize as Alice's sounded at the door, and the girl peeped inside, a mischievous grin dimpling her rosy cheeks. Casting a glance about to ensure their privacy, she quickly slipped into the room and closed the door securely behind her.

"Did you see them?" Rochella asked anxiously, coming to her feet.

"Aye, my lady. I spoke with Bets's beau. You are to come with me the next time I go home. Then you'll meet him and if he approves of you, he's agreed to help you reach France."

Rochella threw her arms about Alice's neck, hugging her exuberantly. "Just think, Alice. One more week and I shall be free."

Alice nodded, swallowing against the sudden constriction in her throat at the thought of her mistress going on such a dangerous journey. She had helped fulfill Lady Devlin's request, but she feared that in doing so, she had sentenced her to death. She had heard about the goings-on in France, and it didn't sound like a good place to be if you were a lady like her mistress.

Sensing Alice's troubled thoughts, Rochella asked, "What is wrong, Alice?"

Tears of misery brimmed in the young maid's eyes. "My lady, I be so worried about you going off over there when there's so much trouble. I couldn't live with myself if something happened to you."

"Alice, France is my homeland. Nothing will harm me there. I appreciate your concern but you have nothing to fear for me."

"But you'll be alone, mistress."

"It cannot be helped. I must return to France."

"Then let me go with you," Alice pleaded. "I'd not be in your way or give you any trouble."

Rochella shook her head. "I am sorry, Alice. I cannot allow you to come."

"Then you must ask Bets's beau to find someone to escort you to your home. You can't go alone."

Surprised she had not thought of such a plan herself, Rochella nodded. "It would solve many of my problems."

Alice smiled her relief. "I'm sure he'll find someone if you have the money to pay him."

Rochella frowned thoughtfully. She had failed to consider the matter of money. If the smugglers agreed to help her, they would expect to be paid handsomely.

"Do you think they will take my jewels in payment?"

Alice slowly shook her head. "They will want gold, my lady."

"But I do not have any money."

"My lady, you're in charge of the funds for the household accounts."

Rochella gave a sad shake of her head. "I have already paid this month's receipts, and until the end of the month there is little remaining in the chest."

"I'm sorry, my lady," Alice sympathized. Without the coin to grease the smugglers' palms, Lady Devlin would never reach France.

"Surely Gareth keeps money at Devil Wind," Rochella mused aloud, her face brightening with the thought. Yes. Her husband would keep a strongbox. If she could find it, all her problems would be solved. Gareth had received a fortune in gold from her father when they married, and she would feel no guilt taking what she needed now. By right it was hers.

"Alice, I want you to take a message to your sister tomorrow," Rochella said. "Tell her I want to meet with her friend as soon as possible. Next week is the new moon and I want everything settled before the time when the smugglers make their run across the channel."

"But, my lady, Hilda would skin me alive if I asked for an extra day off."

"Do not worry about what Hilda will say. I am your mistress, and if I want to give you extra time to spend with your family, that is my business. After I have my breakfast in the morning, you are to go home."

"Aye, my lady. I'll do as you ask."

"Good. Now it is getting late and you need to rest after your long day. You will have another one tomorrow."

Dismissed, Alice eagerly sought out her small pallet in the servants' quarters. Her mission for Lady Devlin had exhausted her and she was asleep as soon as her head hit the pillow.

After breakfasting on hot chocolate and berry muffins, Rochella allowed Alice to coif her hair and help her dress. Unconcerned about the striking picture she made in the pale yellow gown, Rochella turned away from the mirror. "Alice, when you are finished here you may leave for the inn. I have things to do and will not be needing you until this evening, so you have the afternoon to be with your family."

"Aye, my lady," Alice said, giving Rochella a conspiratorial smile.

Knowing Alice would do as bidden, Rochella sailed past her in a flurry of muslin skirts. She flashed the maid a mischievous smile before stepping out into the hallway and closing the door to her chamber behind her. Her satin slippers made no sound on the stairs as she descended to the foyer and turned in the direction of Gareth's study. She would begin her search there. If her husband kept a strongbox in the house, his study was the most likely place. Rapping lightly on the door, she listened for an answer to her knock but heard nothing. She cast a furtive glance about the hallway and then quickly slipped inside the room.

Breathing a sigh of relief, she closed the study door behind her. She took no time to consider her good fortune at finding the room empty, but crossed to the huge mahogany desk and began rummaging through each drawer. Finding nothing in the first two drawers, Rochella reached for the third. She took a steadying breath and said a silent prayer before she slid it open to discover a small box.

Carefully she lifted it out of the drawer and placed it on the shining surface of the desk. She tried the lock but found it would not open without a key. Disappointed but not thwarted, Rochella replaced the strongbox in the drawer and closed it. If she depended on using the key to open the box she would never get the gold she needed. Pondering other means of accomplishing the deed, she failed to hear the study door open.

"May I help you, Lady Devlin?" an icy voice asked from the doorway.

Rochella jumped with a start of surprise and spun about to find Hilda Bronson regarding her suspiciously. She could feel a guilty flush heat her cheeks as she sought to regain her composure. Clearing her throat, she inched her chin up in the air and eyed the housekeeper coolly. "I was looking for my husband and as you can see, he is not here. Do you know where he has gone?"

"Lord Devlin went to Padstow on business," Hilda answered.

The housekeeper's penetrating gaze making her uneasy, Rochella glanced away. Noting the bright sunlight spilling in through the leaded windows, she said the first thing that came to mind. "He chose a beautiful day for his visit."

"It is not for me to say, my lady," Hilda replied, her tone implying it also wasn't Rochella's place to say what Lord Devlin chose to do.

Stinging under the housekeeper's rebuke, Rochella answered haughtily, "You are right, Hilda. It is not for you to say. Now if you will excuse me, I shall let you get back to your duties."

Regally Rochella swept past the older woman and up the stairs to her chamber. She locked the door behind her and crossed to the dressing table. Sinking down on the padded stool, she stared at her reflection. She had succeeded in finding Gareth's strongbox. Now she had to find a way to open it. The only feasible solution was to force the lock open with a knife. Settling the matter in her mind, Rochella smiled. When the moment came for her to leave Devil Wind, she would be ready.

The sun was slipping below the horizon by the time Alice returned from Arthur's Dram. Its rays streaked the evening sky with brilliant golds and mauves, mellowing Devil Wind's harsh lines with its warm light. Waiting anxiously in the small salon, Rochella saw the maid's approach and rushed down to meet her. Drawing her into the garden scented with the heady fragrance of roses in full bloom, she glanced furtively about to ascertain their privacy. "Were you able to get the message to your sister's friend?"

Alice nodded. "Aye, my lady. He said, he'd meet with you tomorrow at Arthur's Dram."

Rochella frowned, wondering what excuse she could make for visiting Arthur's Dram again with only Alice as her escort. Gareth had not been pleased when he found her there on her first visit. Worrying her lower lip, she considered her options. She knew she would need an acceptable reason for such an excursion or he would forbid her going.

"Oh, my," Rochella mused aloud. "Perhaps if I have dinner with Gareth tonight, I can convince him no harm will befall me if I take your mother a basket of food and a few of my old gowns for your sisters. Would your mother be insulted?''

''Nay, my lady. She has too many mouths to feed to find insult in your generosity,'' Alice said, already imagining her mother's relief at not having to worry over clothing her sisters for another year.

''Then we must hurry, Alice. I want to look my best tonight when I dine with my husband,'' Rochella said, turning to retrace her steps to the wide double doors that led out into the gardens.

Gareth handed his coat to the footman and strode into the drawing room. Tired from the long day spent interviewing prospective employees to manage his warehouse in Padstow, he went directly to the cabinet that held the crystal decanter of brandy. Pouring himself a dram, he downed the contents in one gulp. It burned down his throat and into his stomach. Within moments he could feel the tension in his muscles begin to ease.

Refilling the glass, he turned, determined to enjoy a few moments of peace and quiet before venturing into his study to face the work that still awaited him there. He froze at the sight of his wife, sitting demurely in one of the large wing-backed chairs. His gaze moved over her, taking in the golden highlights in her intricately coiffed curls and her moist, glistening lips, before coming to rest upon the creamy expanse of bosom exposed above the provocatively cut décolletage.

Tearing his eyes away from the tempting display, he cleared his throat with an effort and said, ''Good evening, *madame*. I was not expecting the pleasure of your company.''

Rochella smiled up at her husband and felt her heart begin to race. The mere sight of him filled her senses, making it nearly impossible to keep her mind on the reason she had decided to join him for dinner. "Good evening, sir," she replied. "I thought I would join you for dinner unless you prefer otherwise."

"Nay, *madame*. I would enjoy your company. Let me but change and I shall escort you to the dining room," Gareth said, slightly puzzled by his wife's presence. It was the first time since their marriage she had sought out his company and it delighted him.

Rochella gave her assent with a gracious nod of her lovely head and watched as Gareth hurriedly left the drawing room. She clamped her hands together, her knuckles whitening under the pressure. She had to get a grip on her emotions or she would not be able to persuade Gareth to allow her to visit Arthur's Dram with Alice. If she was to escape, she had to use him as he had used her, without thought of his feelings.

Hearing Gareth's footsteps on the stairs several moments later, Rochella braced herself against the effect her husband always had upon her. Drawing in a steadying breath, she raised her chin, firmly believing she had her feelings under control.

Yet when Gareth entered the drawing room, her heart pounded against her ribs and her breath froze in her throat. Her eyes wandered over him, taking in the wide chest beneath his embroidered waistcoat and the muscular neck that contrasted starkly against the white of his intricately tied cravat.

"My lady, shall we dine?" Gareth asked, offering his arm.

Drawing in a deep breath, Rochella placed a trembling hand upon his arm. She could feel the hard muscle beneath the soft texture of his black velvet sleeve. Lowering her gaze away from his penetrating eyes, she swallowed nervously and came to her feet.

Ignoring his own racing pulse, Gareth gallantly escorted Rochella into the dining room. He seated her to his right, then picked up the small silver bell and rang for their dinner. Within a moment the footman had filled their cut crystal glasses with one of France's best wines.

Gareth lifted his glass and smiled at Rochella. "To the lady of Devil Wind. May she find happiness within its walls."

Her cheeks heating with a blush of pleasure, Rochella timidly returned his smile and raised her own glass. Nervously she tasted the ruby wine and her face reflected her surprise to find such an excellent bouquet. "This is wonderful, Gareth. If I did not know better, I would think it came from France."

Gareth smiled, unwilling to tell Rochella she had correctly guessed the origin of the wine. For now he would keep that information his little secret. "We English are not the barbarians the French would have the world believe."

Rochella conceded the point graciously, lowering her eyes to the rich wine in her glass. Everything was going too smoothly for her to point out that the main flaw she found in the Englishman she had married was her inability to understand him from one moment to the next. If all Englishmen were as mercurial as her husband then there were far more faults to them than she had first conceived. However, she was determined not to argue about anything tonight.

Looking once more at her husband, she said, "I know the English are not barbaric, but there are things Englishmen can learn from my country."

"True," Gareth admitted, eyeing Rochella appreciatively. "The French are a sophisticated lot. I have found they also have very beautiful women and excellent wine."

His gaze was like a caress and Rochella swallowed uneasily. Their conversation was drifting toward dangerous ground. Lifting her glass, she drank the wine down in one gulp. The moment her glass was empty the footman refilled it. Praying the wine would stop her insides from quaking each time Gareth looked at her, she again drained her glass. As the footman refilled it, the first course arrived, and Rochella turned her attention to the succulent meal the cook had prepared.

By the time dessert arrived, a luscious pudding topped with caramel sauce and nuts, Rochella sat viewing the world through a pleasant rosy haze.

Surreptitiously studying his wife, Gareth sipped his wine. In the morning she would have a headache from all the wine she had consumed. He frowned as he watched her lift her glass once more to her lips, and wondered at the game she was now playing. Something was not quite right about her this evening, and it was time to find out what it was before she was too inebriated to answer his questions.

"Rochella, don't you think it's time you told me what this is all about?"

Feeling the full effect of the wine, Rochella tried to focus on the image of her husband. "What do you mean?"

"I fear there is more here than meets the eye, or you would not have to drink so much wine to dull the effects of having to dine with me."

"Sir, I am doing as expected of me," Rochella said, drawing herself up as regally as possible and valiantly seeking to look offended by his suspicions. "Have I not played the part of the Lady Devlin as I should?"

Gareth's expression hardened. Before Rochella had time to blink an eye, he pushed himself out of his chair and closed the distance between them. With little effort he pulled her chair about to face him, his hands on its arms successfully blocking any attempt by Rochella to flee. Bending close, he peered into her intoxicated emerald eyes. "All your amicable behavior has been nothing but a game. And had I not watched you consume so much wine, I should never have been the wiser."

Her shining curls falling about her shoulders in a cloud of reddish brown and gold, Rochella adamantly shook her head. "No, Gareth. I did not mean it that way."

Her lower lip began to tremble. All her well-laid plans were falling to pieces before her eyes, and there was nothing she could do about it. She would never get to France if she could not persuade Gareth to allow her to visit Arthur's Dram. Like a small child, she wiped at her eyes with the back of her hand and sniffed. "I— I...know you do not want me as your wife but I—I thought I could...could be the proper mistress of your home."

"You thought that, when you have to get intoxicated to remain in my presence?" Gareth asked, determined to coolly ignore her tears.

Rochella could only shake her head as she looked up into his cold, twilight eyes. How could she tell him that the reason she had drunk so much wine was to still the trembling his presence created within her? How could she explain to this man who had blatantly told her he would keep a mistress that a small piece of her heart died each time she thought of him holding another woman in his arms? This was the man she was supposed to hate. This was the man she was determined to leave. Why at the moment when she needed to be emotionally detached in order to follow through with her plans, did she long for nothing more than to be held in his arms?

Struggling to think, Rochella finally confronted her feelings toward her husband. They jolted her nearly sober and she quickly denied them. She did not love Gareth Devlin. What she felt at the moment was nothing more than the powerful effect of the wine. Pushing his hands away from the arms of her chair, Rochella forced herself to her feet. She swayed precariously for a moment before drawing in a deep breath. "I shall not be questioned like this, Gareth."

Rochella turned, and with what she thought was all the dignity of a queen, she staggered out of the dining room and to the stairs. The floor suddenly lurched beneath her feet like the deck of a ship at sea and she grabbed the stair banister to keep from falling. Holding tightly to the dark polished wood, she placed her foot on the first step, determined to go to her chamber. The step seemed to move of its own accord and she again began to sway.

As Rochella tilted backward, Gareth caught her in his arms before she fell. "You little fool. You would have broken your neck before you made it up the stairs, but you are just too stubborn to ask for help." Rochella firmly clasped in his arms, he took the steps two at a time.

His strong heartbeat soothed Rochella and she lay listening to the sound of it, content with the world. When he reached her chamber, she did not protest when he ordered Alice from the room, and gently laid her down upon her bed.

As if caring for a child, Gareth turned Rochella and unlaced her gown. Easing the garment down her body, he immediately regretted his decision to send Alice away. He had thought it would be much simpler for him to undress his wife, since in her state of inebriation it would be hard for the maid to manage. However, his willpower was not as strong as he had believed. Gritting his teeth, he stripped Rochella of her remaining garments and tossed them aside. She lay naked before him.

Gareth drew in a ragged breath and turned away. He had to find a nightrail to cover her. Crossing to the armoire, he rummaged through laces, satins, velvets and silks until he finally found a sheer bit of a thing that looked as if it were made for using in bed.

Bracing himself, he moved back to Rochella and sat down on the side of the bed. He lifted her into a sitting position and matter-of-factly tugged the nightrail over her head.

The thin material fell over her body like an alluring mist, emphasizing far more than it concealed. The effect was devastating, and Gareth felt his knees go weak.

Knowing his only avenue of rescue was immediate escape from temptation, Gareth made to rise from the bed, only to find himself captured within Rochella's arms. She looked up at him, her eyes the color of the sea on a clear day. "Hold me, Gareth," she whispered in a silky voice, "please."

"Rochella, you need to rest" was Gareth's hoarse answer. He closed his eyes and fought to resist his wife's blatant invitation.

"I am not asking you to love me, Gareth. I just need to be held in your arms for a moment," Rochella said, the wine bringing forth her innermost thoughts.

Hearing the agony in her voice, Gareth surrendered, believing the wine had released the loneliness Rochella had kept pent-up within her. Since coming to Devil Wind she had presented a brave front to the world. Now she clung to him, making him realize she needed love as much as he did.

Gently Gareth took Rochella into his arms and lay beside her on the bed, holding her close and letting her snuggle against his warmth, her face pressed against his chest, her arm encircling his middle. Her breathing became even as she slipped into a sound sleep.

Gareth shifted onto his side and looked down into the face of his sleeping wife. Tenderly he brushed a curling strand of shining hair away from her brow and placed a kiss upon her flawless skin.

Drawing in a deep breath, he folded one of his arms beneath his head and sought to relax. His body still burned from Rochella's nearness, but he felt a wry sense of victory. For the first time he had managed with some effort to lie beside his wife and control his desire to make love to her.

"Perhaps tonight is a new beginning for us, Rochella," Gareth murmured quietly and closed his eyes.

Chapter Eight

The chill of the graying predawn hours came through the open window, ruffling the sheer drapes and making Rochella shiver. Through the blanket of sleep clinging to her mind, she was only vaguely aware of her discomfort and sought out the warmth at her side, snuggling closer. Draping an arm and throwing a leg over the hard masculine form, she cushioned her cheek against his chest, feeling the crisp curls prick her skin.

Shock shattered the remnants of sleep from her mind like a cleansing hurricane. Rochella's eyes snapped open. She shot upright, clutching the sheet to her breasts. Blinking down at the man lying at her side, she could not believe her eyes. Gareth lay staring up at her.

"What are you doing here?" she asked, dreading his answer.

Stretching his arms over his head, Gareth smiled languidly up at his wife. "You asked me to stay. Don't you remember?"

Bracing her knees against her chest, Rochella dug fingers into her hair, pressing down on her skull in an effort to stop the sledgehammer slamming achingly against her temples with each beat of her heart. Through the haze of pain, she sought to recall the events of the previous evening, grimacing as the vague memory of her effort to climb the stairs finally broke through. Beyond that moment, she could recall nothing more. Slowly, to avoid causing herself more agony, she shook her head and managed a weak "No."

Sensing her discomfort, Gareth's heart went out to Rochella and he lifted his arms to her. "Come here, love. You've done nothing to be ashamed of," Gareth said, his voice a soft caress.

Gareth's words were of little reassurance. Great tears brimmed in her eyes and her lower lip began to tremble. "I did not mean for any of this to happen. All I wanted was to be allowed to visit Alice's mother with some food and clothing."

"So that was it," Gareth said, smiling as he reached up and wiped away one glistening droplet. "You could have saved yourself much trouble and a terrible headache if you had only been honest with me, Rochella."

Rochella blinked down at her husband. "You mean you do not mind if I take Alice's sisters a few of my old gowns?"

"Of course not. It is your prerogative to do as you like with your things, and I approve of your thinking of those who need our help. The lady of Devil Wind should be a kind and generous mistress."

"You do?" Rochella asked again, unable to believe how easily she had gotten her way.

"Yes, of course. Now come here and let us get a few more hours' sleep. I have another long day ahead of me. If I am unable to find a man in Padstow to manage my warehouses, I shall have to go to London," Gareth said, once more holding up his arms to her.

Rochella's pulse leaped in her throat. Should his business not go well in Padstow and he did have to travel to London, she would be free to make her escape. After this night she might never see him again.

Her heart suddenly felt as if it had been torn from her body and tossed into a thorn bush. How could she leave this man? Torn, she went willingly into Gareth's arms, her heart and soul telling her to savor their time together for it might be their last.

Before Gareth could protest, Rochella captured his mouth in a kiss that drained any thought of resistance from him. He clamped his arms around her, pressing her thinly clad body to his passion-hardened frame. As her hips arched responsively against him, his flesh throbbed agonizingly against the tight restraints of his silk breeches. All good intentions were once more forgotten, and a groan of anguish blended with one of pleasure as he surrendered to the demands of his weak flesh. He swiftly unlaced his breeches and tossed them aside. Pressing Rochella into the soft down mattress, he gazed into her slumberous eyes. "God, how I need you," he murmured hoarsely. He began a trail of fiery kisses down her throat to the sweet bounties awaiting him beneath the neckline of her nightrail, which he quickly slipped from her shoulders.

Rochella was lost. The mere touch of his lips exploded the embers of her own passion into a raging inferno. She gave herself up to the pleasures of Gareth's hands and lips, savoring his caresses as they began the sensuous journey into the realms of love. Together they climbed to the summit of the hot flowing mountain of passion. The molten heat singed their flesh, uniting them body and soul before erupting into an ecstasy that left them crying out their rapture.

Their breathing ragged, their hearts slowing to normal, they descended from the paradise reserved for lovers, to the land of mortal man where the reality of life's problems still existed.

Confronted once more by his inability to control his emotions where his wife was concerned, Gareth felt a soul-shattering agony grip his heart. Each time he made love to Rochella it was growing more difficult to turn away from her. He now realized what his ancestors had endured and why no one before him had been able to stop the curse by ending the line of Devlin descendants. It was far easier to condemn those yet unborn than to say no to your own heart.

Gareth eased away from Rochella and sat on the side of the bed. He was beginning to believe himself to be the mad Devlin instead of Adam. He could no more control his own emotions than his brother could when beset by one of his fits. Gareth knew the dire consequences of making love to his wife, yet as long as he was near her, he did not have the strength to keep his resolutions. His only recourse was to put some distance between them. He needed time to sort out his feelings and get his emotions under control, or all would be lost.

Turning to look down at her, he placed a gentle hand against her flushed cheek and tenderly brushed his thumb against her chin. "Rochella," he began, but his words were cut short by a graceful finger against his lips.

She shook her head, denying him speech. She wanted no more of his apologies. This morning might be their last time together and she wanted nothing to ruin the sweet afterglow left by their lovemaking. She wanted to carry the memory of that feeling back to France with her. "No, Gareth. Do not say anything. I know how you feel. Let us just savor the moment past."

Gareth gazed down into her sparkling emerald eyes and slowly nodded. Nothing would change what had happened between them now. Only time and distance could ensure his salvation. Without a word, he lay back down and pulled Rochella into his arms. He would hold her for a few hours more and then he would leave for London.

When Rochella awoke she was once more alone. Her head ached with an intensity that threatened to rend her skull. Gingerly she eased herself into a sitting position, only to realize her mistake. Her stomach heaved with nausea. Sliding her feet to the floor, she squinted against the gray light filtering into her room. The clouds gathering on the distant horizon matched her mood.

The events of the previous evening and the early-morning hours descended upon her in one long wave of shame, washing over her with such force she had to clamp her lips tightly together to suppress a cry of pain. Did she have no self-respect? No pride? No power to resist Gareth's attraction?

Torn by questions she could not answer, Rochella slumped back against the satin pillows and stared futilely up at the beamed ceiling. She had accepted the attraction she felt for her husband but she had not expected it to turn into love.

"This cannot have happened," she agonized aloud, hoping the words would make it true. The moment they passed her lips, however, she heard the lie within them. Against her will, she had fallen completely under Gareth's spell. He was unaware of it, but he now possessed her heart.

Rochella clamped her teeth down on her lower lip, a pensive frown marking her smooth brow. What she would not give to know she possessed her husband's love. But that would never be. She would return to France as soon as the smugglers could arrange to take her across the channel and Gareth would find someone else to take her place. She envied the woman whom Gareth chose for himself. If he could give Rochella such pleasure when he felt nothing for her beyond a moment of lust, what would his lovemaking be like with his heart involved? Rochella shivered at the thought.

A brisk knock at the door pulled her from her reveries. She barely managed to cover herself with the sheet before the door opened and Hilda strode in with her breakfast tray. At a glance the housekeeper took in the rumpled bedclothes and a tiny knowing smirk tugged up the corners of her mouth.

"My lady, I've brought your tray this morning. Cook has prepared you a nice breakfast."

"Where is Alice?" Rochella asked, feeling ill at the mere mention of food.

"Alice is too busy washing your gowns this morning to be of service," Hilda said as she set the tray down on the bed.

"Washing my gowns? That is the scrubwoman's duty."

"You are quite right, my lady, but the girl has taken two days off this week, though she is only permitted one. She must be punished. Servants cannot do as they wish, or we shall have no discipline around here."

Rochella pushed the tray away and swallowed hard to keep her nausea at bay. In no mood to soften her remarks, she snapped, "How dare you take it upon yourself to punish my personal servant? You will go now and apologize to her for your impetuous behavior."

Hilda drew herself up and crossed her arms obstinately over her chest. "My lady, it is my responsibility to mete out punishment when necessary."

"And it is my responsibility as mistress of this household to countermand your instructions when I feel they are unjust. I also have the authority to dismiss anyone in my husband's employ should they continue to thwart my wishes, and that includes you, Hilda."

Hilda shifted uneasily. "My lady, I am afraid I've been misinformed."

"You most certainly have been. Now please send Alice to me at once. She has served me well since Babette returned to France."

Hilda lowered her eyes to hide the anger seething through every fiber of her being. "My lady, I apologize for overstepping my authority."

"Your apology is accepted. But the next time please check with me before you take it upon yourself to mete out discipline, especially to my maid. I gave Alice permission to visit her family yesterday, as you would have learned had you consulted me before taking it upon yourself to handle the matter."

"I'm sorry, my lady. I didn't know. I'll go down and send Alice to assist you."

When the door closed behind the housekeeper, Rochella breathed a sigh of relief. Easing her feet to the floor, she lifted the breakfast tray and gingerly set it far enough away from the bed for her to avoid the sight and smell of the food. Her stomach roiling, she managed to stagger back to the bed before collapsing. Stretching out against the cool sheets, she promised herself she would never touch another glass of wine for as long as she lived.

"I will not have long to keep that resolution," Rochella murmured miserably, feeling near to death's door. Swallowing with an effort, she turned her face into the pillow and wondered how soon it would be before the grim reaper came for her.

Thinking it was Alice, she didn't rouse herself when a knock sounded upon the door but merely called out, "Enter." The pillow muffled her words and another knock sounded. Irritated, she inched her head up enough to say, lapsing into French, *"Mon Dieu! Entrez!"* Before the door opened she buried her aching head once more in the softness of the pillow.

A gentle hand caressing her hair made Rochella aware her visitor was not Alice. Slowly she turned and looked up to find her husband bent anxiously over her.

"I would say good-morning, but I can see from your expression that it isn't one," Gareth said, settling himself at her side on the bed.

"I am afraid you are right. It is not a good morning. The weather looks foul," Rochella said, forcing herself not to groan at the misery his movements created.

Gareth smiled. "I don't think the weather has anything to do with making your morning foul, my dear. I fear it's far more likely the juice of the grape that has given you a dim view of the day as well as an unbearable headache."

Rochella struggled to sit up, but Gareth's warm hand pressed her back against the pillows. He shook his head and smiled wryly. "If you want to rid yourself of your headache, you need to rest this morning."

Rochella acquiesced with a nod as another wave of nausea set her stomach to roiling once more.

"I'm glad to see you're going to take my advice," Gareth said. "I won't take up much more of your time.

I just came in to tell you I've reconsidered interviewing the man in Padstow and I'm on my way to London. I don't know how long it will take for me to find the right man so I don't know how long I'll be away.''

Rochella looked at Gareth, her heaving stomach and headache momentarily forgotten. If the arrangements went well with the smugglers, she would be free to leave whenever she wanted. He would be in London and unable to stop her.

A knife seemed to twist in her heart at the thought as she took in Gareth's handsome features, memorizing each one. After today she would have only the memories to give her comfort. She wanted never to forget the piercing eyes that seemed to look into her soul and set her blood on fire, or the sensuous mouth that had given her so much pleasure.

Mon Dieu, how I love him, she thought, restraining the urge to reach out and touch him one last time. Drawing in a deep breath, she finally found her voice. ''I wish you a pleasant journey, Gareth. Come safely back to Devil Wind.''

Gareth abruptly stood. The soft yearning look he'd seen flicker in her eyes was nearly enough to drive all coherent thought from his mind. After clearing his throat, he finally said, ''I shall do my best, *madame*. Now, I shall bid you adieu. I hope when we meet again you will feel much better.''

''Goodbye, Gareth,'' Rochella said, the words sticking uncomfortably in her throat.

Gareth nodded and quickly left the room. When the latch clicked behind him, he leaned back against the closed door and drew in a ragged breath. He wanted nothing more in the world than to go back into his wife's bedchamber and tell her he loved her. But that was the one thing he could never do. Should he ever succumb to the temptation, they would both be doomed.

"My lord, your brother is upset and demanding to be released from the north wing," Hilda said, close at Gareth's side. "Will you come and try to calm him before you leave?"

Gareth's shoulders sagged as he slowly turned to the housekeeper. "Yes, of course. I planned to see Adam to explain about my absence before I left as well as to give you your new instructions."

"I assumed they would be as before," Hilda said.

"This time, I expect you to ensure he doesn't leave the north wing while I'm away. When I return, I shall have decided what must be done in the future."

Gareth and Hilda were surprised when they entered the north wing to find all was quiet. Gareth raised one brow in question at the housekeeper as he unlocked the door and swung it open to reveal Adam sitting calmly by the windows reading.

Slightly disconcerted by Adam's change of demeanor, Hilda shrugged, unable to explain the calmness. The man sitting peacefully in the window seat wasn't the same one she had left earlier, livid with rage after she'd told him of his brother's overnight visit to his wife's bedchamber. His threats to burn down Devil Wind about his brother's ears had frightened her to such an extent that she had gone to Lord Devlin with the hope Adam would vent his frustrations upon his brother instead of following through with his plans.

"How are you feeling today, Adam?" Gareth asked.

Adam closed his book and laid it carefully aside. "Why do you ask, Gareth? I assumed Hilda had already advised you of my state. She's a very reliable prison guard.''

Gareth pulled a chair close to the window and settled himself in it. "She did mention you were upset about something. Is it anything you care to discuss with me?''

"I think not, brother. You would never understand.''

"Give me a chance, Adam. I can't help you if you won't talk to me.''

Adam eyed Gareth cynically. "I have talked to you before, but it has done little good. You still refuse to allow me to leave my prison and act like a normal member of this household.''

"Adam, I promise you'll be allowed to leave the north wing soon, but for the moment I feel it's best for you to remain here.''

"Blast it, Gareth. There is no need to lie. I know you intend to keep me locked away for the rest of my life.''

Gareth's shoulders sagged and he released a long breath. "As soon as I return from London, you will be allowed to join the rest of the household. I just need time to explain things to my wife.''

"Your wife! Damn it, Gareth! You are keeping me locked away because you are afraid she will turn you out of her bed when she learns the truth about us.''

Gareth came to his feet, every line in his body reflecting his tension. "Adam, that is unfair.''

"Unfair? What is unfair is the fact I am locked away while you enjoy frolicking with your wife. Your vow to end the Devlin line didn't last very long, did it, brother?'' Adam ground out between clenched teeth.

Gareth felt as if Adam had hit him in the stomach with a solid fist. He could not deny the truth, no matter how much it hurt. He had kept the secret of his brother from his wife out of fear she would turn away from him in disgust.

The older Devlin drew in a resigned breath. The time for secrets was at an end. When he returned from London he would tell Rochella the entire truth. Should she decide to leave him, he would give her her freedom.

"You are right, Adam. If you will just be patient until I return from London, I shall put an end to this. You will have free rein of Devil Wind."

Adam smiled, enjoying the pain in Gareth's eyes. "I shall be patient until you return, but I make no promises after that."

"I ask for none," Gareth said, extending his hand to his brother to affirm his promise.

Adam shook hands with Gareth. For the moment he was satisfied. He would do as he had promised and remain in the north wing. He had won this skirmish, and by the time his brother returned to Devil Wind, his plans would be set to win the war.

"Goodbye, my love," Rochella whispered softly through a veil of tears as she watched Gareth's coach disappear from view along the winding road.

"My lady, it grows late. If we're to go, we had best hurry," Alice said. Placing a comforting hand on her mistress's shoulder, she glanced up at the overcast sky. "From the looks of it, we'll be drowned by the time we reach Arthur's Dram."

"It does look like rain. Go and tell the footman to have the coach brought round while I dress," Rochella said, needing a few minutes alone to compose herself.

When she heard the door close behind the maid, she wiped at her eyes and turned away from the window. It did no good to mourn over the loss of something you never had. Resolutely she stiffened her spine. Alice was right. It was growing late. She could not allow herself to think of anything except returning to France. She had to concentrate all her energies upon that goal. Once she was assured that her parents were safe, then and only then would she be able to look back and grieve for things that might have been.

The afternoon sky seemed to reflect the emotions Rochella forced herself to ignore. When they were only halfway to their destination, it opened up and wept, drenching the earth and making the road nearly impassable. The rain-cooled summer day left the women shivering from cold by the time they reached the slate-roofed tavern.

Alice's family greeted them warmly and quickly ushered them into the taproom where a meager fire made a valiant effort to consume the damp logs. Smoke filled the room with a blue haze and it was difficult to breathe, yet no one seemed to notice the discomfort as they crowded around Rochella, bringing dry blankets and hot mulled wine to chase away the chill.

When Alice unwrapped the bundles containing the clothing and food, a hush fell over the room. Rochella could see the eager light in the girls' eyes as they looked at the gowns spread across the table, but no one made a sound. Suddenly feeling uncomfortable about her decision to use these hardworking people as an excuse to meet with the smugglers, Rochella turned to the matriarch of the family. Alice's mother stood with head high and back straight, her stance mirroring her pride. A guilty flush spread over Rochella. She had accepted these people's hospitality, and in return she had offended them to accomplish her own selfish goals.

"Please forgive me, Mistress Bibbon. I did not mean to insult you or your family."

A gentle, understanding smile deepened the lines in Alice's mother's work-aged face as she came forward and took Rochella's hand, giving it a warm, reassuring squeeze. "We are grateful, my lady, and we take no offense at your charity. It is welcome."

Rochella smiled her relief as Alice's sisters pounced upon the gowns with squeals of delight. Until that moment she had never truly realized how blessed she was to have been born into wealth. She had taken for granted all the luxuries her family had provided for her believing them her due. Never again would she allow herself to forget there were others less fortunate than she, nor would she take what life had given as her God-given right. Only the accident of birth separated her from Alice and her sisters.

A boom of thunder shook the tavern, and at the same moment the door swung open to reveal a tall, muscular man wearing a shabby rain-drenched cloak and a sailor's cap. A gust of wind showered him with more water as he forced the door closed behind him and turned to the silent assembly. A wry grin tugged up the corners of his lips as he drew off his cap and ran his hand through his wet brown hair. "Didn't mean to dampen the merriment."

Bets was the first to speak. "Oh, Sam. Come look what Lady Devlin has given us. You'll be so proud of me in this." She held up a blue muslin gown in front of her.

"Aye, me Bets. Ye'll be a real beauty in that gown." Sam's keen blue gaze swept over the Bibbon clan and came to rest on Rochella. He tossed away his soaked cloak and nodded. "My lady, since Bets is too preoccupied with her treasures, I'll make the introductions meself. I be the man ye've come to see—Samuel Heath, better known as Sam to me friends and Bets."

"I am pleased to meet you, Mr. Heath. It was kind of you to agree to come out in this weather," Rochella said, extending her hand to him.

He took it within his own callused palm and awkwardly bowed. "May I sit, my lady?"

At her nod, Sam straddled the high-backed chair and propped a hairy arm across its back. He cast only a fleeting glance in the direction of the Bibbons, but it was enough to make one and all suddenly remember other things that needed their immediate attention. Within moments the room was cleared, and Rochella was alone with the smuggler.

"May I ask why it is so urgent for ye to go to France, my lady?" Sam said, unable to change his straightforward manner even when talking to Lord Devlin's wife.

"My parents' lives may be in jeopardy, and my husband refuses to help me return to France," Rochella answered.

Sam tapped his chin with a square-tipped finger, considering her thoughtfully for a long moment before he said, "Ye know it's dangerous fer anyone like yerself to go to France now. That's the reason Lord Devlin has denied your request."

"I understand the situation but I shall not change my mind, Mr. Heath. If you will not help me, then I will keep searching until I find someone who will."

"I didn't say I'd not help ye. I only thought it me duty to warn ye of the dangers ye'll be facing once ye set foot on French soil."

"I'm grateful for your concern but my mind is made up. I cannot worry about my own safety when my parents are in danger."

"It'll cost ye, my lady. Since all the ruckus in France, everything is high, but I'll also be chancing Lord Devlin's wrath if he should ever learn how ye got away from Devil Wind. I'd rather face the devil hisself than yer husband when he's angry."

Rochella nodded her understanding. "I shall pay what you ask, Mr. Heath, and I shall also pay well for an escort, if you can arrange one."

"An escort?" Sam said, raising one bushy brow. "I'm to take ye to France, and that's all I'm to do."

"Mr. Heath, I do not expect you to do more. However, if you know of anyone who would be willing to travel with me to my home in Champagne, I shall gladly pay whatever he asks."

"I suppose I do know a fellow who might be interested in helping ye. He needs the money."

"As I have said, I shall gladly pay for his assistance," Rochella said.

"Even the enticement of yer money may not be enough to persuade him to go back to France, my lady. He'll be taking an awful risk to cross the channel again. He nearly didn't get out of France with his head on his shoulders the last time." Sam snapped two fingers together. "He come that close to the guillotine."

"I shall understand should he decide it's too dangerous for him to travel to France at this time. However, that does not change my plans."

"Then it's settled. If the weather clears we leave tomorrow night. Bring fifty gold pieces for yer passage and meet me at nine o'clock at the inlet near Tintagel

Head. Alice will show ye the way. I'll have a small boat waiting on ye."

"I shall be there, Mr. Heath. And thank you."

"No need to thank me, lady. I'm helping ye fer the gold. It'll mean me and Bets can now get married."

"I wish you and Bets much happiness, Mr. Heath," Rochella said. Coming to her feet, she extended her hand to the smuggler. "Good day, sir."

"Good day, my lady," Sam replied, rising from his chair and graciously bowing over Rochella's hand.

After making their farewells to the Bibbons, Rochella and Alice traveled back to Devil Wind in silence. There were far too many things on her mind for Rochella to make idle conversation. Only one more day and her brief sojourn at Devil Wind would be at an end.

Glancing out the coach window at the black granite castle looming up out of the fog like a many-eyed sentinel, Rochella realized with a start she had come to consider Devil Wind her home. When she had begun to do so, she had no idea. Like her love for Gareth, the feeling had come upon her unexpected and uninvited.

Rochella allowed her gaze to drift toward the cliffs. She imagined Gareth standing there as he had on the many evenings she had watched him from the small salon. She could envision his dark hair ruffled by the ocean breeze that molded his silk shirt to his muscular chest. Dressed in his favorite soft leather breeches, his powerful body poised, his face turned into the wind, he was magnificent.

She felt her throat constrict and tore her eyes away from the cliffs as the coach rumbled to a halt in the courtyard. Her imagination had vanquished all her resolutions to keep her thoughts on her plans to return to France. Now the mere thought of never seeing her husband again made her feel as if her heart were shattering into a thousand tiny pieces. Trembling, she valiantly fought to suppress her feelings as she allowed the coachman to help her down. Without a glance or a word to Alice, she fled up the steps and into the castle. Tears clouding her vision, she passed Hilda on the stairs as she sped toward the privacy of her bedchamber. Wanting to be alone, she locked the door behind her and stumbled toward the bed. She fell upon the soft down, and burying her face in her arms, she wept.

Chapter Nine

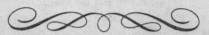

Since awakening that morning to a clear and bright day, Rochella had found she had little energy to set things in order for her departure with Sam Heath. She had allowed Alice to pack her portmanteau, but throughout the day she had done little more than mope about in her chamber, dreading the moment she would leave Devil Wind and its enigmatic master behind.

The sun had already crept below the horizon, pulling the deepening shadows of night over the land, but Rochella still sat with head cushioned on her arms, her knees drawn up to her chest. She had only to dress herself and collect the coins from her husband's strongbox and then she would be ready to leave. She knew it was time for her to go, but she could not force herself to take the first step on the journey that would separate her from the man she loved. For a few brief moments within these walls she had possessed a happiness beyond anything she could have dreamed. Locking the memories away, she turned to the armoire and took out her green riding habit and dark cloak. Stoically, she dressed, picked up the portmanteau and blew out the candle, plunging the room into a darkness that mirrored the feelings in her heart.

Stealthily, Rochella made her way down to Gareth's study and let herself in. She lit one small candle to give her enough light, and after rummaging through her portmanteau, she found the knife Alice had hidden. She opened the drawer, lifted out the strongbox and set it on the shining desk top.

Moistening her dry lips, she lifted the knife and attempted to force the lock. It would not budge. Again she tried and again with the same results. The moments ticked by and her frustration mounted. Nervous perspiration beaded her upper lip as she frantically pried and prodded the metal. Exasperated nearly to the point of picking up the strongbox and throwing it out the window, Rochella jabbed once more at the lock with all her strength. Believing the effort would prove as fruitless as before, she was surprised to see the clasp slip open.

With no time to savor her triumph, she opened the lid. A small gasp escaped her at the sight of the gleaming gold coins. Taking her small reticule, she filled it to the brim. Satisfied with her thievery, she replaced the box in the bottom drawer of the mahogany desk and picked up her portmanteau. She blew out the candle and quietly left the study. With a cautious glance, she slipped down the hall and out into the dark night to meet Alice, who waited in the gardens to show her the way to Tintagel.

Rochella cast one last look at the towering granite walls of Devil Wind. All was silent and dark except for one window in the north wing. Taking no time to wonder what the servants were doing in the unused wing of the castle, Rochella silently said her farewell and turned to follow Alice.

Having grown up exploring the area with her brothers and sisters, Alice knew the shortest route to the inlet. She led Rochella across the wind-whipped heath and along the path down to narrow wave-beaten beach where Sam Heath awaited them with a small dinghy.

He tossed Rochella's portmanteau into the small boat, and brushed his windblown hair out of his face. "It's time fer ye to say yer goodbyes."

Tears of gratitude shimmered in Rochella's emerald eyes as she turned to Alice and pressed several coins into her hand. Alice looked down at them and shook her head. "I can't accept it, my lady."

"Yes. You must. You have been a friend to me and deserve far more than a few coins, but it is all I have to give," Rochella said, pressing Alice's hand closed over the money.

"Ah, my lady," Alice said, her voice filling with tears. "I'm a-goin' to miss you."

Feeling she would burst into tears at any moment if she didn't hurry, Rochella hugged the girl. "Goodbye, Alice. May God keep you and your family safe."

"You too, my lady," Alice sobbed, unable to control her emotions.

Rochella allowed Sam to help her into the dinghy. When he cast off, she glanced one last time in the direction of the granite castle where she had become a woman. She was now free of its cold stone walls, but she feared she would never be free of the memories of the man who had first captured her heart on the day of her arrival.

A dense white mist obscured the receding shoreline as Sam struggled to row the dinghy through the choppy waves. The cold water, as black as the night surrounding them, was still rough from the bad weather the previous day. It tossed the small craft about as if it were a piece of driftwood, making it difficult to control. However, Sam Heath, a seasoned sailor, had faced much worse in his years at sea, and he was unconcerned by the turbulence.

By the time they reached the ship and she was helped on board by one of Sam's cohorts, Rochella little resembled the lady of Devil Wind. The waves splashing against the hull had drenched her riding habit. Salt spray misted her face, and damp wisps of hair clung to her brow beneath the edge of her hood.

Her nerves taut, she stood stiff and shivering as a brisk breeze suddenly dispersed the bank of fog shrouding the vessel within its dark folds. In the dim light from the ship's lantern Rochella viewed the unkempt group of men who comprised the crew and wondered for the first time if she had made a mistake by placing her trust in the smugglers. She knew nothing about Sam Heath beyond what Alice had told her. He could have lured her out here, planning to rob her and drop her body overboard once he and his evil-looking companions had their way with her. No one would ever be the wiser. When Sam returned to Arthur's Dram with his pockets tingling with stolen gold, Alice would believe he had delivered her safely to France.

Rochella shivered again, even as she told herself she was being ridiculous in allowing her imagination to take flight. She trusted Sam Heath. From the first, she had sensed his honesty. He might break England's laws by going against the embargo on French goods, but the man had an air about him that bespoke a certain code of honor.

The thought easing her jittery nerves, she forced herself to wait patiently for Sam to secure the dinghy and climb on board. She did not notice the tall slim man who stepped from the shadows at her side until he spoke.

"Welcome aboard, my lady. I am Dominique Duval. I am to be your escort to Champagne." He bowed chivalrously.

Before Rochella could answer, Sam Heath lumbered over the side of the ship and with the back of a hand wiped the salt spray from his face. He grinned at Rochella when he saw her companion. "I see ye've already met Dom, here. He's agreed to travel with ye to yer home."

"Yes, Mr. Heath and I thank you for your assistance. I will be ever in your debt," Rochella said, smiling at the ruddy-faced seaman.

"Then all's settled. Now it be best if ye let Dom show ye to yer cabin. We're still in English waters and have to be on the lookout for the revenuers."

"Shouldn't we discuss your payment?" Rochella asked.

"We'll settle it before we let ye off in France, my lady. Now please go to yer cabin and be as quiet as possible. Sounds carry a ways on the water, and we don't want to alert the king's men to our presence."

Suddenly understanding the reason for the shuttered lantern, Rochella nodded and turned to Dominique Duval. "Sir, if you will show me to my cabin, we can discuss payment for your services."

Accustomed to using the gifts of his charm and good looks to get what he wanted out of life, Dominique smiled down at Rochella. He'd accepted Sam Heath's offer to help Lord Devlin's wife return to her home in Champagne out of sheer need for money. However, in the past few moments, he'd begun to suspect he might reap other benefits as well. In the dim light he couldn't discern all of Lady Devlin's features, but from the soft sultry tone of her voice and the delicate line of her profile, he surmised her to be a very beautiful woman as well as a rich one.

"Certainement, madame," Dom said, offering his arm to Rochella.

Rochella placed her hand on his sleeve and felt a wave of homesickness at the sound of her own language, after so many months of hearing and speaking English. She had forgotten how sweet it was to the ear. Placing a comforting hand over hers, Dom led her toward the narrow hatch and down the small flight of steps to her cabin.

In a glance Rochella took in the tiny cabin. A black curtain covered the lone porthole, and a narrow bunk and small table were the extent of the furnishings. Crossing to the table, Rochella tossed back the hood of her cloak and opened her reticule. She counted out one hundred gold pieces. "Monsieur Duval, I am grateful for your assistance, and I hope this will be a sufficient amount to cover your expenses."

Dominique, his heart pounding with a certainty that Lady Fortune had once more decided to smile upon him, barely glanced at the gleaming coins on the table. "It is more than enough, *madame*. To what part of Champagne do you wish to travel?"

"To the Château le Lion de Beauvais. It is my home."

Dominique felt like jumping for joy. The lady who stood before him was the heiress to one of the largest and richest estates in France.

Quick of mind, he was already scheming how to get his hands on much more than the money she had already paid him. When he accepted Heath's offer to be her escort, he had planned only to take her far enough into France to get the money he so desperately needed before deserting her. Now the temptation to complete his mission tugged at his conniving brain. If he played the game right, perhaps when he returned to England, he would never have to worry about money again.

"*Madame,* you do understand it will be difficult to travel through France because of the hotheads who are now running the country."

"I know the situation, *monsieur,* but I have no choice. I must reach Beauvais at all cost."

Dominique nodded his understanding. "Then I shall say no more. Rest now. We drop anchor late tomorrow evening, and you will need all your strength once we start to travel across France."

Dominique bowed over Rochella's hand. "Good night, *madame.*"

"Good night, Monsieur Duval," Rochella said.

Dominique left Rochella and returned to the tiny sleeping area Sam had provided for him. In the corner a hammock had been hung from nails for his bed. Engrossed with his plans for the future, he untied his cravat, tossed his coat over a stack of boxes containing English goods for the French merchants and carefully stretched out his lean frame in his swaying bed.

A tiny, devious smile quirked up the corners of his shapely lips as he braced his hands behind his head and stared up at the ceiling. He congratulated himself on having the good sense to chance the danger of returning to France. It could well prove to be a very enriching endeavor for a man who did not have two coins to rub together in his pocket.

Dominique's dark eyes narrowed thoughtfully and his smile faded. Life had never been fair to him. As long as he could remember he had had to scheme and scratch for everything he wanted. His lineage was as ancient as that of the chestnut-haired beauty in the next cabin, yet there had been no money in his immediate family for several generations. As a boy he had starved and stolen to survive, until by chance a distant cousin of his mother's had visited their dilapidated château and taken pity upon him. At first he had been grateful for the man's generosity; however, it had not taken him long to learn what it was like to be an impoverished relative of the rich.

Even servants had the freedom to leave their employer if their treatment became too harsh, but he had not had that privilege. He had been forced to take the abuse his cousin had meted out and act as if he appreciated it. The experience had taught him many lessons, and by the time he reached his teenage years, he had learned those lessons.

Devious and watching for any opportunity to advance himself, Dominique Duval did not care how many people he hurt on his path to success. After years of work, he had managed to bribe and blackmail his way to an appointment as an aide to one of Louis XVI's ministers. At the age of thirty, his position had looked secure.

"Damn the Jacobins to hell," Dominique swore, nearly upsetting himself from the hammock as he shifted restlessly onto his side. The revolution had destroyed everything he had achieved for himself, and he had had to flee France to save his life.

"But with enough money I can live just as well in England," Dominique murmured, his smile returning.

Satisfied he had finally found the means to reach his goal, he closed his eyes. He had much to do within the next few days, and he wanted to be well rested when they reached France the following evening.

Rochella stood by the rail, gazing out over the water at the city of Le Havre. It was only a few months since she had seen her homeland, but she could not stop the ripple of excitement that coursed through her at the sight of the lights flickering from the houses in the darkened city.

Before leaving Beauvais she had felt the world centered around her and those she loved. Now with the maturity that had come from her experiences in England, she realized there was much more to the world than childish pleasures.

She had learned so much, and yet she realized that she actually knew very little about the world she was now entering. The past she had known was now under siege by men who would see her father and those like him destroyed.

Her stomach quivered with apprehension. She prayed she was not too late to save her parents from sacrificing themselves to preserve what would never be again. Should the king accept the new constitution, her family's status in France would be no more than that of the ordinary man. Created on the model of the Declaration of Independence from the United States of America, the constitution would do away with the nobility as known in the past, and impose a constitutional monarchy, where the king obeyed the people's whims.

Engrossed with the images of the France awaiting her when they docked, Rochella didn't hear Dominique Duval's soft footsteps as he approached.

"*Madame,* it will soon be time for us to depart. I suggest you change your gown."

Startled from her reveries, Rochella frowned up at the young Frenchman. *"Monsieur?"*

"It is going to be difficult enough to hide our identities, without your gown proclaiming your breeding," Dominique said. "France as you once knew it is no more. Now is the time of the simple man. Even the wealthy who possess no noble blood in their veins fear to dress too extravagantly."

Rochella glanced down at her elegant pastel blue gown and wondered again at the madness that had seized her country. Smoothing the soft fabric, she nodded her assent and hurried to her cabin to change into the plainest gown she owned, a somber gray silk.

"That is much better," Dominique said, smiling his approval when she reappeared on deck. "Now, *madame,* shall we depart?" He offered his arm to Rochella and escorted her down the gangplank to the wharf. Dominique made no effort to hire a carriage, instead he hurried her along the damp, cobbled streets to a dilapidated building where a sign squeaking over the entrance proclaimed it to be the Auberge Dauphine.

Inside the smoke-filled main room, he introduced himself and Rochella to the proprietor as Citizen Maribe and his wife, who had stopped in Le Havre on their way to Paris to witness the king's signing of the constitution.

Rochella eyed Dominique warily as he signed the register with their fictitious names but made no comment until he had escorted her up the narrow flight of rickety stairs to a small, dusty room. When the door closed behind them, she turned on him with fury blazing in her emerald eyes. "*Monsieur,* how dare you ask for only one room? I cannot stay here with you."

Dominique's lips curved into a smile at the sight of the fire sparkling in her eyes. He raised both hands in a helpless gesture. "*Madame,* it was necessary. Posing as a married couple, we are much less conspicuous. And I assure you, your honor is safe with me. I shall sleep on the floor."

"You are correct, *monsieur.* The floor is exactly where you will sleep," Rochella snapped, still unappeased by his explanation. Yet there was little she could do to change things if she wanted to reach Beauvais. Exasperated to find herself in such a dilemma, she sat down on the bed and folded her arms over her chest. She eyed Dominique coldly. "*Monsieur,* I suggest in the future you make your intentions clear before you act upon them, or you may find yourself in a situation you dislike."

Annoyed any woman would have the nerve to censure him, Dominique's face hardened. He would have liked nothing more than to slap the haughty expression off the woman's lovely face, and had it not been for her wealthy family, he would have done exactly that. However, his greed won out over momentary gratification. "*Madame,* I am sorry to have upset you. I thought you understood I was thinking only of your welfare."

"I do understand, *Monsieur.* However, I am not ignorant, and if you explain your intentions to me beforehand, I shall know how to respond. What would the proprietor have done if I had denied such a relationship existed between us?"

Dominique shifted uneasily. His intentions had been far less than the honorable ones he had spoken of a moment ago. He could have rented two rooms, but he had preferred a more intimate setting to begin the relationship that he hoped would deepen until by the time they reached Beauvais, she could not live without him.

"Again, I must apologize for not warning you earlier. I assumed you would understand the dire circumstances that make it necessary for me to tell such falsehoods. In the next few days we shall have to share each other's company, and we must be convincing enough to keep anyone from suspecting we are not what we say. Should they discover the truth, it would mean our deaths. However, Lady Devlin, if my presence here makes you too uncomfortable, I shall leave."

Rochella lowered her lashes and shook her head. She suddenly felt ridiculous for objecting. Dominique knew far more about the situation in France than she did. She had to trust his judgment. He had put his own life in jeopardy by agreeing to escort her to Beauvais. He would be in grave danger if they were arrested. A blush stole up her cheeks. "I am sorry, Monsieur Duval. I should not have been so hasty with my objections. Please forgive my outburst."

Dominique smiled smugly to himself as he turned and spread his cape on the floor. His back to her, he stretched out his length on the hard, makeshift bed. "I shall accept your apology only if you will call me Dominique," he said softly.

Rochella smiled her relief. "Good night, Dominique." She blew out the stub of the candle that sat guttering in its own wax. Gingerly, she eased herself back against the lumpy pillow, never believing she would actually be able to sleep. However, within a few moments, the sound of her steady breathing filled the tiny room.

Dominique chuckled low in his throat and shifted to make himself more comfortable. He would prefer sleeping beside her, but his patience would be grandly rewarded once they reached Beauvais. His thoughts traveling over his future wealth, Dominique's eyes slowly closed and his soft snore mingled with the sound of Rochella's breathing.

Chapter Ten

Dominique stood gazing down at Rochella. In the soft glow of golden candlelight, she reminded him of the princess in the fairy tale who had been sentenced to death by the witch and slept until her Prince Charming awakened her with a kiss. However, the world Rochella had known before the curse of the revolution would never be the same again. She could not go to sleep for one hundred years and awaken to find nothing had changed. There were no good fairies to change the course of what was happening in France, and after what he'd learned a short while ago down in the taproom, he now had to decide on his own plan of action.

He was at an impasse—unable to choose which direction he should take. He had always been a man who never gambled unless he was sure of the outcome, but after overhearing the inn's proprietor brag to one of his friends that the Jacobins had begun to take control of the provinces and were in the process of confiscating all aristocratic land grants, he could not be certain it would be worth the risk to take Rochella to Champagne. Should Beauvais have already been taken by the Jacobins, she would be as poor as a field mouse after the harvest.

Dominique set the candle on the bedside table and crossed to the window. Through the grimy glass, he stared down at the dark street below, his thoughts returning to the conversation he had overheard. It had been chilling to hear the innkeeper laugh at the efforts of the nobles to raise their own armies abroad to protect their homes. As the man had said with such pride, the plague of the revolution was now spreading from the filth-ridden streets of Paris into the countryside, and it would be dangerous to be caught by the citizens in search of the hated nobility.

Feeling the hair rise at the base of his neck, he glanced once more toward the woman sleeping on the bed. Every instinct he possessed screamed that it was time to leave if he wanted to keep his head attached to his shoulders. The longer he tarried in one place the greater his chance of being recognized became. He was gambling his life against the odds that the marquis of Beauvais would be so grateful for the protection he had given Rochella, he would be generous with his reward.

Dominique had to decide if he wanted to risk the journey to Beauvais on the chance that the Jacobins had not yet taken away the marquis's holdings.

Dominique shrugged. What choice did he truly have? It would take most of the money she had paid him to bribe his way back to England, and from what he had learned downstairs, he would be a fool to place his trust in anyone he didn't know. Friends and relatives were turning on one another in an attempt to save their own lives.

Until he could get himself out of France with all of his members intact, he was determined to hide like a rat in any nook and cranny that provided protection, and when he sensed anyone's suspicion, he would scurry to another dark hiding place. At the moment the best option he had was to take the beautiful marquis's daughter to her papa. If his luck held out, he would come away a rich man as well as a live one.

His decision made, Dominique crossed to the bed and shook Rochella lightly by the shoulder. Rousing with a start, she came alert with a cry of fright.

"*Madame,* it is only I. It is time we leave. We must make as much progress today as possible. I have already hired a coach."

Rochella yawned and rubbed the sleep from her eyes as she glanced toward the dark windows. She sat up and slid her feet into her slippers. Her stomach rumbled with hunger. She would have enjoyed a light breakfast before they set out on their journey, but the urgency in Dominique's voice indicated her wish was in vain. Running a hand through her tousled curls, she turned to her escort to see him holding her cloak.

"I'm sorry we cannot tarry, but we must make haste. I fear our good proprietor suspects we are not what we have said."

Rochella found herself hurriedly draped in her cloak and propelled down the inn's back stairs to the refuse-filled alley. The stench of rotting garbage and human waste blanketed the air and made it hard to breathe. Several times she felt her foot sink into the quagmire but refused to even contemplate what she had stepped into.

Nausea rose in a sickening wave as she sought to keep up with Dom's long strides along the dark alley. After what seemed an eternity, they emerged into the gloom-shrouded street, where a rickety coach awaited them. With its mud-caked wheels and cracked windows, the vehicle looked as if it would not travel a mile without disintegrating.

Her stomach still heaving, Rochella caught a fleeting glimpse of the driver. Perched atop the coach, he sat hunched against the chill like a huge vulture. Dominique gave her no time for further inspection, but propelled her up the wobbly wooden step and inside the dimly lit vehicle. The light from the flickering, soot-smudged coach lantern illuminated the rat-chewed padding on the walls as well as clumps of coarse cotton and horsehair protruding through the holes in what had once been elegant velvet seats.

Too ill to care about the condition of the coach, Rochella sank down on the lumpy seat opposite Dominique. She laid her head back and closed her eyes, taking several deep breaths in an effort to quell her rioting insides.

The moment the door closed behind them, the crack of the whip sounded and the coach jolted into motion down the cobbled street. The unsprung ride did little to help her queasy stomach, and swaying back and forth, she prayed she would not shame herself by throwing up all over Dominique's shiny boots.

Soon the clicky-clap of steel against stone turned to soft thuds when the coach left the city streets behind and took to the country roads.

"*Madame,* are you ill?" Dominique asked. He had been too concerned about escaping Le Havre to note his companion's pallor. Now, in the gray light of dawn, he could see the white line about her lips and the ashen cast of her skin.

"I shall be all right," Rochella said, her voice hoarse.

With a frown Dominique leaned forward and placed his hand against her brow. Cold sweat dampened his fingers. Worry lines etched his eyes and lips. Lady Devlin was ill.

Drying his fingers on the leg of his breeches, he mused grimly, All I need now is for her to sicken and die on me. If that should happen I'll be left with nothing to show for the gamble I've taken.

"I fear you are unwell," he probed.

Rochella raised her head and gave him a wobbly smile in an attempt to reassure him. "Truly it is nothing. The stench in the alley and the swaying of the coach made me nauseated, but I am fine now."

"I fear our means of transportation is not what you arc accustomed to," Dominique replied, "but it was the best available for hire. We are lucky to have it."

Rochella looked at him sharply. "Do you mean the situation in France is so bad that one cannot even rent a decent coach?"

Dominique nodded as the shadowy gray sky began to lighten, turning to rose with the rising of the sun. "I fear conditions are far worse than even I imagined when we left England. The entire country is now under Jacobin control, and the nobles are fleeing France to save their lives."

Rochella felt a chill of fear ripple down her spine. Her parents would not be among those fleeing France. Her father, stubborn and proud, would never surrender Beauvais to the mercy of the Jacobin rabble. He would stand and fight. And, she feared, he would die.

"My God, we must reach Beauvais before it is too late. I must convince Papa that his life is more important than a pile of stones," Rochella said, unaware she had spoken aloud.

"Try not to worry. I am sure your parents are wise enough to seek safety should things become too dangerous. And we have no proof any violence has occurred in the region of Champagne. I know only what

I overheard from the innkeeper and his friends. There may be no truth in their gossip."

"You are right," Rochella said with more assurance than she felt. A sense of foreboding shadowed her, dimming the bright sunlight spilling in through the coach window.

Dominique could only nod his agreement. His own doubts had suddenly returned.

As the miles and hours passed with the constant drum of horses' hooves pounding through the day, Rochella's fear mounted. She had seen little along their route to raise her spirits. The estates they had passed were overgrown with weeds and looked deserted. Nor did her feelings improve later in the afternoon when they stopped at an inn to eat their first meal of the day. When Dominique questioned the innkeeper about the regiments of armed soldiers passing by, the man wiped his pudgy-fingered hands on what had once been a white apron and answered with gusto, "France is at war."

Rochella felt faint. Her appetite, already on the wane, vanished completely. She forced the last bit of hard cheese down her throat and rose unsteadily to her feet. Her voice quavered as she said, "I should like to go now," before turning to the door.

Dominique felt the last of his hopes evaporate into the hot afternoon air. Gulping what remained of the bitter wine, he slowly came to his feet and followed in her wake. He caught up with her just as she attempted to climb into the coach. "Shall I tell the driver to return to Le Havre?"

Rochella gave a vehement shake of her head as she allowed him to assist her into the coach. "No. I must reach Beauvais now at all costs."

"Surely you cannot mean to go on. You have just heard that France is at war. It is best for us to return to Le Havre and then take the first ship back to England and safety," Dominique cajoled as he settled his lean frame on the seat opposite her.

"I said I was going to Beauvais, *monsieur*. If you feel you must return to Le Havre then do so. I shall not stop you. However, you will have to go there on your own, because I shall need the coach."

"Very well, *madame*. It is your decision and your life you risk. But I shall not desert you, no matter how foolish I believe your choice is," Dominique answered in frustration. He had come too far to change his plans now.

"Thank you, *monsieur*. I shall see Papa pays you well for your consideration."

As twilight deepened into night, Dominique ordered the coachman to stop at a small inn outside of Compiègne. Exhausted from the long day's travel, Rochella made no protest when he once more told the innkeeper they were man and wife. All she wanted at that moment was to rest. She was far too tired to care about proprieties.

However, the sleep she so desperately sought eluded her when her head hit the smelly pillow. Her eyes would not close nor would her mind shut out the images of what might even now be transpiring at Beauvais.

How can all of my countrymen have gone mad? Rochella wondered, suddenly realizing that in a few short months France had become an alien land. She did not understand how her own people could turn on one another.

Gareth had tried to explain the situation, but she had not listened; she had had only one thing in mind, and that was the welfare of her parents if they ventured to visit Paris. In her naiveté she had never considered that the danger would spread to Beauvais.

Suddenly afraid of what the future would bring, Rochella covered her face with her hands and wondered at her own stupidity. She had foolishly left the safety of her home in England to come here to this mad world. She had thought herself brave enough to face any challenge. Now she wondered if she had the courage to face another day. At the moment she desperately needed to feel Gareth's arms about her.

Tears stung her eyes with the reality of her situation. Drawing in a shuddering breath, Rochella stared up at the cobwebbed ceiling. She had known before she left her husband that she loved him. Now in this shabby little room with Dominique's light snores filling the air, she regretted one thing more than anything else. Gareth would never know that he would hold her heart until the last breath of life left her body. From what she had already learned of her homeland, that might not be very long.

During the next days, Rochella saw the revolution in action. On the outskirts of Reims, a mob attacked their coach, and had it not been for Dominique's quick actions they would have been dragged from the vehicle and torn apart. When Dominique saw what was taking place, he ordered Rochella to do exactly as he bade. Dressed in somber black, he opened the coach door and swung himself down to face the angry group.

"Vive la révolution," he shouted at the top of his lungs. His words surprised the canaille, giving him enough time to posture dramatically with hands spread wide as he again shouted so everyone could hear, "Down with aristocrats who take from the people."

A hush fell over the mob as he continued. "Citizens of Reims, you who are true to France, do you attack your own—a poor merchant who cannot feed his children because of the taxes levied on him? We are all united in this revolution against corruption. We all want full bellies for ourselves and our children. We are tired of hearing their cries of hunger. You must not turn away from our glorious cause. Seek out the aristocrats and make them pay with their lives for the atrocities we have endured, but bid this humble merchant and his wife a fond and safe farewell. I go now to join our men to fight for France's freedom."

A rumble sounded through the mob as they eyed Dominique for a long tense moment. Then a shout went up from the back of the crowd, *"Vive la révolution."* It was an infectious cry, and soon everyone was cheering as Dominique was helped back into the coach and they were sent on their way with a bottle of wine, a loaf of fresh bread and a round of cheese.

Dominique wiped the nervous perspiration from his brow as he settled himself in the seat opposite the trembling Rochella. Believing she trembled from fear, he placed a comforting hand over her tightly clenched fists. "Now you see why you could not gown yourself in your finery and travel through France."

Rochella raised her head and looked at him, her eyes flashing. "How dare you say such horrid things? You incited those madmen to murder."

Chagrined by Rochella's censure, Dominique stiffened and drew away from her. No one spoke to Dominique Duval in such a way. Especially a bit of fluff who didn't have enough brains to realize that their lives had been at stake since the moment they arrived in France. His voice was chilly when he answered, "And had I not said what I did, you would now be dead yourself, *madame.* I did the only thing possible to ensure our survival. It is now left to others to do the same for themselves."

"But did you have to turn on your own kind? Do the lives of others lie so lightly upon your shoulders that you can toss them away?"

"*Madame,* it was your life I was trying to save," Dominique snapped, his face hard. "I thought I would have your gratitude instead of your censure for my efforts."

"I am grateful and I understand your reasoning. However, I wish you had been able to refrain from encouraging the canaille to murder. I cannot stop thinking of what will happen to the next people who cross their path," Rochella said.

Dominique drew in a deep, quelling breath in an effort to retain his composure. Rochella's life meant nothing to him, but he treasured his own neck and would eagerly toss her to the canaille if it became necessary. At the moment, however, he had to remain the proper gentleman and make amends if he wanted to get his hands on any of the Beauvais gold.

"Do you think I liked what I had to do? I was thinking only of your welfare. I know I should never have said what I did, but I needed to make them believe we were their own. Forgive me, Lady Devlin. I am afraid I didn't consider the consequences of my actions.'' The lies fell easily from his lips.

Contrition filled Rochella. He had risked his own life to protect her, and she repaid him by chastising him for telling the rabble what they wanted to hear. She did not agree with his methods, but she knew that he had done the only thing he could to save them. "I am the one who should apologize, *monsieur*. You did what was necessary. I fear my worry colored my judgment."

Gloating over her apology, Dominique leaned forward and took Rochella's hand within his own. His face reflected none of his inner feelings as he sympathized. "I understand. I should feel the same in your position. Let us now try to put all this behind us. We have only a few more hours of travel before we reach Beauvais, and you will see all your worry has been for naught."

"I pray you are right," Rochella said, easing her hand away from him and fighting to control the shiver of revulsion that his touch aroused within her. He had Gallic good looks with dark hair and eyes, but there was something about him that made her wary. She would truly be glad when the last few hours passed, and she was free of his company.

Sensing her withdrawal, Dominique settled back against the tattered seat. Arms folded over his chest, he laid his head back and closed his eyes, feigning sleep. She would rue the day she had snubbed him. All his life fine, aristocratic ladies had turned up their delicate little noses at him. He would endure her company until her father's gold was in his hands. Then she would meet the true Dominique Duval and suffer the full extent of his revenge.

As the coach rumbled over the last miles of the winding dusty road toward Beauvais, Rochella's apprehension mounted. A sickening wave of nausea churned her insides as she viewed the devastation that had been wrought upon the countryside. Scorched and blackened earth had replaced the once verdant pastureland that had fed the prime stock of the estates adjoining Beauvais land. The softly rolling fields that she had ridden over with her father and their neighbors lay bare and untilled. The world she remembered with such fondness had vanished within a few short months.

White-lipped, Rochella sat on the edge of her seat as the coach wound its way along the graveled drive to her home. She held her breath, straining for the first glimpse of the château. As the coach rounded the last bend, she saw her home and her spirits soared. The château still stood. Eager to see her parents, she overlooked the overgrown gardens and the blackened rows of grapevines.

When the coach circled to a halt in front of the château Rochella did not wait for Dominique to assist her down but exited on her own and ran up the flagged walk. She hammered on the massive front door but received no answer. Turning the latch, which had grown rusty, she was shocked to feel the door tremble as it slowly swung open.

Rochella blinked at what had formerly been her home, and felt her hopes crumble. She took several steps inside, unable to believe what she saw. Tatters of what had once been finely worked tapestries swayed before her eyes as black shadows swirled her into the safe void of unconsciousness. Her last thought before she sank to the floor was, They have burned my home.

Rochella fought the hands that slapped her lightly on the cheeks. "No, no, no," she murmured as she fought to remain in the safety of the dark world of unconsciousness. She did not want to come back to face reality.

"Madame?" Dominique asked anxiously when he saw Rochella's eyelids flicker. "Wake up."

Unable to avoid conscious thought, Rochella slowly opened her eyes and looked up at Dominique. Great sobs were wrenched from her as she clung to his coat and wept. *"Mon Dieu,* what has become of my parents?"

Dominique glanced about the charred ruins and shook his head. "I don't know, but we must leave here. It is far too dangerous for us to tarry."

Sniffling, Rochella pushed herself away from him and tried to compose herself. She smudged her cheeks as she wiped away her tears and gazed about her. "I shall not leave until I know of my parents."

"You speak foolishness," Dominique said. Getting to his feet, he looked contemptuously down at Rochella. "As you can see, there is no one here, and I tell you, it is much too dangerous to remain."

Rochella stubbornly shook her head. "I shall not leave! This is my home, and until I know what has happened to my parents, I shall remain."

Dominique's gaze swept over the burned-out interior of the once proud Château le Lion, and all his hopes for a rich future evaporated. His gaze came back to the lovely woman before him, and his eyes narrowed. How he would love to have the time to show her exactly how he felt about her and her kind, but the coachman was impatient. After seeing what had happened at the château, the man refused to wait for long. Dominique glanced toward the open door. His revenge would be knowing he had left this beautiful destitute woman to the mercy of the canaille.

When Dominique turned to leave, his foot crushed Rochella's reticule. He bent and picked up the purse. When he opened it and saw its contents, he smiled. His efforts had been worth something, after all. He glanced toward Rochella and furtively slipped the purse into his pocket. "If I cannot change your mind, *madame*, I shall take my leave. I have fulfilled my duty by bringing you to your home as you wished. Now I shall bid you adieu."

Still in a state of shock, Rochella did not completely grasp the meaning of Dominique's words. She looked up at him and nodded. "Thank you for your help."

Bowing gracefully from the waist, Dominique Duval, the born scoundrel, patted his pocket with assurance as he said, "Good luck, *madame*." Turning on his heel, he left the Château le Lion and its fair mistress behind. He felt only a flicker of conscience when he entered the coach and saw Rochella's portmanteau. Tossing it out onto the graveled drive, he ordered the driver to whip the horses to their fastest pace. At least he was leaving her with something, he told himself, and settled back against the rat-chewed seat.

Rochella stood by a heat-shattered window and watched the dilapidated coach pass from view, only vaguely aware that she had been left to fend for herself in a homeland that was devouring its own children. Her reason numbed by the horror surrounding her, she was only aware of the pain tearing at her heart. Tears blurred her vision as she turned away from the window. No longer possessing the strength to stand, she sank to the blackened floor and drew up her knees to her chest. Through misty eyes she peered at the fallen timbers. This place had housed two centuries of the Beauvais family under its gabled roof.

Rochella bowed her head against her knees and wept until nothing was left except dry, racking sobs. Then sniffling, her eyes red and swollen, her slender body trembling with small shudders, she raised her head and looked once more at her home.

Drawing deeply from her well of strength, she forced her mind to focus on the present. There was nothing left here for her.

She got slowly to her feet and made her way through the vast chambers filled now with the charred remains of broken furniture. She had almost decided it was useless to go any farther when she realized the fire had miraculously been contained. Only the east wing and the main hall had been destroyed. Her hope flaring and her heart pounding with a burst of excitement, she rushed through the quiet halls calling, "Mama, Papa."

There was no answer to her urgent cries. When she at last came to her parents' bedchamber, she knew she would never receive one. Even here in the master suite nothing had been spared. The down mattress had been slashed into pieces and torn from the huge four-poster bed. Feathers littered the floor and floated into the air when she moved. The dust curtains where she had hidden as a child were shredded beyond recognition, as were all the other drapes. The doors to the armoire hung lopsided from their hinges, revealing an empty interior. Ripped and burned, the remains of her mother's clothing blackened the hearth.

"Mama, Papa," Rochella whispered futilely, unable to tear her gaze away from the devastation. "Where are you?"

Again no answer came.

Her shoulders bowed under the heavy burden of her grief, Rochella made her way back to the main foyer and stepped out into the encroaching twilight. The evening shadows deepened, and a shiver passed down her spine as she realized she was now totally alone. Wrapping her arms protectively about her, she drew in several deep breaths in an effort to still the sudden trembling that beset her limbs. New tears threatened, but she refused to give way to them. She had to remain in control if she hoped to survive.

Dragging in a ragged breath, Rochella swept her gaze over the burned vineyards to the cottages used by the vintagers. A small spiral of smoke wound its way skyward from one thatched roof. At the sight Rochella's heart leaped into her throat. Giving no thought to the danger, she gathered up her skirts and ran toward the first sign of life she had seen since returning home.

In her haste she stumbled and fell over clumps of grass and bushes but was back on her feet in an instant, heedless of the pain her frantic pace caused her. Her chest heaving from the exertion and her hair falling in her eyes, she banged on the rough wooden door, calling, "Mama, Papa."

The door swung open and from the shadowy interior emerged the tines of a wooden pitchfork. Unable to see who threatened her with the crude weapon, Rochella quickly backed away from the door. "Please, I mean you no harm. It is I, Rochella de Beauvais."

"*Mamselle?* Is it truly you?" Babette asked as she tossed her weapon away. Stepping from the shadows she stood staring, openmouthed, unable to believe her mistress had returned to France.

"Babette," Rochella said, throwing herself into the maid's arms. Laughter mingled with tears of relief, making it impossible for her to say more.

"*Oui, mamselle.* But what are you doing here?" Babette managed to say at last. Casting a wary glance about, she quickly drew Rochella inside. She closed the door and secured it with a wooden peg.

"Babette, where are my parents, and why has my home been burned?" Rochella asked, too anxious with worry to answer the maid's questions. Sinking down on a rough-hewn, three-legged stool before the meager fire, she watched Babette nervously twist the hem of her apron until it was a tight roll.

"*Mamselle,* the peasants banded together and burned your home," Babette said at last. Unable to look Rochella in the eye, she shifted her gaze to the rush mat at her feet.

"But where are my parents?" Rochella asked, needing to hear the answer yet also dreading the news it might bring.

"*Mamselle,* I don't know where they are now, but I heard several men laugh when they said the marquis would find little welcome in Paris should he go there."

"Then they were not killed when the château was burned?" Rochella asked to reassure herself she had not misunderstood.

"Oh, no, *mamselle.* Your parents were forced out of the château by the peasants, but they were not killed. They had already fled by the time the looting and burning began."

Rochella closed her eyes and savored the relief sweeping over her. Her parents lived. Her father had wisely chosen to escape instead of standing to fight. But where had they gone? It would be too dangerous for them to go to Paris. But where else would they go? Rochella shook her head. Her father possessed many friends in Paris, and he would seek them out first for help. The marquis was far too stubborn to completely abandon Beauvais land. He would retreat until he could muster enough help to reclaim his estate from the rabble.

Settling the matter in her mind, Rochella looked up at Babette. "You said the peasants burned my home but I saw no one. Where have they gone?"

"They also fled when the news came that the Austrian army had crossed the border into France. They were afraid to be caught between the two armies."

"Are the Austrians so close then?" Rochella asked, her eyes widening in alarm.

"*Oui, mamselle.* They are now at the border of Beauvais land. Soon the French army will arrive and the fighting will begin."

"*Mon Dieu,*" Rochella breathed.

"My Jacques says our army will defeat the Austrians, and then the world will recognize that Frenchmen are free to choose their own destinies instead of allowing a weak king to determine our fates," Babette said with pride.

"Babette, you speak as if you agree with the canaille," Rochella said, surprised by the vehemence in her voice.

Babette raised her chin in the air. "I do, *mamselle.* Jacques has made me see how foolish I have been to believe one person is born better than another. We are all born of the flesh and it makes us equal. Your blood is no better than mine."

"I see," Rochella said, coming to her feet. She had thought herself safe with Babette, yet now she was not certain. She glanced uneasily toward the locked door and asked, "Where is Jacques now?"

"He has gone to organize our men to fight for France. When the Austrians arrive, they will not find only French soldiers but also the citizens of France," Babette answered, her voice mirroring her newfound pride.

Rochella felt a momentary reprieve. She was sure Babette would not intentionally harm her, but she could not trust Jacques. Though Babette had not said so Rochella suspected that Jacques Benoir was behind the peasant uprising at Beauvais.

"Babette, I must go before Jacques returns."

Babette nodded. "I know, *mamselle*. It would not do for you to be here. I fear my Jacques does not have a soft spot in his heart for you and your family as I do."

"Then will you help me?" Rochella pleaded. "I have to find my parents."

Babette shook her head. "*Non, mamselle*. I cannot help you. I will not jeopardize what I have found with Jacques for anyone, even you, *mamselle*. He is my life and should I lose him, I could not live."

"I understand," Rochella said. It hurt to lose Babette's friendship, yet in some small way she envied her. She had not let anyone sway her from the man who held her heart. Her loyalty was to him, and only him. Rochella turned toward the door and opened it. She hesitated briefly upon the threshold and looked back at the maid. "May God keep you safe, Babette."

"May he do the same for you, *mamselle*. Goodbye."

Rochella closed the door behind her and stepped out into the black night, once more alone. At the sight of the flickering campfires in the distant forest a chill of fear rippled through her. Soon the peaceful countryside would ring with the sound of battle. Muskets and cannon would drench Beauvais land in French and Austrian blood.

Rochella drew in a shaky breath and turned her gaze to the eerie, blackened skeleton of the château. Tonight for the last time she would stay in her home. Tomorrow she would collect her reticule and set out for Paris to find her parents.

Chapter Eleven

Rochella peered through the broken glass at the activity in the vineyards. Where workers had once pruned and cultivated, soldiers now marched in straight lines, armed with bayonets and muskets. Their heavy boots trampled the charred remains of the grapevines into dust, leaving a gray cloud hovering over the gently rolling hills.

Since dawn when the sound of their movements had roused her from her restless sleep, Rochella had watched them pass. Behind the uniformed soldiers she had recognized Babette's Jacques, leading a group of volunteers. Armed with pikes and a few crudely crafted weapons, they marched proudly off to battle.

Her eyes glued to the scene, Rochella leaned weakly against the window casing, wondering how she had managed to get herself stranded in the middle of a war.

She knew she could not remain at the château any longer without chancing being caught. Her only hope now was to find her reticule and pray that the money it contained would be enough to bribe her way to safety.

An hour later, sitting back on her heels, her face and hands black with soot, Rochella felt completely vulnerable for the first time in her life. Her purse was no-

where to be found, and she was without means to help
herself in any way. She had no money, no food, no
place to hide and no friends to help her.

The sound of a cannonade broke through Rochella's
despair, shaking her out of her lethargy and causing the
blackened timbers to tremble overhead. Realizing the
danger of remaining in the château, she was instantly on
her feet. As she fled, she heard an explosion behind her
and paused only long enough to glimpse the château's
charred walls crumbling from the blast of the cannon-
balls. Had she remained a moment longer, she would
have been crushed to death. Taking no time to savor her
good fortune, Rochella sped toward the shelter of the
woods.

Tree branches tore at her clothing and hair, yet panic
urged her on deeper into the forest. The sound of cannon was only a distant rumble when she stumbled over
a rotting log and went down with a crash. Gasping for
breath, she struggled to regain her footing, only to find
her strength had at last deserted her. A whimper of defeat escaped her pale lips as she sank back to the moist,
leaf-strewn ground. She could go no farther. Here,
upon the land that had nurtured her family for generations, she would die. Wrapping her arms about her
knees, she curled into a ball and waited for the destiny
that Gareth had foretold when he had denied her wish
to come to France.

Tears stung her eyes at the thought of her husband,
of the life they could have shared had he loved her, of
the children they could have made from that love. Had
he only loved her, she would never have left his side to
come to France. She knew she could not place the blame
on Gareth for her own reckless decisions. However, had

things been different between them, they might have been able to find a way together to help her parents.

"*Mamselle,*" a soft voice whispered. "Are you hurt?"

Rochella remained silent.

"*Mamselle,* are you hurt?" This time the question was accompanied by a light shake on Rochella's shoulder.

Slowly Rochella was roused from her stupor and stared up into the gentle eyes of a peasant girl.

The girl knelt at her side and smiled timidly down at her. "Can you sit up?"

Rochella nodded, and with the aid of the girl's arm about her shoulders eased herself upright. Again her efforts earned her a smile. Tenderly the girl brushed the leaves and twigs from Rochella's chestnut hair. "What is your name and where are you from, *mamselle?*"

"I am—I am—" Rochella stuttered, suddenly cautious of revealing her true identity after what Babette had said. This girl could be her enemy. At last she murmured uncertainly, "I am called Marie, and I once lived near here."

The girl patted her hand with understanding and said kindly, "I am Colette Dubois, Marie, and like you, I have been driven from my home. But these woods are no place to be. It is far too dangerous. I come here only when it is necessary to hunt for food. Come," Colette said as Rochella got to her feet. "I shall take you back to my hut near the edge of the woods. I have snared a rabbit." She retrieved the limp carcass of the furry creature and held it up proudly. "We shall eat well this day."

With Colette's help Rochella managed to traverse the well-trampled path to the hovel the girl called home.

Gazing about the tiny, thatch-roofed hut with its mud-plastered walls so thin you could see the sunlight through them, Rochella realized the dogs at Beauvais had lived in better shelter than this kindhearted girl. A pile of rags to serve as her bed, an iron pot and a carved wooden bowl were the extent of her worldly possessions, yet she was willing to share.

Rochella blinked back a rush of blinding tears. It was easy to be generous when you were rich, but when you possessed so very little, a gesture such as Colette had made revealed something money could not buy—a heart of pure gold.

Seeing the brightness in Rochella's eyes, Colette urged her toward the pile of rags. "Here, sit down. You are not well."

Rochella accepted the seat amid the rags and brushed at her eyes. "I am not ill, just tired and hungry. I have not eaten since yesterday."

Colette nodded and smiled. "Then our rabbit will soon remedy your problem. Rest here while I skin and clean him. We shall have you feeling better in no time."

"Thank you, Colette," Rochella said, her voice wobbly with emotion. "I do not know what would have happened to me, had you not come to my rescue."

"God watches over his children, Marie," Colette said, and she ducked out the opening where a tattered blanket served as a door.

Rochella lay back and stared up at the straw ceiling overhead. How could Colette still believe that God would take care of her? From everything Rochella had seen and heard, God had deserted France and the devil now reigned in his stead.

A shudder shook Rochella. It would be so easy to hate the French people, yet Colette's kindness made her realize it was not they who were at fault but those in power. The government had brought the terror down upon their heads by ignoring the pleas of its own people.

Colette's return with a steaming bowl of rabbit eased Rochella's hunger and buoyed her flagging spirits. She might be the prey, and the canaille the hunter. However, like the fox, she intended to survive by using her wits. She would not fall meekly into the clutches of the mob, no matter how terrified or uncertain she was. She would go to Paris and find her parents. Then together they would go to England. For now she would not consider the prospect that her return might not be welcomed at Devil Wind.

Forcing any negative thoughts from her mind, Rochella fell asleep curled against Colette for warmth.

Great booms of thunder roused her the next morning. Groggily she opened her eyes and squinted against the bright sunlight streaming in through the cracks in the walls. Another large boom caused the hut to vibrate, jarring her from her languid stupor. The sound she had heard was not thunder but cannonade.

"Colette, wake up," Rochella said, shaking the girl's shoulder.

Colette blinked up at her for several moments and then came alert with a start. "What is it, Marie?"

"We are in danger if we stay here," Rochella said, getting to her feet. Again the earth vibrated from the blast of cannon.

Colette was on her feet in an instant, collecting her few meager possessions. "We must make for the woods. The trees will protect us."

The girls turned in unison to the door, but their exit was blocked by two burly figures. Before Rochella could react, Colette threw aside her bundle, retrieved the knife she kept at her waist and faced the intruders.

"What is the meaning of this?" Rochella began, taking a step forward. "I—"

Colette quickly intervened, cutting off Rochella's next words before she could say anything to endanger herself. "I am Colette Dubois and this is my sister, Marie. What is it you want with us, citizens?"

Rochella realized the mistake she had nearly made and eased herself back to Colette's side. Her surprise had made her forget her ruse. She flashed Colette a look of gratitude and saw again the look of understanding. The girl had known all along that she was lying to her, and yet she had freely shared all she possessed.

The two men grinned at each other and stepped into the tiny hut. Their heads touched the straw ceiling and their wide girth blocked any avenue of escape. "*Mesdemoiselles,* it is our pleasure to find such lovely ladies. I am Pierre, and this is my friend Gage."

Colette waved the knife threateningly. "We have no need for introductions. Be gone with you. This is our home and you have no rights here."

Gage raked Colette with his leering gaze and took another step forward, undeterred by her meager weapon. "Now, *mademoiselle,* is that any way to treat soldiers of France?"

"Soldiers of France," Colette scoffed. "I smell the scent of desertion about the two of you. Begone before you are found and hanged for your cowardice."

At Colette's bravado Rochella felt terror grip her insides. An angry glint entered Gage's eyes, and his evil laughter shook the thin walls of the hut.

"*Mademoiselle,* you are a feisty little pigeon—one I shall consume in one bite." He took another step toward Colette.

"We shall not hurt you, if you be good to us, *petite,*" Gage said, snaking out a hand and capturing Colette about the throat. "But if you resist us, then we shall make you suffer. It has been a long time since my friend and I have had a woman."

"Take your hands off me," Colette ordered, bringing her knife up to strike. Before the words were out of her mouth, Gage had captured her wrist and twisted it until the knife fell unheeded to the floor.

"It is no use to fight," he said. Grinning down at Colette, he ripped the thin material of her bodice from neckline to waist. A cry of outrage on her lips, Colette sought to defend herself. She slapped and beat at him with her fists.

"Leave her alone," Rochella ordered. Determined to help her friend, she launched herself into the fray, kicking and scratching.

With one large hairy arm, Gage thrust Rochella away from him. "Get her out of here while I take care of this one," he said to Pierre.

Pierre grabbed Rochella about the waist, swinging her off her feet, and hauled her outside, kicking and screaming. Intent on battling each other, neither of them heard the sound of approaching hoofbeats.

"Hold, I say," a deep masculine voice ordered.

Giving Rochella a rough push into the dirt, Pierre snapped to attention and saluted. "Sir, we have found a traitor."

A stocky, middle-aged colonel dismounted and strode toward them. His gaze swept over the scene, taking in

Rochella and her disheveled state, before once more coming to rest on Pierre. "A traitor?"

"She is an aristocrat pretending to be a peasant. That makes her a traitor."

Rochella felt a new wave of fear wash over her as the colonel stood regarding her for a long, thoughtful moment. At the sound of a struggle coming from inside the hut, the officer looked back at Pierre through narrowed eyes.

Pierre swallowed hard and shifted uneasily. He feared the colonel was one of those soldiers who did not appreciate the spoils of war or understand it was a soldier's right to take what he found upon the land whether it be a woman or a horse.

"Sir, you've got to believe me. She is an aristocrat if I've ever seen one," Pierre nearly whined. He caught himself about to wring his hands and quickly stuck the offending members in his pockets.

Ignoring him, the colonel disappeared into the hut. It was only a moment before the sound of a pistol ripped through the air, and he stepped once more into the sunlight, his face pale.

When she saw the expression on the officer's face, Rochella's heart froze. She clambered to her feet and ran toward the hut. The colonel stopped her before she reached the door. "*Mademoiselle,* it is not a pretty scene."

Rochella looked from his haggard face to the cottage and cried, "Let me go! I have to see Colette."

The colonel shook his head. "You can do nothing, *mademoiselle.* The girl is dead."

Her eyes widening, Rochella stared up at the colonel in shock. When she spoke her voice was a whisper of agony. "How can it be? It has been only minutes since he took her."

"The bastard slit the young woman's throat," the colonel said in disgust. "But he will harm no one else."

Rochella's stomach heaved with revulsion, and her knees threatened to give way beneath her.

Pierre held up his hands in supplication as he began to back away. "I didn't know he intended to harm the girl."

"Sergeant, you are under arrest," the colonel said, taking his pistol from the holster at his side and aiming it at Pierre.

"We meant only to bring the two back to headquarters, Colonel, nothing more. But they fought us and we had to subdue them. We did nothing else, I swear."

"You can tell your story at your court martial," the colonel replied, and then looked at Rochella. "*Mademoiselle,* you will have to come back to headquarters with me. It will be decided there what to do with you."

Rochella closed her eyes and nodded. The very thing she had feared had come to pass. Drawing once more from her well of courage, she looked at the colonel. "Will you allow me to bury Colette before we go?"

"I shall send back some men to see to it," the colonel said. Taking Rochella by the arm he led her to his horse and helped her mount. Climbing up behind her, he took the reins and motioned the sergeant forward with his pistol.

Gareth stepped down from the coach and drew in a breath of the crisp, clean sea air. It felt good to be home where he could retreat from the outside world. It had taken only a few days for him to grow weary of the London that his peers seemed to enjoy with such zest.

He had no need for London, filled with its squalid odors—from the smell of the butcher shops, where the blood of slaughtered animals ran freely into the gutters, to the many chimneys belching smoke that left a heavy gray haze hanging like a caul over the city.

Yet after today, Devil Wind might no longer be my sanctuary, Gareth agonized. Turning to look out across the glistening sea, the expression in his dark eyes reflected his dread of the reception he would receive when he told Rochella about his family.

Again, he filled his lungs with the fresh clean air and resolutely took the steps to the wide double doors. Perhaps she would turn away from him when she knew the truth, but he could not go on living the lie. Rochella deserved better. She had been honest with him and now it was time for him to be so with her.

"Where is my wife?" Gareth asked, handing the footman his cape.

The footman's eyes widened and he stuttered nervously. "M-my Lord—ah, I'm afraid Lady Devlin isn't here. Mistress Bronson can explain things to you."

Gareth frowned at the footman, wondering at the man's hesitation and evasiveness. He seemed afraid of something. "Then tell her I want to see her immediately," Gareth said.

Bemused by the apprehensive look on the footman's face, Gareth shook his head and strode down the hallway to his study. He crossed to his desk and opened the bottom drawer. Intent on leaving his extra coins in the strongbox, he lifted it out. His brows lowered into an ominous frown at the sight of the broken lock.

"I shall have someone's hide for this offense," he vowed. Flipping open the lid, he stared down at the remaining coins.

"My lord?" Hilda said from the doorway.

His eyes flashing with ire and his swarthy complexion deepening in hue, Gareth slammed his fist down upon the desk. "I have been robbed!"

Hilda stepped into the study and quietly closed the door behind her. She had been looking forward to this moment, yet she had also been dreading it. She moistened her lips nervously and cleared her throat several times before she managed to speak. "My lord, I fear I know the culprit."

Gareth's angry gaze locked upon Hilda. His voice was low and full of menace as he asked, "Who was it?"

Unable to control the prickle of fear that raced up her spine, Hilda cleared her throat again before she finally said, "It—it was your wife, Lady Devlin."

"Don't be ridiculous," Gareth snapped. He was in no mood to hear anyone besmirch his wife.

"It is true nonetheless."

"Why would my wife steal from me when she has only to ask for anything she wants?" Gareth asked, glaring at the housekeeper.

"Lord Devlin, you will have to receive your answer from Lady Devlin."

"Then go and tell her I wish to see her immediately."

"I cannot do that, my lord."

"Hilda, I am in no mood for disobedience. Do as I bid you."

"My lord, I would do as you bid if I were able."

Gareth drew in a deep breath and sought to keep a rein on his temper. At last he asked, "Hilda, is there a reason for your reticence?"

"My lord, Lady Devlin is not at Devil Wind."

Gareth relaxed and a wry grin tugged up the corner of his mouth. "Then as soon as she returns, tell Lady Devlin I wish to see her."

Hilda shifted uneasily. "My lord, I fear Lady Devlin has no intention of returning. She left almost two weeks ago."

"What?" Gareth said, unable to believe what the housekeeper was telling him.

"Lady Devlin left the day following your departure to London. No one was aware of her intentions until the next morning when I found this note in her chamber. It is addressed to you." Hilda handed the letter to Gareth and quickly stepped away from the desk.

Gareth's hand closed about the note. "That will be all, Hilda."

"Yes, my lord," Hilda said and swiftly exited the study. Adam wasn't the only member of the Devlin household who possessed a temper, and she wanted to be far away from Lord Devlin's when it exploded after he read the note.

Hilda smiled confidently. Everything was working out well. Rochella had returned to France where she belonged, and when Lord Devlin read the note she'd forged after forcing Alice to tell her where Lady Devlin had gone, he would not be too eager to have her back. If anything, he would never want to see her again. Brushing her hands together at a job well done, Hilda ascended the stairs to the north wing. Adam was going to be well pleased with the way she had handled the situation.

Unable to open the letter right away, Gareth sank back into his chair and stared at the crumpled missive in his hand. He desperately wanted to know what it said, yet once he read it, he would be unable to deny that Rochella had left him. As long as he didn't see the words, he could believe she was still safely upstairs in her chamber or walking in the gardens or riding across the heath enjoying the beautiful day.

Gareth laid his head back and squeezed his eyes closed against the sudden sting of tears. How easily she had found her way into his heart. She had come to him unwanted, yet she had managed to break down all the barriers he had erected to protect himself. She had made him love her despite all his vows, and then she had left him without a thought to the pain he would suffer when he returned home to find her gone.

Nostrils flaring, Gareth drew in an unsteady breath and looked once more at the letter in his hand. After a long moment he tore it open. His eyes scanned the hurriedly scribbled handwriting before focusing his attention to the words his wife had written.

Dear Gareth,
Our marriage has been a mistake from the beginning. I am returning to France where I can be happy. Do not attempt to follow me. I shall never return to Devil Wind.

Rochella

Gareth's expression hardened at the curt message and his anger rose. His eyes narrowing and his lips pressed into a thin line, he crumpled the note in his balled fist. If she thought to end their marriage with a few terse sentences then she was sorely mistaken. He deserved far more. He would be damned if he would allow her to walk out of his life without an explanation. Perhaps their marriage had been a mistake in the beginning, but the moments they had shared had not been. Rochella was now a Devlin, and if she thought that he would not follow her and bring her back, she was sorely mistaken.

With the thought of what was happening in France, Gareth's anger drained from him as suddenly as it had arisen. His heart began to pump violently against his ribs as he experienced true fear for the first time in his life. "My God!" he breathed. "She is in the midst of a revolution."

Thinking only of the danger in which his wife had so foolishly placed herself, Gareth jerked a piece of paper from the desk drawer and hurriedly scribbled a note to his cousin Robert, asking him to come to Devil Wind to oversee Gareth's affairs while he was away.

After sending the messenger to Robert's estate, Gareth took only enough time to change into his riding clothes before he, too, was mounted on his fastest steed and on his way to London. In order to travel freely in France, he would need the king's permission and the protection of the English government.

Chapter Twelve

The army regiment had made camp in the meadow where Rochella had often played as a child. However, like so much else she had seen since her return to France, it had been destroyed by the revolution. Trampled and churned by the heavy boots of the infantry and the hooves of cavalry horses, the ground lay bare, and the area was a hive of activity as soldiers scurried about preparing for the coming battle.

Rochella felt a chill run up her spine as the colonel maneuvered his mount through the scores of tents and campfires to the center of the encampment. Though surrounded by her own countrymen, she felt she was in the midst of enemies. The men who paused in their duties to watch them pass would eagerly see her hang because of the blood in her veins. She wondered how long they would have to wait to do so, once the colonel turned her over to his commanding officer.

The officer reined his mount to a halt in front of a large tent where two red-coated soldiers stood guard. After dismounting, he turned and helped Rochella to the ground. "Please ask the general if he will see me," he said to one of the guards as he returned their courtesy salutes. "Tell him I have found an aristocrat hiding in a serf's hovel in the nearby woods."

The wait was brief. The guard returned and held open the tent flap for the colonel and his hostage to pass into the humid shadowy interior. The colonel came to attention before the large desk and saluted the man seated behind it. "Sir, one of my men found this girl in a hut nearby. He claims she is an aristocrat."

"What is your opinion, Colonel?" the general asked. Getting to his feet, he came around the desk.

"Sir, I can only say she denies it."

"Then that will be all for now, Colonel. I will question the young lady further," the general said.

Dismissed, the colonel saluted once more and left Rochella alone with his imposing commander. He mounted and rode back in the direction he'd come. It was now time to see to Pierre's punishment.

Folding his arms over his chest, the general leaned back against the heavy desk and turned his attention to Rochella. He studied her thoughtfully for a long moment, taking in her appearance, his keen gaze missing nothing. Her simple gray gown was in tatters and her thick chestnut-colored hair tumbled about her shoulders in a riot of reddish-brown curls, yet he noted the fine quality of the material of her clothing as well as the sheen to her hair. A man accustomed to the best that money could buy, he instantly recognized his own.

"Won't you be seated, *mademoiselle?*" he asked courteously, indicating the canvas camp chair with a graceful wave of his long-fingered hand.

Gratefully, Rochella sank into the chair and nervously moistened her lips.

"Allow me to introduce myself. I am the Marquis de Lafayette, the commanding officer of this regiment and of the National Guard of France," General Lafayette said. When Rochella made no move to introduce herself, he smiled. "May I know your name, *mademoiselle?*"

Rochella shifted, ill at ease. She had heard a great deal about the Marquis de Lafayette, yet after everything she had seen and heard, she did not know whom to trust. At last she lied, "I—I am, ah, Marie Dubois."

The general arched one brow skeptically. "*Mademoiselle,* I understand your reasoning, yet you have nothing to fear if you tell me the truth."

"I am telling you the truth," Rochella insisted, lowering her eyes to the earthen floor. She jumped with a start when the general reached down and took her hand. Her gaze fastened upon his handsome face with its high forehead, straight brows and long, aquiline nose as he turned her hand palm upward and inspected it carefully.

A smile tugged at his well-shaped lips. "The softness of your hands belies your words."

Rochella released a long breath, stiffened her back and raised her chin in the air. Her ruse was at an end. She would face whatever the future brought with courage and pride. "*Monsieur,* I am Rochella de Beauvais from the Château le Lion de Beauvais."

General Lafayette chuckled his admiration. "Ah, de Beauvais. I remember the marquis well. Are your parents still on the estate?"

"*Non, monsieur.* They were driven away by the rabble who came to take our home."

Lafayette arched a curious brow. "Then why were you hiding in a peasant's hut? Why did you not flee with your parents?"

"I have been away from France until recently. I did not know what had transpired until I returned to find my home burned and my parents missing." Rochella struggled to keep the pain from her voice.

Seeing the quick flare of anguish in her emerald eyes, General Lafayette nodded and once more took his seat behind the desk. He understood her pain far better than she realized. Of late he had wondered how he himself would fare in the near future. France was turning on even those who were loyal to it. "Do you know where your parents are now?"

Rochella saw the flicker of compassion in the general's eyes and struggled to keep her composure. "No. I fear they have gone to Paris to seek help from Papa's friends."

"Then what are your plans, *mademoiselle?*" the general asked.

"I must try to find my parents."

"Surely you do not mean to go to Paris yourself?" The general's voice reflected his astonishment at her answer.

"I must" was Rochella's resolute answer.

The general shook his head. "It is impossible. Paris at the moment is far too dangerous, especially for a young noblewoman alone. And you must remember, I still have to deal with you."

Rochella stared at the general, suddenly uneasy. She had momentarily forgotten the marquis's position. He was still a general in the service of France. She swallowed hard and her words were barely audible as she asked, "What do you mean? Am I under arrest?"

General Lafayette held up one elegantly manicured hand and shook his head. "No, Mademoiselle Beauvais. I am not placing you under arrest, but I must make certain that my men do not learn what I have done. However, at the moment, I can offer you no protection. We are engaged in a war and this is no place for a young woman of your breeding.''

"Can you not just allow me to leave?'' Rochella asked.

General Lafayette's lips curved into a beautiful smile, but he shook his head once more. "I am afraid not.'' He studied her thoughtfully for a long moment before taking a pinch of snuff from an intricately worked silver box. He sneezed lightly into a soft linen handkerchief before he continued. "Perhaps I do know what to do with you. However, it will not be very pleasant, *mademoiselle.*''

Rochella glanced down at her tattered clothing before looking once more at the general. "I assure you, *monsieur,* of late I have had to deal with much unpleasantness.''

General Lafayette threw back his wigged head, and his laughter filled the tent. "I believe you, Mademoiselle Beauvais. My proposition is against my better judgment, for I honestly feel I should send you in the opposite direction. However, I shall send you to Paris if that is your wish. A supply wagon leaves at dawn for the city, and you may travel with it. I shall tell my lieutenant I am sending you back to Paris to stand trial.''

Rochella came to her feet and dropped into a low curtsy. "You have my gratitude for life, *monsieur.*''

General Lafayette rose and moved around his desk. He pulled Rochella to her feet and kissed her hand. "*Mademoiselle,* do not say such a thing. You may regret your words once you reach Paris. I shall send a letter of introduction to a friend in the city. Perhaps he will be able to help you locate your parents if they are in Paris.''

"I will never regret your help," Rochella said, her eyes filling with grateful tears.

The general wondered what she would find in Paris, when even at this moment the king of France himself was in danger. He prayed that he had not just sentenced her to death.

"I shall have one of my guards escort you to your tent for tonight. Rest, my dear. I fear you will need all your strength in the coming days." He summoned the guard and gave him instructions. Rochella dropped the marquis another curtsy and followed the guard out.

General Lafayette settled himself once more behind his desk and picked up the map he'd been studying when the colonel had arrived with his beautiful prisoner. France had a hundred thousand troops, but with the raw volunteers that filled its ranks, the army was ill prepared to face Austria's trained soldiers on the battlefield. Running his fingers over his smoothly shaved chin, the general considered all the lives that would be lost in the encounter with the Austrians. His troops were as poorly equipped as the colonials he had commanded in America. After picking up the quill pen, he dipped it into the inkwell and began to write to the king of Austria. Perhaps he would be able to stop the senseless loss of life before it was too late.

Rochella awoke at dawn from a sound and restful sleep. Stretching her arms over her head, she stared up at the canvas and smiled. She would go to Paris under the protection of the French soldiers, and with the letter to General Lafayette's friend she would have help in locating her parents. The world looked much brighter on this warm summer morning than it had only twenty-four hours earlier when she had awakened to horror.

Rochella closed her eyes against the memory of Colette. She could not allow herself to dwell upon the death of the young woman. She had to focus all her energy on reaching Paris and finding her parents. She was caught in a sea of unrest, and no matter how hard she struggled to keep her head above the waters of the terror engulfing her country, the rushing tides threatened to pull her down. She knew that if she wanted to survive she had to remain strong and not allow her emotions to weaken her.

Resolutely Rochella tossed back the blanket and sat up on the narrow army cot. Standing, she straightened her tattered gown. She had come a long way from the elegantly dressed daughter of one of the wealthiest men in France. She released a resigned breath and shrugged. The gown would have to do. It was all she had. She opened the tent flap and stepped outside.

The guard on duty smiled at her. "*Mademoiselle*, General Lafayette thought you might need this," he said, holding up her scuffed portmanteau.

Rochella's mouth fell agape at the sight of the baggage.

The guard grinned at her pleased surprise. "The general sent me back to the château to see if I might be able to salvage a few articles of your clothing. Fortunately, I found this just outside or I fear you would have nothing left. The château has been completely destroyed by cannon fire."

"Thank you so much. Please also convey my appreciation to the general," Rochella said, her voice husky with emotion.

"I shall do so when he returns, *mademoiselle*. He rode to the front several hours ago." The guard glanced down at the bucket of water at his feet. "The wagon will be leaving for Paris within the hour, and I thought you might like to wash and change before you set out."

"I would love to, thank you," Rochella said, giving him a dazzling smile.

The guard cleared his throat. "Then I shall leave you to your ablutions and see to your breakfast."

A bemused smile tugged up the corners of Rochella's lips as she watched the young man stride away. Some things did not change even in times of revolution and war. Her future looking somehow brighter, she picked up the bucket of cherished water and her portmanteau, and strode into the tent.

Less than an hour later, Rochella, dressed in a soft muslin gown, stepped from the tent to find her guard waiting to escort her to the supply wagon. He cast a furtive glance about before hurriedly handing her a paper sealed with the waxed crest of the Marquis de Lafayette. "The general asked me to convey his wish for your success, *mademoiselle*."

Rochella glanced down at the name of Monsieur Talleyrand-Périgord, written in an elegant script across the front of the missive, and felt her spirits soar. She had often heard her father and mother speak of the illustrious Talleyrand when they returned from their visits to court. And she knew if anyone would be able to help her, Talleyrand would be the person.

Placing the letter of introduction safely in her portmanteau, Rochella extended her hand to the young guard. "Thank you for everything."

He nodded and without another word escorted her to the wagon, where two rough-looking soldiers waited.

They eyed her suspiciously as the guard helped her into the back of the wagon and she took her seat on a pile of canvas. They had heard from their companions that an aristocrat had been captured and was being sent back to Paris to stand trial, but they had received no such order. On the contrary, they had been instructed to show the utmost respect to the girl and to ensure her protection on the journey to Paris. When they reached the city they were to release her. The two suspected something was not quite right, but knew they had to obey their orders, no matter how they felt about them.

At the end of eight horrendous days Rochella at last saw the gates of Paris. General Lafayette's prediction of an unpleasant journey to Paris had been mildly understated. She ached from head to toe and had bruises in places no lady of good breeding would mention. The roads had been little more than trails trampled out by the booted feet of the hundreds of soldiers marching toward the eastern front. Like a ship at sea the wagon had swayed and dipped constantly into the deep ruts, jarring every bone in Rochella's body with each bumpy jolt.

Her guards had done little to ease the discomfort of her situation. They had followed their orders to the letter. They had seen to her protection but not to her comfort. They had kept to themselves, never speaking unless it was necessary. The long, silent summer days had given Rochella much time for contemplation of her past as well as her future. With the oppressive heat of the midday sun bearing down upon the canvas overhead, she had found her thoughts often turning to the cool, misty days at Devil Wind and the handsome visage of its master. At those times she could not stop herself from wondering if Gareth was relieved she was gone. Or did he miss her in some small way?

Evening was settling over the city by the time the guards had maneuvered the wagon through the maze of buildings that had been constructed outside the walls of Paris. Peeping through the slits in the canvas cover, Rochella saw the armed guards at the gates and felt a chill of fear at the thought of her fate should her silent companions venture to expose her presence.

The two men sat in the front of the wagon with heads close together. They talked quietly to keep her from hearing their conversation, yet she did overhear her name mentioned. The breath caught in her throat and her heart began to pound uncomfortably against her ribs as she realized their intention. She had seen the suspicious looks they had given her and did not doubt that they suspected all was not as the general had indicated. Her instincts suddenly compelling her actions, Rochella eased to the back of the wagon, grabbed her portmanteau and jumped down to the dusty road. The weight of her portmanteau combined with the momentum of her jump nearly sent her headfirst into the roadway, but she managed to regain her balance, staggering like a drunk to the side of the road. Breathing heavily, she ran into an alley between two cottages where the deepening shadows sheltered her escape. Heart pumping furiously, she cautiously eased her way along the rear of the cottage and watched as the supply wagon stopped at the gates.

A moment later her suspicion about the soldiers' intentions was confirmed. She held her breath as she listened to them tell the guards about their orders to take her to Paris. She smiled at the astonished looks on their faces when the guards searched the wagon and found no sign of her. Both men clambered down from their seat to make certain, shaking their heads in bewilderment.

"She was there a short while ago," the spokesman of the two said, scratching his chin. "There's something strange about all this. In camp we heard rumors the girl was an aristocrat."

"We'll keep an eye out for her," the guard at the gate said. "She might be a spy. There's been too much desertion lately to trust anyone."

The spokesman cocked a bushy brow and pushed back his tall hat. "What do you mean?"

"Haven't you heard?" the guard asked. When the two in the wagon again shook their heads, he continued. "When our forces were ordered to advance on the enemy, several officers resigned and three cavalry detachments went over to the enemy. We received word of what was happening at the front by special communiqué only yesterday."

"Then you'd best keep your eyes open. The girl was friendly with General Lafayette, and his sympathies for the king and his own kind are well known."

The guard nodded, and the two soldiers returned to their perch and whipped the horses into motion.

Rochella watched the wagon pass through the gates and wondered how she would gain entry to the city. A breeze from the Seine made her shiver then, and she rubbed absently at her arms as she thought desperately how she could pass the guards unhindered. Nothing feasible came to her mind.

Spotting her movements in the shadowy alley, a stray dog let out a loud baying bark, startling Rochella. "Go away," she whispered, shooing the mongrel. The dog let out another loud bark. Her heart in her throat, Rochella cast a frantic glance toward the gates.

"You skinny beast," she hissed. She picked up a small stone and tossed it at the animal. "Get going." She breathed a sigh of relief when the dog tucked his tail and fled.

Looking once more toward the gates, she eased deeper into the shadows and watched a group of soldiers come through with several women clinging to them. They all laughed and talked as they passed the sentry without question. Rochella smiled to herself as a plan began to form.

She would enter the city with the returning soldiers. No one would ever know she was not one of their women, if she chose the right moment to join them. Satisfied her plan would work, Rochella glanced down at the portmanteau at her feet. She would have to leave it behind but she needed the letter of introduction to Talleyrand. After retrieving the letter, she slipped it inside her bodice and patted it. The parchment rattled at her touch. Should she be stopped and searched, she would be arrested immediately if the letter were found upon her person.

Resigned to the fact she would have to leave the precious document behind, she replaced it in the portmanteau and swiftly hid the bag beneath the bushes edging the cottage, covering it with loose dirt and leaves. Dusting the dirt from her hands, she gazed down at the hiding place. She did not like the thought of leaving the letter behind, but she had no choice. She could only pray it would be there when she returned for it.

Carefully, she made her way back in the direction she had come, settling herself in the deepest shadows near the edge of the road. She glanced up at the sky, grateful for the black night.

Several hours later when Rochella was beginning to doubt the wisdom of her plan, a group of merry-makers came staggering toward the city gates. Silently she slipped from her hiding place. She followed at a safe distance until the group neared the sentry. Quickening her pace then, she eased herself among the intoxicated revelers, mingling with the soldiers like one of their doxies. When the guard on duty called out a friendly greeting to his comrades and the group slowed to exchange ribald comments about the pleasures to be found in the night, Rochella thought her heart would stop. A few moments later, however, the guard, still laughing, waved them on their way without checking their papers.

As soon as they were away from the gates, Rochella detached herself from the group and dashed into the nearest alley.

Knees quaking with relief, she paused for a moment to draw in great breaths of air. Warily, she clung to the protection of the shadows and peered out at the activity in the street beyond. A crowd had gathered around a wagon where a short, dark-haired man with a large head spoke with a fervor that excited his audience. His skin was flushed and his eyes glowed with his zeal. His voice was strong and passionate as he raised his hand and shook it threateningly.

"Lafayette has retreated and the Austrian army is now preparing to destroy us while our good King Louis awaits their help in his luxurious palace. The time when the aristocrats crushed us beneath their high-heeled boots is at an end. We, the citizens of France, must rise up and build our own army to protect all we have worked to achieve."

A rumble of agreement passed through the crowd and their excitement mounted as they shouted, *"Vive la nation! Vive la liberté! Vive Marat!"*

From her dark haven, Rochella listened to the man arouse the crowd into an angry mob. Cold terror washed over her as she realized the extent of the danger surrounding her on all sides. The mob had begun to break up into groups, dispersing in all directions as they vehemently shouted, *"Vive la liberté!"*

Suddenly panicking, Rochella fled back in the direction she had just come. Running out into the dark street, she looked frantically all around, searching for a safe haven. She saw none, and her panic drove her on. Her chest began to ache from the exertion, making it difficult for her to catch her breath, and she stumbled over a loose cobblestone and fell to her knees. Gritting her teeth against the burning pain from her scrapes, she forced herself back to her feet. Her blood drumming in her ears, she realized she could run no farther. She staggered forward into the black shadows of a doorway and huddled on the step to regain her breath.

Warily she searched the darkness for any sign of danger, before she allowed herself to relax enough to rest her weary muscles and take in her surroundings. Slowly her terror began to ebb and she realized she could not remain in the doorway forever. She had to find Monsieur Talleyrand.

Seeing a faint light at the end of the street, Rochella forced herself back to her feet and began to walk toward it. She had no idea how she was going to find Monsieur Talleyrand's residence in a city filled with bloodthirsty madmen, yet she knew she had to try. She had no money to secure lodgings or to buy food, and she was without any friends in the French capital.

The bells of Notre-Dame de Paris cathedral rang out the hour of midnight as Rochella wandered through the quiet streets. The stupidity of her impetuousness was slowly beginning to sink into her fatigued mind. It had been a child's folly to believe she could find her parents in a city where she would be imprisoned should she be caught. She had not listened to those far wiser and now she feared she would pay dearly for her foolishness.

Weary to the bone, she sank down in a doorway. She intended to rest only a moment, but her exhaustion overcame her as she laid her head against her knees and went to sleep.

Chapter Thirteen

"What have we here?"

A deep masculine voice startled Rochella awake. Shielding her eyes against the early-morning light, she squinted up at the young, uniformed army officer. The blood slowly drained from her face as she realized she had been caught.

When he saw her look of fright, the young man's brows knit with a frown. He bent forward and extended his hand to assist her to stand. "*Mademoiselle,* may I be of service?"

A lump of fear making it impossible for her to speak, Rochella rose unsteadily to her feet.

"*Mademoiselle?*" the young officer asked again, his blue-gray eyes mirroring his concern when she didn't answer.

Feeling suddenly ill, Rochella swayed and her legs threatened to give way beneath her. Her face ashen, she leaned against the wall for support and gulped in air to try to keep from fainting.

"*Mademoiselle!* You are ill," the young officer said as he quickly assessed the situation and acted upon it instinctively. He lifted Rochella carefully into his arms and carried her up the short flight of stairs to his tiny apartment. After kicking the door open, he strode briskly across the room and deposited her in a chair. Without a word, he turned to the small table, which held a bottle of brandy and two glasses. He poured a small amount into one of the glasses and handed it to her. "Drink this. It will give you strength."

Rochella managed to mumble a grateful thank-you before she raised the glass unsteadily to her lips. The fiery liquid took her breath as it burned all the way to her empty stomach. She gasped and felt a sudden rush of blood heat her cheeks.

The young officer, standing with hands braced behind his back and shoulders slightly hunched, smiled at Rochella's reaction to the brandy. "It should make you feel better. At least it has put the color back in your cheeks."

"I am grateful for your help, but I cannot impose further upon your kindness," Rochella said, silently praying he wouldn't stop her from leaving. She got to her feet, and felt the floor suddenly shift beneath her. As abruptly as she had come out of the chair, she went back into it.

"*Mademoiselle,* you are in no condition to be on the streets," the officer said. Bending over her in concern, he touched his hand to her brow. A look of relief flickered in his gray eyes when he found her skin cool.

"But I cannot stay here," Rochella answered. Frantically she sought any excuse to get away from the army officer before he began to question her reason for sleeping on his doorstep. At last she said, "We are strangers."

"That situation can easily be remedied, *mademoiselle.* I am René Valdis from the province of Loire. Now, may I know your name?"

"I—I—" Fear clogging her throat, Rochella stuttered to a halt.

An understanding smile tugged at the corners of René's lips. "Perhaps now is not the time for introductions. I see no reason why I have to know your name for you to rest here for a while."

"I am grateful for your hospitality but I cannot accept it," Rochella answered, unable to trust René's kindness. She attempted to stand once more and found her legs still would not support her.

"It would seem for the moment you have little choice, *mademoiselle.* Please rest. I assure you no harm will come to you here."

René turned and poured himself a brandy. Relaxing back against the edge of the table, he studied Rochella thoughtfully as he sipped the amber liquid fire. When he finished his drink, he set aside the glass and looked again at his guest. *"Mademoiselle,* you remind me of my sister, Thérèse. She is very beautiful and very stubborn, yet she is an intelligent woman who realizes the value of placing her trust in those who might help her in a time of need."

Rochella shifted uneasily and lowered her eyes to her hands, unable to meet his kind gray eyes any longer.

Seeing his comparison would not reap the reward of even her name, he smiled and shrugged. "Well, no matter. Your secrets are yours to keep, *mademoiselle.* I only want to know if you slept in my doorway all night?"

Her eyes still on her tightly clasped hands, Rochella's answer was barely audible as she nodded and said, *"Oui."*

"Mon Dieu! It is far too dangerous for a young woman to be on the streets of Paris at any time of day

but it is worse at night. What possessed you to sleep in my doorway?'' René asked, forgetting his vow to let her keep her secrets. However, her lack of response quickly refreshed his memory. His cheeks flushing crimson, he cleared his throat. "I am sorry. Your reasons are your own."

René strode across the room to the small cabinet and slid back the curtain that concealed his meager supply of food—a bottle of wine, a precious loaf of hard, crusty bread and a round of rich, yellow cheese. Taking down the bread and cheese, he sliced several pieces of each and placed them on a cracked china plate. He put the bottle of wine and the plate on the rough-hewn table and with a graceful sweep of his hand, gestured for Rochella to join him. "It is not much, but in these times it is the best a man of my station can offer his guest. Please join me. I think you will feel much better after you have eaten."

Rochella's stomach growled in response to the sight of the food. She knew she should not accept anything from René Valdis; he was a stranger as well as an officer in the French army. Yet she was too famished to resist.

His meager meal quickly finished, René settled back in his chair. He sipped a glass of wine and quietly watched his guest devour her food. The girl intrigued him. She was starving, yet she ate with the manners of a lady. René smiled to himself, as he downed the last of his wine. She was obviously not a peasant. He suspected that she was an aristocrat hiding from the tribunal. René was disgusted with the recent turn of events in France. How could everything have come to such a pass in his country? he wondered. He was a loyal officer in the French army, but he did not approve of the way Robespierre and his cohorts on the tribunal were achieving their goals. He firmly believed in the cause of justice for the common man, yet he had hoped to see France governed by a constitutional monarchy.

Now, from what he had heard from his brother in the tribunal offices, Louis XVI would soon lose his head on the guillotine, as had so many of his subjects from the nobility in the past months.

Disturbed by the thought, René set down his glass with such force it jarred the table. His actions startled Rochella away from her meal. She looked at him warily.

"*Mademoiselle,* I have given you my word no harm will come to you," he snapped, unable to contain his exasperation.

Rochella lowered her eyes back to her plate as her cheeks flamed. "I am sorry. I did not mean to stare."

"No, I am the one who should be sorry," René said, rubbing a hand tiredly over his face. He had been on duty all night and was weary to the bone. It had been his squad's responsibility to guard the transport of flour from the warehouses to the baker's shops. Flour was in such short supply that thieves had begun raiding wagons carrying the precious commodity. There was already a shortage of bread, and if things did not improve he feared there would be bread riots. The revolution was a grand thing to the common man until it took away his already meager supply of food.

Looking once more at Rochella, he gave her a weary smile. "I should not have snapped at you."

René pushed himself to his feet and crossed to the small window overlooking the street. He looked down at the people crowding the thoroughfare. They looked normal as they went about their daily business, yet he knew beneath each calm facade fermented a member of a bloodthirsty mob that Robespierre could inspire to do his bidding.

He squeezed his eyes closed against the memories of the recent weeks. He had been a soldier since his teens and had witnessed death many times. Yet what he had seen in Paris since being transferred here from Nantes sickened him far more than the worst of war. These people were slaughtering their own as revenge for all the past transgressions of the aristocracy. René firmly believed in equal rights for all men, but that also included those who were being sent to their deaths with only the tribunal's condemnation.

His heart went out to the young woman whom he had found on his stoop. If he did not learn who she was and why she was wandering the streets of Paris alone, he would not be able to help her survive.

René took a seat at the table and leaned forward, bracing himself on his elbows and clasping his hands in front of him. "*Mademoiselle,* do you now feel well enough to tell me who you are and why you are in Paris?"

Rochella stared down at her plate and did not answer.

"Since you refuse to trust me, I fear my only choice is to take you to my commanding officer."

Rochella's head snapped up. "No, please."

"But, *mademoiselle,* I cannot in good conscience allow you to wander about Paris alone. As I have said, it is far too dangerous."

"Please just allow me to leave here," Rochella begged.

René shook his head. "I am sorry, *mademoiselle.* Should anything happen to you, I would feel I was to blame."

Rochella eyed René uncertainly, unable to decide what she should do. He had befriended her, sharing what little food he possessed and offering her his protection, yet she did not know if she should trust him with the truth. Intuitively she sensed he meant her no harm, yet after all she had experienced in the past weeks, she was afraid to rely on her instincts.

Seeing the skeptical look in her eyes, René shook his head. "*Mademoiselle,* I do not know what else I can do to make you understand. Should you be an aristocrat as I suspect, it is in your best interest to trust me. I can only assure you that I have no great love for what has been going on in France, and I would see you safe if you gave me the opportunity."

Rochella gazed at René across the table, and her defenses cracked. She desperately needed to trust someone in this, or she feared she would never find the man who could help her locate her parents. She released a long breath and nodded. "All right, *monsieur.* I shall tell you who I am."

René leaned forward, eager to solve the mystery about his beautiful guest.

Rochella took a deep sip of the wine before she said, "I am Rochella de Beauvais from the province of Champagne, and my father is the Marquis de Beauvais."

The lieutenant's eyes widened, and he let out a low whistle. He had suspected her origins but he had never dreamed they would be so illustrious. Even he knew of her family and the excellent wines produced from the Beauvais vineyards.

"*Mademoiselle,* I know of your family," René said, his look of astonishment fading into a frown of concern as he suddenly comprehended the dire consequences that would follow should anyone else learn her true identity. In the eyes of the tribunal such a distinguished family name would be enough for them to convict her of treason, and she would be sentenced to prison or even worse.

"And I fear you have been very foolish to come to Paris. We must find a way to get you back to your family in Champagne immediately."

Touched by his kindness, Rochella felt tears brim in her eyes as she sadly shook her head. "*Monsieur,* I fear it is impossible. I no longer have a home and I came here in search of my parents."

René covered her hand with his own and gazed across the table at her sympathetically. "Would you tell me what has happened?"

Rochella nodded and began her story with her father sending her to England as the bride of Lord Gareth Devlin. When she finished, she looked up to see René shaking his head.

"Madame Devlin," he said, using her English title awkwardly, "I fear you should have remained in England. This quest you have set for yourself is doomed to failure. There is no way you can hope to find your parents without help from someone in authority, and I, for one, have no idea who would be willing to put himself in such jeopardy to help you."

"If I can only reach the Monsieur Talleyrand, he will help me."

"Talleyrand," René gasped, his eyes widening in horror. "*Madame,* surely you cannot mean to go to that rogue. He sits on the tribunal with Robespierre and Danton."

"But I have been told he is the only man who might be able to help me find my parents," Rochella said, undeterred by René's shock.

"*Oui,* he is the only man who might help you, yet you risk your life if he feels such action would benefit him in some way. The man is a chameleon. His colors and loyalties change with the breeze."

"But he is the bishop of Autun. Surely we speak of two different men."

"I fear not, *Madame.* Talleyrand is the man who was responsible for the National Assembly taking control of all church property to help solve the problems of the French treasury."

"I am afraid nothing you have said has changed my mind. It does not matter what kind of man Talleyrand is. If he can help me find my parents, then I must see him."

René shook his head. "Can I not make you understand the danger you are putting yourself in?"

"I shall not rest until I find my parents."

René released an exasperated breath. "Even if you manage to find Talleyrand, there is no guarantee you will be allowed to speak with the man. Without a letter of introduction, you will not be admitted to his presence."

"I have a letter of introduction," Rochella said, smiling for the first time.

"May I see it?" René asked, slightly flabbergasted.

"I do not have it with me now. I hid it with my portmanteau before I entered Paris."

René ran his fingers through his dark hair in exasperation. "Then the first thing we must do is to find your letter," he said, resigned to the fact that he was already involved in her scheme whether he liked it or not. His conscience would not allow him to do otherwise. "Once that is done, we shall see what we can do to help you meet Talleyrand."

Rochella pushed back her chair and stood. "If you will escort me, I shall show you where I hid my portmanteau."

René shook his head once more. "*Non, madame.* That is impossible. You must remain here while I go and look for your portmanteau. It is for your own safety. You have no papers, and should you be stopped and questioned, you would immediately be arrested."

Seeing the wisdom in René's reasoning, Rochella gave him instructions. When she finished, she held out her hand to her new friend. "You will never know how grateful I am to you, René. I do not know what would have become of me, had you not taken pity on me."

Blushing from the praise, René took Rochella's hand as he came to his feet. He gave her a comforting smile. "I feel confident you would have managed somehow to get what you want, Madame Devlin. Now rest while I go find your letter of introduction."

Tension made it impossible for Rochella to follow René's order to rest. Instead, she tidied the tiny room, washed herself in the small, chipped porcelain bowl and combed the tangles from her hair with the comb she had found among René's personal articles. Then she paced back and forth until she thought she would wear holes in the already balding carpet.

The afternoon shadows darkened the cobbled Paris streets when René returned. Having had no rest since the previous day, he was exhausted. His eyes red-rimmed and shoulders slumped, he sank into the straight-backed chair and sadly shook his head. "*Madame,* I have bad news. Your letter is gone."

He reached for the bottle of wine and poured himself a drink, downing the contents of the glass in one gulp before he continued. "When I reached your hiding place there was nothing there. I questioned the inhabitants of the cottage, and they said a small boy had discovered the bag and given it to one of the guards at the gate. I am afraid we will now have a difficult time in securing an audience with Talleyrand. The guards will have taken your letter to the Assembly, and they will have questioned Talleyrand about the missive. They will be searching for you."

Bitter tears sprang unbidden to her eyes as Rochella's hopes once more faded into the Paris night. Her question when it came was barely audible. "What shall I do?"

"I would suggest you accept my hospitality until we feel it is safe to approach Talleyrand. He will be kept under surveillance until the authorities find other prey more to their interest. As for them searching for you, there are too many things taking place at this time for them to spend much time looking for one woman."

"Will not my presence cause suspicion to fall on you?"

"It is nothing unusual. Many soldiers keep women companions," René said, putting it as politely as possible. He had to suppress a smile when Rochella's eyes rounded with understanding before she flashed him a suspicious look. René chuckled at her suspicions. Madame Rochella Devlin would be surprised to learn that though he found her very beautiful, he preferred the camp followers. This girl reminded him too much of a member of his own family, and he could no more take her to bed than he could take his sister. "*Madame,* I assure you I have nothing devious in mind. You are my guest and friend while you stay in my humble dwelling."

"Thank you, René," Rochella said, flushing with embarrassment for even having considered this kind man would have an ulterior motive for his invitation.

René smiled as he stood and straightened the red coat of his uniform. "Then I shall bid you a good-night. It is time I returned to duty."

Chapter Fourteen

A gentle breeze stirred the tattered curtains beside her as Rochella leaned out the window seeking to catch a touch of coolness from the summer air. She had been René's guest for more than two weeks, and the tiny room they shared was like an oven. Beads of perspiration ran unhindered down her back, dampening the fabric of her dark blue gown and making it stick uncomfortably to her skin.

Gazing down at the quiet avenue, she grimaced. The pedestrians went about their business as if only a short while ago they had not been seized by a fit of madness that had driven them to attack the baker. From her vantage point she had watched as the angry women went to his door demanding bread. When the man tried to explain there was no bread because of the flour shortage, the women had attacked him with their knives, leaving only a bloody body lying in the street.

Since coming to Paris she had witnessed other such sights from her second-story window. She had seen husbands turn on wives, and children turn on parents. She had heard shouts for the republic and liberty echo down the cobbled lane as armed guards invaded households where suspected supporters of the monarchy lived.

Shaking her head, Rochella turned away from the window and wiped the perspiration from her brow. She pulled at the dark material about her waist to ease the itching that had set in as the heat increased. She gazed at her reflection in the cracked mirror René had found for her use. She was dressed in a blue Directoire gown with a small ribbon of red and white—the colors of the revolution. René had bought the dress on the second day of her stay and insisted she wear it, saying it would be far safer for her to be dressed like a good republican when they went out.

The sound of rapid footsteps on the stairs froze Rochella's breath in her throat. Anxiously she waited, nerves drawn taut, fear curling her insides, as the door swung open. Relief swept over her when she saw René filling the doorway, with a wide smile on his handsome face.

"I have news," he said, quickly closing the door behind him. "I was visiting my brother today at the Hôtel de Ville. I asked him if I might have an audience with Monsieur Talleyrand, and he arranged it. Talleyrand will see us tomorrow."

Rochella flew into René's arms and showered his face with kisses. Between each kiss she said, "Thank you, thank you, thank you."

René tensed momentarily before his arms came about Rochella, drawing her against him. During the past two weeks he had managed to keep his distance, but now at her touch desire flamed red-hot within him before he could stop it.

Unprepared for his sudden display of affection, Rochella stiffened in his embrace. Sensing her withdrawal, René quickly brought his own emotions under control and let his arms fall away from her. He cleared his throat and stepped to the table to fill his glass from the half full bottle of wine. His shoulders slumped as he downed the ruby liquid and looked once more at Rochella. "Forgive me."

Seeing his agony, Rochella crossed to René and hugged him. "There is nothing to forgive. Friends do not apologize for sharing their feelings."

René raised a hand and gently brushed his knuckles against the curve of her soft cheek. "I should not have reacted in such a way, but you are so beautiful, Rochella. It is hard for a man to resist your loveliness."

"I fear such is not always true," Rochella said, her eyes filling with misery as she turned away.

René caught her and drew her back into his arms. "We have never spoken of your husband in England. Did you love him very much?"

Rochella nodded, unable to voice her feeling for Gareth.

"Then why did you leave him? Surely he would have helped you find your parents."

Tiny crystal droplets beaded Rochella's dark lashes as she looked up at René and whispered brokenly, "The love was one-sided."

René held Rochella close and let her weep. Her tears touched his heart as had her courage. "Hush now," he murmured softly. "Let us not dwell upon the past but look to the future."

Wiping at her damp eyes, Rochella nodded and cleared her throat. "*Oui.* Now is not the time to think upon things that cannot be changed. I chose my path and now I must follow it."

"Oui, chérie," René said, unable to offer any advice to comfort her aching heart.

The noonday sun bore down upon the city, baking the streets of Paris with its heat, and Rochella hurried to keep up with René's long strides. As they neared the center of the city, their progress was slowed by the crowds that packed the cobbled thoroughfare. It seemed to Rochella all the residents of Paris were making their way toward the palace, Les Tuileries. Sensing trouble, she glanced apprehensively up at René and saw his handsome face marred with a frown. "What is it, René? Why are all these people going toward the Tuileries?" She clung to his arm to keep the jostling crowd from separating them.

René bent his head close to her for privacy. "I have heard only snatches of conversation, but I surmise these people are angry with the king and intend to take their complaints directly to him. It seems they have been inspired by the recent speeches of Robespierre and Marat."

Rochella glanced anxiously around her. She knew from the expressions on the angry faces around her that something terrible was about to take place.

Suddenly the crowd surged forward, tearing Rochella away from René and forcing her along in its wake. Panicking, she tried to push her way through the mass of bodies but found herself carried like a flotsam on a wave of humanity. Terrified of being crushed should she lose her footing, she could do little but struggle to keep her balance as the throng of people forced its way into the courtyard of the palace and they began shouting their demands.

Rochella felt a hand take her firmly by the wrist and begin to pull her through the crowd. Gratefully she saw that her savior was René. He shouldered his way past the barrier of bodies, maneuvering them closer to the edge of the mob on the Palais Royale until they were finally free. He did not release his hold on her nor slacken their pace until they reached the Café de Foy.

Winding his way through a maze of tables and chairs, he found them a small table in a dimly lit corner. Seating Rochella, he ordered wine. After a middle-aged, potbellied man served their wine and left to tend his other patrons, René turned to Rochella. "I shall send Monsieur Talleyrand a message. It will be safe for you to await him here."

Rochella looked up at René, puzzled. "You aren't going to be with me?"

René shook his head as he bent and placed a tender kiss on her brow. "From what we have just witnessed, I fear I am needed at the Tuileries."

Rochella clutched René's hand. Fearing for his safety, she pleaded, "René, you cannot go back into that mob."

"It is my duty as a soldier of France. Until things are settled one way or the other, I must do my best to protect our king." René cupped Rochella's chin and gave her a reassuring smile.

"René, please do not go. I feel something terrible will happen if you do," Rochella pleaded again. Every instinct she possessed told her she would never see René again if he left her now. She had to try to prevent such a tragedy from happening.

René eased his hand away from Rochella. "I have no choice."

Before she could frame the words to keep him at her side, he turned and left her. He paused at the entrance of the café, gave a boy a folded piece of paper, glanced back at her as if to say farewell and then turned in the direction of the Tuileries.

Rochella came halfway out of her chair and then sat back down, defeated. She wanted to rush after René and drag him away from the danger, but she knew she could not. Like herself, he had made his decision and nothing she could say or do would alter it, even in the face of death. Tears welled in her eyes, and her lower lip quivered with suppressed emotion as she stared at the vacant doorway.

Rochella did not know how long she sat staring at her untouched glass of wine in the Café de Foy. The afternoon shadows were already beginning to creep across the rooftops when a young man approached her table and tipped his cockade.

"*Citizen,* I have been sent to escort you to the Hôtel de Ville."

Rochella rose unsteadily to her feet. Her worst fears had finally been realized. She was being arrested. Determined to put on a brave front, she swallowed back the uncomfortable lump in her throat and stiffened her spine as she followed the young man without protest.

Rochella clasped her hands tightly in front of her and felt her stomach lurch at the sight of the building looming ominously up ahead. On one of their frequent walks, René had taken her past the Jacobin headquarters where Robespierre and his cohorts had planned the revolution. It now took every ounce of willpower she possessed to follow her guard up the flight of steps and enter the Hôtel de Ville.

The guard led her to the end of a long corridor and tapped lightly upon the huge double doors. They immediately swung open to reveal a shadowy room. The messenger gestured for her to enter, and when she had stepped inside he closed the door behind her, leaving her alone.

"Citizen Beauvais, please be seated," a pleasant voice commanded from the shadows.

Startled, Rochella swung about to see the outline of a tall man.

"Please, rest yourself," he said, studying his beautiful guest for a long thoughtful moment before moving toward the large intricately carved desk.

Fearing her legs would soon give way beneath her, Rochella moved toward a chair and gratefully sank down upon the damask-upholstered seat.

She moistened her dry lips as the man limped into the circle of light provided by the candles in the silver candelabras on the desk. She could not take her eyes off his face. Delicately arched brows rose above his mesmerizing blue eyes, which flashed with intelligence. The clean lines of his straight nose only emphasized the perfect shape of his mouth.

"It is my understanding you wanted to see me," Monsieur Talleyrand said, bestowing one of his devastating smiles upon Rochella. At the age of thirty-eight, he knew the effect his looks had upon women and used it to his advantage. He also used the limp, from an injury he had received at age four, to work upon the hearts of the fairer sex. Women loved to mother him all the way into his bed.

Leaning casually upon his gold-headed cane, he assessed Rochella's merits and waited for her to speak. Rochella shifted uneasily under his intense gaze and sought to collect her thoughts. She had been unprepared to meet Monsieur Talleyrand in the heart of the Jacobin club. She cleared her throat and then hesitated only a brief moment before she said, "Monsieur—I mean, Citizen Talleyrand, I am Rochella de Beauvais. I have come to ask your help in locating my parents, the Marquis and Marquise de Beauvais."

Calmly, Talleyrand retrieved a gold snuffbox from his velvet waistcoat and took a pinch of the pungent powder. He sniffed several times, then raised a lace handkerchief to his nose and sneezed. Delicately, he replaced the handkerchief in the cuff of his sleeve before he looked once more at Rochella. "Citizen Beauvais, do you realize I know nothing of you save the letter I was shown by the committee? Why do you now seek out my help?"

Rochella's emerald gaze met his unflinchingly. "I was told by your friend, the Marquis de Lafayette, that you alone would have the power to help me in my search."

"Fortunately, Lafayette is right," Talleyrand said, easing his tall frame into a chair. He propped the cane between his legs and leaned forward. "The marquis is also well aware of my penchant for beautiful women."

"I do not understand," Rochella lied, praying she had misunderstood Talleyrand's insinuation. Lowering her eyes from his, she could not stop the blush that heated her cheeks from his intense scrutiny. A moment later Rochella jumped with a start when the marquis placed his hand over hers. Her eyes flew to his face and he gave her another charming smile.

"In these times, *chérie,* what you ask could well cost me my life. I must know what I shall receive in return for my favors," Talleyrand said, his voice silky.

"Monsieur Talleyrand, I have nothing to give you. Everything I owned was destroyed when the peasants set my home ablaze. However, once we find my parents, I am sure my father will be very generous for your help in reuniting us."

The corners of Talleyrand's lips curled upward as he allowed his gaze to drift slowly down Rochella's length. "*Mademoiselle,* it is very rare to encounter one who possesses such beauty. I have no need for your father's gold. The price I require is you."

Rochella felt her face flame and she swallowed against the sudden constriction in her throat. Her words were a husky whisper as she said, "*Monsieur,* surely you jest."

"*Non, mademoiselle,*" Talleyrand said, relaxing back in his chair. "I seldom jest when the stakes are so high. My life means much to me."

Frantically, Rochella sought to change the subject to safer ground. "*Monsieur,* if you are willing to help me find my parents, then why are you at the Hôtel de Ville?"

"At the moment I am in favor because of the services I rendered the state by securing the church property," Talleyrand said and chuckled. "But I fear Rome did not agree with my ideas and excommunicated me." Rochella's horrified expression made him laugh aloud. "*Chérie,* don't look so stricken. I have lost little from the pope's decision. I am quite pleased to be free of life in the church. However, my standing in the church or in the Jacobin Club has little to do with our conversation."

"Monsieur, I am afraid such is not so," Rochella said. Eyes flashing, she raised her chin at a haughty angle. "I cannot accept your proposal. I am already married. And were I free to accept your offer, how do I know you would fulfill your end of our bargain?''

Talleyrand chuckled at her show of spirit. ''*Mademoiselle*—or should I say *Madame*—you astonish me. If I were not prepared to execute my end of our bargain, I would have you here and now, and then turn you over to Robespierre.''

The mention of Robespierre dampened Rochella's spirit. She wanted nothing to do with the man who was fast becoming the leading influence in the Assembly.

Seeing his ploy had worked, Talleyrand leaned forward. ''What is your answer, *mademoiselle?*''

Sitting with hands clenched into fists in her lap, bitterness rising like bile in her throat, eyes sparkling with rancor, Rochella regarded Talleyrand through narrowed lids. ''*Monsieur,* were I a man, I should call you out for this insult.''

''Were you a man, I assure you, I should not have made such a proposal. And you may not feel it an insult once you are in my arms. I have often been told women do not easily forget my lovemaking.''

Rochella fought to control the urge to scratch out the man's beautiful eyes. It was in her best interest not to anger him, yet she had to find a way to avoid agreeing to his dishonorable proposition. ''*Monsieur,*'' she said, striving to keep her voice calm and even, ''I have already told you I am married. I am not free to accept you should it be my wish.''

A cunning expression entered Talleyrand's eyes. He took her hand once more and raised it to his lips. ''*Madame,* would you agree if you were free?''

Sensing victory, Rochella felt she could agree without fear. She was legally married by the laws of France and the church. Nothing on earth could change that fact beyond an annulment by the pope himself. She nodded meekly. *"Oui, monsieur.* I would do anything to find my parents."

Rochella hid her triumphant smile at how easily she had managed to avoid such an unsavory situation. Her feeling of victory faded a moment later when Talley-rand said, "Then you will have to get a divorce."

"D—divorce?" Rochella stuttered. *"Monsieur,* you know the laws of the France forbid such a thing. I am bound to my husband until one of us dies."

Relaxing once more in his chair, Talleyrand studied his victim. With each statement she uttered, he was tightening the noose. When he was through with her, she would willingly come to his bed. "Yet if you could divorce your husband, would you do so? And after-ward would you agree to become my mistress should I agree to help you find your parents?"

"This conversation is of no consequence, *mon-sieur,"* Rochella said, feeling her confidence surge. "I am bound to another by the laws of our land. But you have my word you will be justly rewarded should you help me locate my parents."

"Madame, you did not answer my question. Would you become my mistress were you a free woman?"

"Oui, monsieur. I would make such an arrangement if it would help my parents," Rochella said, secure in the fact even a powerful man such as Talleyrand could not change laws that had stood for centuries.

Talleyrand's even white teeth gleamed in the candle-light. "Then I shall petition the assembly to grant you a divorce immediately."

Stunned, Rochella stared at the man smiling at her like a cat ready to pounce. Feeling a sinking sensation in the pit of her stomach, she sought desperately to find a way to avoid being a feast for this man's passion. "*Monsieur,* divorce is illegal in France!"

Talleyrand's smile broadened. "*Non, madame.* The Assembly has made it as easy to obtain a divorce from one's spouse as it is to marry."

Rochella felt the trap close about her and knew there was no way she could easily extricate herself from this situation. She had blindly followed his lead without question.

Talleyrand stood with the help of his cane and offered his arm to Rochella. "Come, I shall personally escort you to my home."

"*Monsieur,* I said I would agree to your proposal should my divorce be granted and you kept your end of our bargain by helping find my parents. I do not choose to fulfill my part of our arrangement until I have proof you are doing likewise."

Talleyrand smiled down at Rochella. She intrigued him, unlike other females of his acquaintance who would be eager to come to his bed. She was no fool, and he would have to handle her with care.

"*Madame,* I do not expect to become your lover so easily. I merely wanted to ensure your safety by offering my house as your place of residence until the time I can prove to you I intend to honor our agreement to the letter."

"I am sorry, *monsieur.* I shall remain with my friend until I see your evidence. Then, and only then, shall I permit the liberties you request for your help," Rochella said, her voice husky with ire. The words she uttered were like balls of prickly wool in her throat. It was hard to speak them though she knew she had no choice. Until she found a way to extricate herself from their agreement, time was her only ally.

Before Talleyrand could protest her decision, a sharp rapping sounded at the door. He turned to see his assistant rush white-faced into the chamber. Without a glance at Talleyrand's guest, he burst out, "Rossignol has murdered the Marquis de Mandat and the fighting at the Tuileries has turned into a massacre. They have butchered the king's Swiss Guard like pigs at market. Even some of the soldiers from Brest have been cut down in the melee because their red uniforms resembled those of the Guard. Now they have built bonfires to burn the remains."

Talleyrand paled. He had known what was going to transpire today; it had been well planned. Yet he had not expected it to turn into such a bloodbath. "The king and queen? What of them?"

"They remain unharmed."

Talleyrand breathed a sigh of relief. At least for the moment the king still lived. Yet he feared the events of the day would alter that situation. Talleyrand limped behind his desk and hurriedly scribbled a message. After folding the missive, he sealed it with wax and handed it to his assistant. "Take this to Danton. The Commune must secure the king and queen immediately. They must not lose their lives to the rabble."

When the door closed behind his assistant, Talleyrand turned to Rochella, a smile curving his lips as if nothing out of the ordinary was happening beyond his office doors. "Now, *madame,* where were we before we were interrupted?"

"I must go," Rochella said, ashen with worry. Coming to her feet, her thoughts only on René, she turned to the door.

Though his limp impeded his speed, Talleyrand moved swiftly to block her exit. "*Madame,* we have not finished our business."

"I have no time to discuss our arrangement, *monsieur.* I must go to the Tuileries. I fear for my friend's life," Rochella said. She tried to step past him to the door.

"Are you mad, *madame?* You cannot go to the Tuileries. Did you not hear a word my assistant said? The protest has turned into a massacre."

"I must find René," Rochella said and again tried to step around Talleyrand.

He took her by the arms and held her fast. "Look at me, *madame,*" he ordered. Rochella obeyed. "Will it help your parents for you to allow your emotions to get you killed over this friend?"

Rochella seemed to wilt. "But I must know about René. Were it not for him, I would not be here now."

Talleyrand loosened his grip. "If you will wait here, I shall send someone to find your friend. And then I shall escort you to my home."

Rochella opened her mouth to protest, but Talleyrand shook his head. "*Non, madame.* I shall not allow you to stay with your friend as you suggested. You will reside in the safety of my home until I prove to you that I am honoring our agreement. When that time arrives I shall expect you to honor your end of the bargain."

Unable to find an argument against Talleyrand's proposal, Rochella allowed him to escort her back to her chair in front of the desk. She waited tense and anxious, hands clasped, while he sent out several of his men to find René Valdis. The search set into motion, he escorted her from the Hôtel de Ville to his elegant carriage. From there they drove swiftly to the rue de Bac, where he owned one of the elaborate, pink-bricked, three-storied town houses that lined the cobbled street.

Accustomed to such elegance from birth, Rochella paid little heed to the richly paneled walls or the crystal chandeliers that hung from the elaborately molded ceilings. Yet she did flash Talleyrand a look that expressed her feelings about a man who sanctioned the revolutionary acts of the common man to bring down other wealthy men like himself.

Leading her up a gracefully curved staircase, Talleyrand shrugged off the look with a smile and said, "A man should have a few pleasures in life."

His answer nearly made Rochella choke. She should not have expected anything more from Charles Maurice de Talleyrand-Périgord. From his own lips she had heard that he had been excommunicated from the church because of his vile actions. She flashed him a look of loathing as he opened the door to a beautiful room.

Talleyrand stepped back to allow Rochella to enter and waited for her praise when she took in the delicately carved furniture of white and gold, the thick soft yellow carpet that covered the shining parquet flooring and the pale green velvet drapes accenting the double French windows. The scent of flowers filled the air from the vases on the bedside table and the mantel of intricately sculpted Italian marble.

Rochella entered the chamber and crossed to the dressing table, where three large glass mirrors reflected the elegance of the room behind her. Absently she lifted the silver-backed hairbrush and turned it over in her hand. How long had it been since her hair had been properly cared for? How long had it been since she had slept in a feather bed with no worries to rouse her from sleep? It was hard to remember.

Talleyrand came up behind her and placed his hands on her shoulders. He looked at her pensive reflection in the dressing table mirror. "I knew the moment I saw you, this room had been created for you."

His words reminded Rochella of her situation, and she turned on him, emerald fire flashing in her eyes.

"I must remind you, *madame*," Talleyrand said, "it was your own words that placed you under my protection. I have not forced you here."

"Then you will help me locate my parents should I decide not to remain under your protection?"

"You are no fool, *madame*. But then again, neither am I," Talleyrand said. "We have an agreement and I expect you to fulfill your part. I want you to consider your options very carefully so you will not make the wrong decision. Much rests upon your word—your life as well as your parents', and now, should he be still alive, René Valdis's life. I shall leave you to ponder upon our agreement. I give you my word, I shall accept whatever choice you make."

Talleyrand limped toward the door. He paused, hand on the latch, and looked back at Rochella. "I shall have my housekeeper summon the seamstress so you can rid yourself of that ridiculous garment. You, my dear Rochella, were made to wear bright colors, not that drab rag."

"But they are the colors of the revolution. Will it not be dangerous for me to be seen in frivolous apparel?" Rochella asked sweetly, though the venom of her contempt dripped from every word.

"In my home we dress as we please, and it does not please me to see you dressed like a fishwife at market.

Good day, *madame.*'' Talleyrand limped from the room.

Rochella sank into a soft, damask-covered chair and wearily leaned back her head. "Gareth," she whispered, "I sought to be free of you and now my wish has been granted, I do not like the pain it leaves my soul."

Agitated, Rochella came out of her chair and crossed to the windows overlooking the gardens. A dull ache began to throb in her temples and she rested her forehead against the cool panes of glass. Despair filled her as she stared down at the profusion of roses in neat beds. By the look of the tranquil garden, no one would ever suspect what was occurring only a short distance away.

Rochella glanced up at the clear blue of the late afternoon. She had left the man she loved to return to her parents. Now she was not at all certain that everything she had done was not in vain.

"I shall have lost my husband, my parents and my honor," she murmured disconsolately. She knew her parents would not have wanted their freedom at the price she would pay to Talleyrand, but she also knew she had no other choice to make.

Tears brimming in her eyes, Rochella turned away from the window and crossed to the large bed. She lay down and closed her eyes. "Papa, please forgive, but it is something I must do." Her softly spoken plea broke the silence of the room. Her heart cried out for her husband's forgiveness as well, yet she knew that Gareth would care little about how she felt at that moment. The ache in her throat mounting, she rolled onto her side and curled into a ball in an effort to shut out the pain. Yet nothing could shield her against the agony in her mind and heart. She wept herself to sleep.

* * *

Talleyrand found Rochella sound asleep when he returned several hours later, laden with boxes of the necessities he thought she would need. Looking down at her, lying innocently unaware of his presence, he noted the streaks left by her tears. An uncommon twinge of guilt pricked at his heart. He had done little to ease her pain.

Unaccustomed to such feelings, Talleyrand quickly shrugged aside the emotion. He led his life with his own best interest in mind, and he would not change it now for Rochella de Beauvais. Her reluctance to share his bed had made him want her, yet no woman had ever succeeded in snaring his emotions. She would serve well enough until he found something more enticing.

Setting aside his packages, he lightly shook Rochella by the shoulder. "*Madame,* it is time to wake and see the gifts I have brought you."

Rochella stirred and slowly opened her eyes. Disoriented, she blinked up at Talleyrand. When her mind registered his identity, she abruptly sat up. "Forgive me, *monsieur.* I did not mean to fall asleep."

"There's nothing to forgive, *ma chérie,*" Talleyrand said. Smiling, he gestured to the packages at the foot of the bed. "Come, I have brought you several gowns from which to choose."

Listlessly, Rochella did as bidden. She opened each package but could muster no enthusiasm for the exquisite silks, satins and laces revealed. She mumbled a dull thank-you and began to rewrap Talleyrand's gifts.

Her lack of response rankled Talleyrand's temper. He captured her chin and turned her face up, forcing her to look at him. His cool blue eyes sparkled with ire. "*Ma-

dame, there is one small item I forgot to mention when we made our agreement earlier today.''

Rochella regarded Talleyrand cooly yet didn't give him the pleasure of hearing her ask what more he expected of her. From what she'd already seen of the man, she knew he'd soon tell her.

Talleyrand gazed down at Rochella through narrowed lashes and his fingers tightened on her smooth skin. ''Since you seem reluctant to ask, I shall tell you. When we are together you will be civil and show a certain amount of affection toward me, no matter how you feel to the contrary.''

Her own temper simmering, Rochella jerked free of his hand. *''Monsieur,''* she said, ''I have agreed to become your mistress when you find my parents, but I did not agree to fawn over you with feigned pleasure.''

Talleyrand could not stop his smile of admiration. The petite beauty looked like an angry lioness ready to attack. Stepping a safe distance from the bed, he took his lace handkerchief from the cuff of his sleeve and lightly dabbed at his nose. He gave her a smug look. ''It seems I shall have to purchase your warmth with small tidbits of information instead of frivolities.'' He shrugged and paused for effect. ''Will you perhaps give me a kiss should I tell you what I have heard of your parents?''

Rochella regarded Talleyrand warily. It was only a few shorts hours since he had left her. How could he have gleaned any information so soon? She said as much to him.

''Perhaps a small kiss will reward you with the answer you desire.''

Rochella released a long breath and gracefully accepted defeat. She rose on tiptoes and placed a sisterly kiss upon Talleyrand's smoothly shaved cheek. When he did not respond to her actions, she said, exasperated, "You have the kiss, *monsieur*. Now I would have your news."

"*Ma chérie,* I was not referring to a kiss from a nun," Talleyrand said before he captured Rochella in his arms and his mouth descended over hers. His lips devoured the sweetness of her mouth and she was left gasping for breath when he calmly released her.

"*Monsieur—*" she began to censure, but he held up a silencing hand.

"Since we reside under the same roof, I prefer you call me Charles. It is so much more intimate. Do you not agree?"

Rochella drew in a steadying breath, squelching the urge to slap Talleyrand's handsome face. "Charles," she said hesitantly, "must I remind you, you said you had news of my parents."

"Ah, yes, I have. While I was out I stopped to pay a visit to my friend, Madame de Staël, at the Swedish embassy. I mentioned in passing that the de Beauvaises had come to Paris but I had not been fortunate enough to see them. Madame de Staël said the Marquis de Beauvais was a friend of her father's and usually paid his respects to the family when he visited Paris. Unfortunately, they had failed to visit on this occasion."

Exasperated, Rochella snapped, "Is that all you learned?"

"Calm yourself, my dear," Talleyrand said. "Things like this take time. I have planted the seeds and now we must watch until they come to fruition. Madame de Staël's own curiosity will be our best ally in locating your parents should they be in Paris at the present time.

Have you considered the fact that they might have fled the country instead?''

Rochella lowered her sooty lashes. She did not want Talleyrand to see the uncertainty his question roused.

He cupped her small chin within the palm of his hand and forced her to look into his eyes. ''*Ma chérie,* should we learn that this is true, our agreement still holds. I shall have fulfilled my end of our arrangement. Do you understand?''

Rochella nodded.

''Good. Now that is settled, I shall tell you what else I have done this evening for another kiss.''

Rochella didn't resist as he lowered his mouth to hers once more, nor did she respond to the soft pressure of his lips against hers.

Talleyrand arched one brow as he looked down at her. His next words deviously played upon her emotions. ''Does my limp repulse you? Is it the reason you do not want to touch me?''

''*Non.* You only asked for a kiss and I have given it,'' Rochella said.

Talleyrand chuckled under his breath, accepting her answer. ''I have met with Danton. He assures me you will be a free citizen of France within the week.'' He chuckled again. ''After telling me how much it would cost me to gain your divorce without anyone knowing he was helping a woman wanted by the authorities, he said no honest Frenchman could abide knowing a *citoyenne* was bound to an Englishman.''

Rochella turned away at his words. ''I am tired and would like to retire early this evening.''

''As you wish, *madame,*'' Talleyrand said. ''Just remember I am fulfilling my commitment.''

''And I shall fulfill mine,'' Rochella said.

"Then I shall leave you. I have other commitments this evening at the Hôtel de Ville. Good night, *madame*."

Talleyrand's hand was already on the latch when Rochella asked, "Did you learn anything about René Valdis?"

"I fear not, *madame*. My man could find no trace of him. He was not at the Tuileries, or at his post or his lodgings."

"Do you think he's—" Rochella could not say the word *dead*.

Talleyrand shrugged. "I know not, *madame*. It is most certainly possible after what transpired today. Now I shall bid you adieu." With that he left the room.

Rochella pushed the packages from the bed and pulled off her gown. Weary with grief, she climbed into the large tester, wearing only her chemise. Yet when she snuggled down into the soft feather mattress sleep alluded her. Near morning she finally drifted into an exhausted slumber only to dream of a blue-eyed demon with a limp who frightened her far more than the revolutionary tribunal.

Rochella awoke with a cry on her lips and sweat beading her brow, her heart drumming furiously within her breast. Shaken, she lay back against the pillows and prayed that somehow she would escape Talleyrand's evil clutches.

Chapter Fifteen

Anguish filling his soul, Gareth stared at the black-ened ruins. Since leaving England, he had prayed he would find Rochella safe and sound at Beauvais. Now, looking at the charred remains of the château, he felt his hopes of finding his wife unharmed turn to ash.

"Rochella, why could you not have waited only a few more days," he murmured softly, and felt the tears burn his eyes. Swallowing back the urge to cry his misery out aloud, he slowly withdrew the letter he had received before he sailed. It had come to Devil Wind the day after he had left for London.

Gareth crumpled the missive in his palm, visualizing the marquis's bold script asking him to explain the de-velopments in France to Rochella and to assure her that he and the marquise were safe with friends in Austria, and promising that as soon as events allowed, they would travel to England for a visit with their daughter and son-in-law.

"Why in the name of God did you not write sooner?" Gareth ground out between clenched teeth. "Now it is too late. Rochella is gone." He threw down the letter, furious with the marquis and himself for not having been truthful with Rochella from the onset.

Weary in body and mind, Gareth ran a hand through his dark hair and turned away from the skeletal remains of the Beauvais legacy. He mounted his horse, fully conscious of the fact that it was doubtful he would ever find a trace of his beautiful wife. All he could do now was pray she had been wise enough to flee to Austria like her parents.

His heart feeling as if it were being ripped out of his chest, Gareth maneuvered his horse along the overgrown drive that led to the road. He glanced toward the horizon, noting the last rays of the sun spreading through the distant stand of trees. A movement to his right caught Gareth's attention, and his hopes soared anew when he saw a woman dash into a nearby cottage.

Spurring his mount, he galloped toward the structure and reined his horse to a skiddering halt. In a flash he had dismounted and was banging on the haphazardly hung door. It swayed precariously and threatened to fall as it slowly opened to reveal the shrunken Babette. Gaunt with hunger, her eyes wide with fear, she cowered when she recognized Gareth. Shaking her matted head from side to side, she raised a hand in defense. "Go away, devil. I have already lived through hell, and I have no need of you here."

Gareth's dark brows drew together in puzzlement. The girl seemed to have lost all her wits. "Babette, it is I, Lord Devlin. I have come to find your mistress, my wife—Lady Devlin."

"I said, go away. Cease your punishment. You have taken my Jacques in your cruel war, now leave me to grieve."

Gareth stepped into the small cottage, his girth making it seem to shrink in size. "Listen to me, Babette. I am no devil, I am Lord Devlin. I am here to find Rochella. Do you understand me?''

A snarl curled Babette's lips. ''I understand. Until *mamselle* married you our lives were good. All that has happened is your fault. Were it not for you, we would still be living in the château, happy and safe.''

Gareth took Babette by the arms and gave her a light shake. ''Listen to me! Have you seen my wife? Do you know where she has gone? Is she still alive?''

Babette gave a shrill laugh and looked smugly up at Gareth through mad eyes. ''She escaped you, and you will never find her in Paris. She will not suffer your devil's wrath like my Jacques did.'' Her voice began to quaver and she slowly shook her head from side to side. ''Why did you have to let him die? He was all I had. He was all I had.''

Gareth released his hold on Babette and she slowly folded up into a ball on the earthen floor. ''He was all I had,'' she murmured again and again as she rocked to and fro.

Gareth dug into his pocket and withdrew several gold coins. He bent and pressed them into her hand before he turned and left. There was nothing more he could do for the woman. After closing the door behind him, Gareth mounted his horse. It was sad to realize there was little he could do about Babette. He hoped the coins would help her survive.

Turning his thoughts once more to his wife, he urged his horse into a gallop. He wanted to put as many miles as he could behind him before he had to stop for the night. If Babette's wild raving was correct, Rochella was alive and in Paris. He hoped that with the help of the king's letter he would be able to find her.

* * *

A sultry breeze stirred the velvet drapes and the sheer lace underpanels as it entered the chamber through the double French doors. Beyond the glassed panels an intricately crafted wrought-iron balcony overlooked the gardens. The fragrance of the brilliant blossoms wafted upward on the warm current of air and filled the room as did the sweet melody of the birds chirping in the nearby trees. Rochella, however, was in no mood to pay heed to nature's beauty. Nausea roiled her insides and she silently paced the chamber like a caged beast.

It had been more than a week since she came to live in Talleyrand's luxurious mansion, yet she had found no way to extricate herself from the situation. She was in a constant state of agitation, never knowing exactly what to expect from him. He kept her totally off balance by subtly attacking her defenses with extravagant compliments and gifts that would have made most women swoon with pleasure. He had not tried to force her to his bed but had cunningly played on her honor. Each day he would visit her with a small tidbit of information and each time Rochella would have to pay with a kiss to receive it.

Rochella stopped and gripped the back of a white-and-gold Louis XIV chair. Her nails dug into the wood, marring the smooth painted surface as she squeezed her eyes closed against her own stupidity. How could she ever have allowed herself to agree to become his mistress?

"What a fool I was to have believed I could match his cunning," Rochella whispered to the still room. Talleyrand had brought the divorce papers for her signature the previous night, and she had signed them with a quivering hand. When he took the papers back to the

Assembly she would be free of the only man she would ever love.

Anguish filled her as she opened her eyes and gazed at her silken prison. She still could not understand how she could receive a divorce without the tribunal learning of her whereabouts. However, Talleyrand had assured her he had arranged everything so as not to jeopardize her safety. He had boasted that well-placed bribes could arrange anything one desired in life.

Another bout of tears threatened, and she drew in a shuddering breath in an effort to quell them. It seemed all she had done in the past months was cry, yet she could not stop the tears from coming when she thought of her husband and her parents.

Irritated with herself, Rochella wiped at her reddened eyes. She had to be strong. She could not show any sign of the weakness she felt in front of her jailer. He was far too clever and would use it against her. She suspected he had already done so by manipulating her own need of comfort to his advantage.

Consumed with her thoughts, Rochella did not hear Talleyrand enter the room. The sound of his voice startled her from her reveries, and she spun about to face him. Her wide-eyed expression reflected her surprise. "*Monsieur,* I did not hear you enter."

"So I noticed," Talleyrand said. With a smile he limped across the chamber. Exuding all his charm, he handed Rochella a small bouquet of rosebuds. "What thoughts occupy your lovely head so deeply?"

Rochella gazed up into his handsome face and knew she must extricate herself from their agreement. "*Monsieur,*" she began before pausing briefly to draw in a steadying breath. "Charles, I am grateful for all the help you have given me, but I can no longer stay in your home. I should never have agreed to your proposal. I am sorry, but I cannot fulfill my part."

The warmth vanished from Talleyrand's eyes and they became cool as ice. "Though I have done everything possible to fulfill my end of our agreement, you now feel you cannot honor yours?"

Rochella nodded uncomfortably. "I should never have agreed to it. At first I thought I could become your mistress, but now I realize you have asked something of me that I cannot do. Your revolution has taken everything from me except my dignity, and I shall not surrender that as long as I have a breath left in my body."

Talleyrand, always able to sense the vulnerable spot in the armor of his enemies, smiled to himself. He would maneuver his attack to aim in a different direction. His voice was like a caress as he asked softly, "Why do you feel this way?"

Rochella turned away, instinctively feeling the web he sought to weave about her. She laid the rosebuds aside. "I cannot surrender the last thing I possess to you when there is no feeling between us. We would only be using each other to gain our own ends. It is wrong and I cannot continue with our agreement. You speak of honoring my word, yet if I do, I shall have no honor left."

Talleyrand crossed to her and placed his hands gently on her shoulders, turning her to face him. Warmth now melted the coldness in his eyes as he looked down at her and whispered huskily, "You are wrong, *chérie.* I do have feelings for you. Do you think I would risk my life in an attempt to find your parents were it not so?"

"You speak of your feelings now, yet you agreed to help me the first time we met. You felt nothing for me then."

Talleyrand bestowed a captivating smile upon Rochella. "*Oui*. I made our agreement without emotion. In my greed I wanted to possess your loveliness. However, I did not expect you to touch my heart. You have enchanted my soul, Rochella, as no woman has ever done. Stay here with me, Rochella. I shall help you find your parents. You are now a free woman and have no need for guilt over our relationship. Let me love you the way I desire, and I will see no harm ever befalls you or yours," Talleyrand whispered, pulling her close against him. Always the diplomat, he knew exactly what to say to manipulate matters to his advantage. It had been a means of survival and he had mastered the art of the game. Seldom did he not come out the victor.

"I cannot," Rochella murmured, shaking her head.

Talleyrand ground his teeth in angry frustration. He had wanted this woman since the day she walked into his office. To have her, he had gone to great extremes to make her believe he had risked his own safety to petition the Assembly for her divorce. The proof of his trouble lay in his jacket pocket. The paper that granted her a divorce had been forged by an expert in his craft, and few would ever know it was not the real thing. Such a ploy was the only means to get her to freely surrender herself to him, for his pride in his own seductive prowess would not allow him to physically force himself upon her.

He knew she would never come to him without being legally separated from her husband, and an actual divorce was an impossibility, especially now, when the letter from Lafayette had reached the Assembly. No one in his right mind would publicly link himself with the lovely Rochella. Even he, who sat on the tribunal, would be in jeopardy of losing his head should anyone learn she now resided in his home.

Since the proclamation from the Duke of Brunswick, threatening military execution to all Paris residents should the king be harmed, a new wave of antiroyalist fever had spread through the city. The Commune was avidly searching every house suspected of harboring anyone who held opposition to the Assembly.

Talleyrand curled one long strand of chestnut-brown hair about his finger and for a fleeting moment felt the urge to vent his frustration by strangling Rochella with it. Yet he did nothing. Time was in his favor, and should things not change, he could always make the grand gesture of showing his loyalty to the republic by turning her over to the tribunal.

A smile touching his lips, he bent and placed a kiss upon Rochella's brow, murmuring his understanding. "I shall try to be patient, *chérie*. I care too much to force you."

"Thank you, Charles," Rochella murmured. She brushed a stray curl away from her brow and wondered why the warm, sunny room suddenly seemed cast in shadows.

"This is for you, *chérie*," Talleyrand said. Taking the forged divorce decree from his pocket, he dropped it into Rochella's lap before placing another kiss upon her brow. Then he left her to ponder his strange behavior.

Rochella's hand shook as she lifted the paper. Paling, she read the decree granting her a divorce from Gareth. Once more the nausea rose sickeningly in her throat. Trembling, she lay back and stared up at the ceiling, unable to think about her future now that her life had been severed from Gareth's. Rolling onto her

side, she covered her face and allowed a wave of defeat
to spread over her. If only she could die from the
strange illness that had plagued her for the past weeks.
Then all her worries and heartbreak would be over.
Rochella buried her face in the pillow and wept herself
to sleep.

Screams and shouts roused Rochella. Frightened
from a sound sleep, she was out of bed before she was
fully awake. Barefoot, she ran onto the balcony, but the
garden below was tranquil. A moment later another
shrill scream brought her completely alert, and made
her aware of the terror taking place in the two-story,
brick mansion across the avenue. The sansculottes were
herding the members of the household into carts as if
they were sheep going to slaughter.

Unable to watch the scene, she started to turn away
but stopped abruptly at the sight of Talleyrand, standing on the balcony outside her bedchamber. He stood
with arms folded over his chest, calmly watching the
brutality.

His lack of emotion triggered Rochella's indignation
against the man who had agreed to assist her in finding
her parents. It rose in a blinding wave, blocking out all
the excuses she'd made to ignore Talleyrand's part in the
revolution. Now she faced the truth head-on. Talleyrand's actions had helped create the terror that was
racing across France on a wave of blood, and she could
no longer abide the sight of him.

Nearly choking on the bitterness rising in her throat,
she stared at Talleyrand coldly as he slowly turned to
look at her. He smiled as if nothing unusual were taking place only a short distance from the balcony where
they stood.

"I had hoped you would sleep through the little disruption across the way," he said calmly.

"Sleep!" Rochella exploded. "How can anyone sleep when the world has gone mad?"

Talleyrand shrugged. "It would have been better for your peace of mind, *chérie*. I can see you are distressed by what you witnessed."

"Distressed, *monsieur?* I am far more than distressed. I am appalled that you can stand and watch such a thing."

"I cannot change what the Commune has chosen to do. Since the king and queen were arrested and imprisoned, more than a thousand people have been taken into custody. Of late, I have begun to worry about my own neck as well as yours. Now come inside and rest. You are far too pale."

Talleyrand moved to escort Rochella back into her chamber, but she jerked away before his hand could touch her. Repulsed, she eyed him as if he had suddenly turned into a snake. How could she ever have been fool enough to allow him to touch her so intimately?

"Until now I had not realized that you are truly one of them."

"*Chérie,* you must not link me with such rabble. I do only what I have to do," Talleyrand said.

Angry tears brimmed in Rochella's eyes. "You, an aristocrat, have condoned the arrest of your king and queen without raising a hand in protest." Seeing a look of denial on Talleyrand's face, Rochella shook her head. "Do not attempt to deny the part you have played in all of this," she said with a wave of her hand in the direction of the bricked mansion. "You must accept your blame for allowing men like Robespierre and

Marat to rouse the populace into such a frenzy they forget they are human.''

Talleyrand's handsome features flushed a dull red. ''I do what I must.''

''That is a poor excuse, *monsieur.*'' Rochella stepped into her bedchamber. Her gaze swept over the silk-covered walls, the luxurious furnishings and the thick carpet at her feet. Suddenly everything seemed to come crashing down upon her and she knew if she stayed a moment longer in her exquisite prison, she would go completely mad. She had to get away from Talleyrand. She turned to the armoire and took out her Directoire gown.

''What are you doing?'' Talleyrand asked, limping across the chamber to where she had placed the gown on the bed.

''I am leaving here, *monsieur.*''

Talleyrand reached out to take her by the arm and she turned on him. ''Do not touch me. There is blood on your soft hands.''

''*Chérie,* I cannot allow you to leave here. It is far too dangerous at this time,'' Talleyrand said, a light film of nervous perspiration dotting his upper lip and brow. Should she be arrested, he knew there would be too many uncomfortable questions to be answered.

''I am willing to take my chances.''

Talleyrand grabbed Rochella by the arm and jerked her against him. His cold eyes glittered with contempt. ''Foolish girl. I have risked my own life to offer you protection and how do you repay me? If you were caught, you would jeopardize everything I have worked to achieve. I cannot allow that to happen.''

"You need not fear I shall divulge your duplicity to your grand cause. Be assured I shall keep my own counsel," Rochella said, freeing herself of his hold.

Talleyrand, always the statesman, stepped away from Rochella. "I trust you to keep your word, *madame,* or those dear to you may pay the price with their lives."

"What do you mean?" Rochella asked, her heart beginning to pound against her ribs.

"Only what I said," Talleyrand replied with a confident smile. "The young man who befriended you—" Talleyrand paused for effect and tapped his chin thoughtfully with a finger as if searching for the man's name "—ah, yes, René Valdis, is it not?" He nodded. "I fear the tribunal would be most interested to learn of his association with you, should you dare to reveal where you have been hiding of late."

"You told me René was dead," Rochella said, stunned.

"Non," Talleyrand said, flicking the lace at his wrist, "I never said so. It has come to my attention that he was only slightly wounded in the battle with the mob and has since returned to his duties."

"Why did you not tell me?" Rochella asked, knowing the answer to her question before the words had completely passed her lips. The knowledge of someone to befriend her would have given her a reason to leave his house before he managed to woo her to his bed.

"You are vile," she whispered, fighting to contain the urge to lash out physically at Talleyrand.

"Chérie, there is no need for us to part on unfriendly terms. As I have told you several times, I do what I have to do," Talleyrand said with no show of remorse. "It is the way we succeed in life, the way we get what we want."

Rochella raised her chin in the air. "Thank God, you did not get me."

His eyes narrowing, Talleyrand's expression hardened until his perfect features looked sculpted out of stone. "*Madame,* you are free to leave my home. Do not press your good fortune too far. I could have the servants hold you down while I take you and then turn you over to the authorities without a blink of an eye."

Talleyrand knew his threat was in vain. Should he be foolish enough to tell anyone of harboring Rochella, he also would pay for his folly. He turned and limped out of the room without a backward glance. He knew when to cut his losses and look to the future.

Taking Talleyrand's threat to heart, Rochella swiftly changed into the dark blue gown she had arrived in. The moment she stepped out onto the street, she realized with startling clarity what severing her relationship with Talleyrand meant. She was once more destitute and without friends. She could not return to René's without placing him in jeopardy. Now all that was left to her was to try to find a way to escape Paris with her life.

The thought made Rochella pause. She had come to the city to find her parents, but nothing she had seen or heard since coming here had given her any hope. It was time to face the reality that she had sought to ignore since returning to France. She could do nothing to help them should she even find them still alive.

Accepting defeat, Rochella gazed down the long avenue at the elegant mansions that lined the cobbled street. Her heart cried out for her to find her way back to England and Gareth. Following its call, she turned, envisioning the end of the day and the gates of Paris well behind her.

Chapter Sixteen

"Your papers, *mademoiselle?*" the guard said, seizing Rochella by the arm and halting her progress through the crowd of farmers leaving the city with their empty carts.

Rochella swallowed and feigned a search through the pocket of her dark blue gown. She fumbled briefly in the emptiness and then looked up at the guard with a sheepish smile, her voice quivering. "I must have lost them."

The guard grunted his disgust. "*Oui,* you lost them like so many others who have tried to pass here. And like all the rest you never had any papers to lose."

"*Non,* I do have p-papers—or I did have papers this morning when I came here to sell the few vegetables I grew in m-my garden," Rochella stuttered.

"It will go much easier with you if you tell me the truth, *mademoiselle,*" the guard said, forcibly maneuvering Rochella through the crowd toward the guard post.

"I do not lie. I am but a poor farm girl who came into the city to sell her goods."

The guard raked an assessing gaze over Rochella and smiled. "*Mademoiselle,* your goods would be well worth what you ask, and were I not on duty I would be more than happy to pay your price."

Rochella flushed with humiliation. "*Monsieur,* I sell only carrots and peas, nothing more."

"*Oui, mademoiselle,*" the guard chuckled skeptically. "However, it does not matter what goods you sell. Without the right papers, you go nowhere but the Hôtel de Ville."

Rochella shook her head vehemently and pleaded, "Please, *monsieur.* Do not arrest me. My poor mother is bedridden and will starve if I do not return home this eve. I beg of you, have mercy."

"You beg well, *mademoiselle,* but your pleas for mercy fall on deaf ears. My duty is to the Commune. I have orders to take everyone, even lovely farm girls who do not have the correct identification papers, to the Hôtel."

Knowing it was useless to argue further, Rochella quietly allowed the guard to lead her through the crowded streets to the Hôtel de Ville. He ushered her up the flight of steps and into the foyer. However, this time she was not led down the corridor to Talleyrand's office but to a tiny, bare chamber with benches lining the walls. Several men and women sat, shoulders slumped, heads bowed, in dejected silence. Consumed with their own troubles, they showed no interest in the new arrival when the guard seated her among them and ordered her to wait.

Rochella glanced at the quiet group and felt her spirits sink even deeper. This was her second visit to the Hôtel de Ville, and this time she seriously doubted she would leave a free women.

Shifting uneasily, she hid her trembling hands in the pockets of her gown. The same kind of fear she saw written across the haggard faces of the other occupants gnawed at her insides. The urge to scream vibrated in her throat, yet she fought to suppress it. If she ever gave way to the terror gripping her, she would never stop screaming.

The deathly silence in the antechamber was broken only by the sound of a heavy-set man's labored breathing. Nervously he loosened his cravat and shifted on the bench. Sweat beaded his flushed features as he glanced toward the antechamber door and then at Rochella. He quickly looked away, lowering his gaze once more to the planked floor. Yet in the moment their eyes met, Rochella saw the stark terror in his look and knew he had already been apprised of the fate awaiting him beyond the door to the interrogation chamber.

The hours crept by, and Rochella finally found herself alone in the antechamber. She looked at the vacant benches and wondered what had transpired beyond the door. One by one the men and women had been called, yet none had come back through the door to freedom. Rochella fought to quell the quaking in her limbs, but no thought or deed stilled the shivering that had beset her.

"I have to be brave," she muttered when the door finally opened and the guard stepped into the room. She made an effort to stand, yet her limbs would not obey her. The guard, used to such ploys by the prisoners, jerked her roughly to her feet and propelled her before him into a chamber almost entirely in shadow. Only a small space in the center of the room was illuminated. The guard shoved her into a circle of light provided by several candelabra strategically placed to hinder the prisoner's vision.

Rochella raised a hand to shield her eyes, but the guard pushed it roughly back to her side. He drew a hard, straight-backed chair into the circle and forced her to sit, remaining behind her to ensure she made no attempt to escape.

When her eyes began to adjust, Rochella vaguely discerned several shadowy figures seated behind a long table. She jumped with a start when a booming, masculine voice announced, "Citizen, you have been brought to the Hôtel de Ville for questioning because you attempted to leave the city without the correct papers. It is our duty to France to discover the reason behind your action."

"I lost my papers at the market today," Rochella lied.

"What is your name, citizen?" the man said again, ignoring her answer as if she had not spoken.

"Marie Dubois," Rochella said, unable to stop the quiver in her voice.

A chair scraped against the floor, and a moment later a shadowy figure rose and moved around the table into the light. Rochella looked up into a broad, flat face, deeply pitted from the pox. A white wig with two powdered, rolled curls adorned the man's large head. Neatly dressed in a dark blue waistcoat, he fumbled briefly with a gold snuffbox as he squinted down at her through his spectacles. "The girl lies," the man said, gauging her reaction to his words.

The booming voice came again from the shadows. "Citizen, do you lie?"

The spokesman leaned forward, giving Rochella a brief glimpse of his face. Heavy-jowled with a short pug nose and thick lips, his face was scarred deeply as if he'd once suffered a terrible accident.

Forcing herself to sit perfectly still under the interrogators' penetrating assessment, she cleared her throat and fought to keep her voice even as she said, "I do not lie."

"Citizen Danton, I say she lies to us," said the man standing in front of Rochella. "This is the girl we have sought for these past weeks. Her name is Rochella Devlin, no matter what she tells us to the contrary. The description the soldiers gave us is identical to this girl. She is the traitor Lafayette sent here." He pointed a bony finger at her. "Speak the truth, *madame,* and we shall show mercy."

Rochella shook her head in denial but knew the man did not believe her. The pulse in her throat beat frantically as she sought a reprieve from the third man seated at the table. She strained to see through the shadows. An audible gasp escaped her when she recognized Talleyrand, sitting quietly as his companions discussed what should be done with her while they confirmed her identity. His cool blue eyes and handsome face were unreadable as he looked through Rochella as if she did not exist. Staggered that he had not already divulged her identity to the two men, she watched him intently and tried to understand why he had not exposed her.

The first man turned from his heated discussion with Danton. "I think, citizen, that you are a traitor, and you will be tried as such. When you are found guilty, you will be executed to show others what happens to those who try to help émigrés against France and the republic."

"Citizen Robespierre," Danton said from the shadows. "I agree she should be tried, but first we need to find everyone connected with her. Then we will know for certain her true identity. Should she be involved in a plot against the revolution as we suspect, it would be best to delay her trial until all have been found.''

''I'm not involved in any plot, Monsieur Danton. I am innocent of what you believe.''

Robespierre narrowed his green, bespectacled eyes and bent forward. He was so close Rochella could see his eyes were thickly mattered with mucus. ''If you are truly innocent, you will tell us your real name, as well as who has harbored you during the past weeks.''

Rochella glanced once more at Talleyrand, then, remembering his threat against René, quickly averted her eyes. She could not jeopardize her friend even to make Talleyrand suffer. She remained silent.

A malicious grin spread over Robespierre's thin lips. ''You condemn yourself with your silence. Guard, take her to La Force. Perhaps the rats and vermin will help her find her tongue.''

''I am innocent of any crime,'' Rochella cried, resisting the guard with all her strength. Yet she did not have the power to stop herself from being bodily dragged from the chamber.

Satisfied with a day's work well done, Robespierre rocked to and fro on the balls of his feet. ''We shall find her conspirators and they will pay with their lives.''

Neither Danton nor Robespierre noted Talleyrand's thoughtful expression. The former bishop was already making plans for his departure from France. The events of the past hour had only hastened the moment by a few days. He would be in England within the fortnight.

The guard cuffed Rochella on the chin, stunning her into submission, then dragged her limp body to the prison cart and tossed her inside. The cart, already filled with men and women who had sat in the antechamber awaiting judgment, jolted into motion. In her dazed stupor Rochella was only vaguely aware of the mud and refuse thrown at them by the patriots whom they passed along the way to La Force. The crowd's violence revealed the contempt the populace felt for anyone the Commune suspected of crimes against the state.

No light illuminated the night when the cart squeaked into the prison yard. The prisoners were herded into La Force and locked into their cells, where they found a meal of watery gruel and stale bread. Cold and slightly disoriented Rochella sank into a corner of her tiny cell. She wrapped her arms tightly about her knees and pressed her back against the wall in an effort to protect herself against the rats she heard scurrying in the darkness at her feet. They squealed angrily at one another as they fought over the crumbs from the stale bread, and when she heard a light splash she knew they'd turned their attack to the gruel.

Her stomach churning, she laid her head against her knees and wondered if her death sentence had already been carried out and she was now in hell.

Exhausted from the pace he had set, Gareth rode through the cobbled streets of Paris toward the English ambassador's residence. It had been a hazardous journey from Beauvais. On several occasions he had been stopped by French as well as Austrian soldiers. Fortunately, King George had given him diplomatic immunity, and the papers had saved his skin.

On the long road to Paris, he had seen things to chill his soul. As the miles passed beneath his horse's hooves, he chided himself for being a fool. He had allowed the only woman he had ever loved to leave him without knowing of his feeling. And he could not stop blaming himself for her flight. Had he been honest with her from the beginning, perhaps he would not have lost her.

Now, with so little hope of finding her, he wished he had told her what was in his heart. Regret tore through him like a cold wind. He found no warmth under the summer sun as he reflected upon fate's intervention in his life. By sending Rochella to her death, fate had saved him from breaking his vows to end the Devlin curse.

Disheartened, Gareth reined his lathered mount to a halt in front of the ambassador's elegant mansion. He slid to the ground and took from his saddlebag the packet King George had given him. For a long moment he stood gazing down the street, which was lined with the gracious residences of the rich. Soon, if men like Robespierre and Marat had their way, all this would be destroyed to satisfy their lust for power. Gareth frowned and turned toward the steps leading up to the intricately carved front door. In the past days he'd grown to hate this land and its mad people.

A liveried servant answered Gareth's knock. After receiving his calling card, he ushered him into a small antechamber to await Henry Stafford, the British ambassador. Gareth had to wait only a short while before the ambassador came hurrying into the room, his hand outstretched in greeting. "Lord Devlin, it is a pleasure to see you again. What brings you to Paris?"

Gareth took the folded parchment from the leather pouch and handed it to the ambassador. "Sir, the king asked me to deliver his missive personally to you. He thought it would be better that I bring it than that he send it through regular channels."

The middle-aged statesman pursed his lips and nodded his bewigged head. He took the parchment from

Gareth. "Come into my study. We may talk in private there."

Once the doors were closed securely, the ambassador poured himself and his visitor a brandy. His face reflected the gravity of the situation as he said, "You do know Louis in now in prison?"

Gareth nodded. "I heard the news from our agents in Le Havre. If Louis is harmed, Britain means to break diplomatic relations with France. We cannot condone such actions. It is far too dangerous."

"I suspected as much," the ambassador said, seating himself in a plush leather chair. He swirled the brandy about his glass as he gave his guest a rueful smile. "Should England take such a stand, it will mean war. The Legislative Assembly is now controlled by the radicals, and I fear to think what will happen to the royal family."

Gareth allowed his tired muscles to relax as he leaned back in his chair and stretched his long legs before him. "Do you not think the Prussians will come to the king's rescue? Longwy and Verdun have fallen to the duke's army. Near Champagne I saw a great many French soldiers fleeing to save their own lives."

The ambassador took a long swallow of the fiery liquid before he spoke. "Perhaps, but there is a madness in Paris at the moment. I fear the Duke of Brunswick will be too late if he does succeed in making his way to the city. There are executions every day and the number sentenced to death grows by the hour."

Noting his friend's worried expression, the ambassador leaned forward and asked, "Lord Devlin, my orders were not the only reason for your journey to Paris, were they?"

Gareth ran a hand over his beard-stubbled cheek, and the pain that tore through him was reflected in the look he bestowed upon his friend. He shook his head. "No, Henry. I have come to France in hopes of finding my wife. Up to now however, I have failed."

The ambassador clicked his tongue sadly as he set his glass aside on the nearby table. "I am sorry to hear that. Was she in Paris?"

"No, she would have gone first to her home, the Château le Lion de Beauvais."

The ambassador gaped at Gareth. "You mean Rochella de Beauvais is your wife?"

Gareth sat upright in his chair and leaned anxiously forward. "Yes, Rochella is my wife. Do you know something of her?"

"She is here in Paris. There has been a warrant for her arrest for the past few weeks."

A mixture of relief and concern washed over Gareth as he asked, "Rochella is here? Where?"

"My lord, I fear I do not have that answer."

Gareth shook his head. Rochella was known to be in Paris, yet how would he find her when no one would willingly admit to knowing of her whereabouts?

He said as much to the ambassador, who replied, "There is only one place I can think of at the moment where you may find any information about your wife. It is the Jacobin Club. However, it would be dangerous to have them know of your relationship with the Beauvais family and your reason for coming here."

Gareth got to his feet. "How do I get to the Jacobin Club?"

The ambassador held up one pudgy hand to stay Gareth. "It is not so simple, my friend. You need to know one of the leaders of the Assembly."

Seeing the look of frustration that crossed Gareth's face, the ambassador continued. "I would suggest you go with me to Madame de Staël's salon. I, myself, have visited there on several occasions and Danton is a frequent visitor. She supports the Girondin party, yet she is favored by several of the Jacobins because of her wit and intelligence. Rest here for a few days while I try to find out what I can about your wife. When I hear that Danton means to pay a visit to the lovely Madame de Staël, we shall also drop by to pay our respects."

Gareth leaned back in his chair and briefly closed his eyes. Knowing Rochella was within mere miles of him, he found it hard to suppress the urge to rush out in search of her. However, reason held rein over his emotions. If he was to get Rochella and himself out of France alive, he must be patient.

The sound of the key turning in the rusty lock roused Rochella from her fitful slumber. Throughout the past night and day of her imprisonment, she had sat huddled in a ball, her back braced against the cold damp stone wall, on guard against the prison's furry, long-tailed inhabitants, which fought over the meals of bread and gruel the guards brought. Weak from lack of food and the fatigue from her long vigil, she had finally fallen asleep.

Slowly she raised a trembling hand to shield her eyes against the torchlight as the door swung open.

"Come with me, Citizen," the pug-faced jailer ordered.

Bracing a hand against the wall, Rochella tried to obey his command but found her limbs too numb to move. Giving a sullen grunt, the jailer grabbed her by the scruff of the neck with one large, calloused hand

and jerked her to her feet. Her knees wobbled beneath her but she managed to stay erect.

"I don't have time to be your servant," he growled. "I got other duties to attend to." He propelled her roughly out of the cell and along the dark passageway to a flight of narrow stairs. Heedless of her small size, he took the steps two at a time, dragging Rochella along in his wake. At the landing he opened a door and thrust her forward.

Without support of his hand, Rochella stumbled to her knees on the floor. Her lips trembling from pain, she brushed her tangled hair from her face and looked up into the face of Robespierre. Feeling ill but determined not to cower in front of the vile man, Rochella struggled to her feet. She swayed unsteadily, yet she would not allow him to know how she had suffered from his treatment.

Robespierre eyed Rochella in distaste. Her odor insulted his sense of smell and his nostrils contracted as he took a neatly folded linen handkerchief from his pocket and dabbed at his thin nose. Tiny lines etched his pursed lips as he asked, "Are you now ready to be honest with me, Citizen Beauvais?"

Feeling too ill to lie, Rochella said, "I am Rochella de Beauvais."

Robespierre nodded triumphantly. "As I knew from the beginning. Now are you ready to tell me who else is involved in the conspiracy against the republic?"

Rochella took a steadying breath and looked at the lawyer through fever-bright eyes. "I have already told you, I am innocent of what you charge. The only reason I came to Paris was to find my parents. There is no conspiracy."

Robespierre casually seated himself in a wooden chair and crossed his white-stockinged legs. His bony fingers smoothed his immaculate cravat and a semblance of a smile touched his lips. "You have lied about your identity and now you expect me to believe your reason for being in Paris." He shook his head at the ridiculous idea. "Before you entered the city, you carried a letter from General Lafayette to Talleyrand. It is well known where the general's sympathies lie. As for Talleyrand, he has denied any knowledge of you, but your reaction to the gentleman last eve leads me to believe otherwise. Now I shall ask you once more, Citizen Beauvais. What is your reason for coming to Paris? Are Talleyrand and Lafayette in collusion to help the king?"

"I have answered your questions already. I know nothing of any plot," Rochella answered with as much dignity as she could summon. Her skin felt hot and she moistened her dry lips.

"You risk your life to protect those who will not lift a finger to help you. Do you not think it is a very foolish decision on your part?" Robespierre asked, glaring at Rochella through his spectacles.

"I have spoken only the truth," Rochella said, her voice quavering.

"We shall see how you feel about your so-called truth," Robespierre said, coming to his feet. He crossed to the door and called for the jailer. "Guard, take her back to her cell. We shall see what she has to say after a few days without food and water."

Giving her no chance to walk ahead of him, the guard gripped Rochella by the upper arm and dragged her through the passageway and once more down the darkened stairs. He thrust her into the black hole of her cell and slammed the door. Defeated, Rochella sank down to the floor and pulled the moth-eaten blanket about her shoulders. She shivered as she laid her head back against the slimy stone and sent a prayer toward heaven for her rescue, though she knew it was hopeless. She had no friends or family who knew where she was. And even if they did, they could not come for her without risking their own lives.

Having found himself a quiet corner to await Danton's arrival, Gareth sipped a glass of wine with the hope of quelling the feeling of desperation that had seized him when he awoke that morning. All day he had been plagued by images of Rochella crying out for his help. He knew she was near, yet not knowing her whereabouts made it seem she was at the other end of the earth. And for all the ambassador had learned during the past few days, she very well could be across the world from him.

Gareth drained his glass and set it aside. It was more than three hours since he had arrived at this circus the ambassador called Madame de Staël's salon, and he had yet to learn anything of importance. It was taking every ounce of willpower he possessed to remain in the company of those responsible for the terror he had witnessed across France.

His dark gaze swept over the room. The elite of France's newest society were gathered here to discuss the happenings of the day and the grand cause of the revolution. As in many homes in English society, Madame de Staël's salon was *the* place to be seen and heard. The revolution had been founded on the grounds of equality for all men, yet Gareth saw none of that equality within the silken walls of Madame de Staël's elegant home. Only those who were in power were in attendance. Members of the political parties associated freely, debating political and philosophical issues while each tried to convince the others of the righteousness of his cause.

Gareth frowned and turned away. He was in no mood for conversation. All he wanted was to find his wife and be done with France once and for all.

"Monsieur Devlin," a soft feminine voice said at his side, "Henry tells me you have come here to meet Danton."

Gareth turned to find Madame de Staël smiling up at him. She was a tall woman, yet the top of her head came only to his shoulder. He nodded. *"Oui, madame.* I came here expressly to meet Monsieur Danton."

Madame de Staël arched a curious brow. "Is there a special reason you need to become acquainted with my friend?"

"Madame, the matter is of a personal nature."

Madame de Staël's gaze swept the chamber and she lowered her voice. "Monsieur Devlin, only last eve I heard of a very beautiful young woman who was imprisoned at La Force. Could she be the reason for your visit to my salon?"

Gareth paled. Fine lines of tension etched his eyes and mouth as he looked at the lovely woman before him. "You seem well informed, *madame.* Do you perchance know the identity of the lady incarcerated?"

Again Madame de Staël cast a furtive glance around them to ascertain their conversation was not overheard. She spied her husband speaking with the English ambassador near the gaming tables, while several members of the Assembly argued over their wine nearby. The few women present had their heads together, chatting quietly among themselves. Madame de

Staël looked once more at Gareth. "*Monsieur,* I know only what the gossips have said. Today Talleyrand fled the country under suspicion of harboring the young lady of whom we speak. She is thought to be in collusion with him and Lafayette to reinstate the king."

"*Merci, madame.* I am grateful for your information," Gareth said, raising Madame de Staël's beringed hand to his lips.

When their eyes met, she smiled sympathetically at him, understanding the torment she saw within the dark depths. She knew what it was like to love someone the tribunal thought a traitor to the revolution. The father of her unborn child now hid in her wine cellar awaiting the time when she could find a way to help him escape Paris. "You must love her very much."

"I do, *madame.* She is my life."

"I hope you find her, *monsieur.*"

"Germaine," came a booming voice from across the room. "I need a drink."

Madame de Staël looked uneasy as Danton approached her. She said, "It would seem you have already had your share of drink this evening."

Wrapping a powerful arm about Madame de Staël's shoulders, he hugged her against him. "And I need far more to appease my thirst."

Madame de Staël glanced toward Gareth as she eased her friend down into a chair. "Georges, it is not like you to drink so much."

"*Non?*" Danton said, looking up at her. He paid no heed to the tall stranger standing near the window. "Then tonight will be different, Germaine. I need to forget what tomorrow will bring."

"What do you mean?" Madame de Staël asked, casting a worried glance in Gareth's direction.

"The sansculottes plan to massacre all of the prisoners in the Paris jails."

"What?" Madame de Staël said, horrified.

"It is true," Danton muttered, shaking his big head, his scarred features screwed up into a frown. He was feigning a distress he did not truly feel. He did not divulge to his friend that he had told the minister of prisons that the prisoners could fend for themselves. He knew Germaine would never understand such actions. It was better to place the blame for what would take place on others' shoulders if he wanted to return to her salon in the future. "The sansculottes are afraid to leave the city to fight the invaders, because they fear the prisoners will be set free to slaughter those left behind. So they intend to see such a thing does not happen."

"My God!" Gareth said. "Rochella could be murdered before I have a chance to help her."

"Please, *monsieur,*" Madame de Staël said, shaking her head to silence Gareth before Danton's inebriated mind took in what he had revealed. "Georges," she then said to Danton in a rush, "I should like to introduce to you a visitor to Paris, Monsieur Devlin. He is an envoy to the British embassy."

Slowly Danton turned his massive head to look at Gareth. He was intoxicated, yet his keen eyes missed nothing as he took in the tall, well-built Englishman. Nor was his mind too drenched in wine to have missed what he had just heard. He eyed Gareth suspiciously. "So, *monsieur,* is it possible that you are acquainted with Rochella de Beauvais?"

Madame de Staël felt her spirits sink at Danton's harsh tone. "Georges, Monsieur Devlin is *madame*'s husband. She is innocent of any crime save the one of loving her parents too much. She came to Paris only to find them.''

Danton turned his cold, calculating eyes on Germaine de Staël. ''We have a letter from Lafayette connecting her with Talleyrand. Robespierre is positive she is involved in a plot to save the king.''

''Then Robespierre is mistaken,'' Gareth said, stepping forward. ''My wife is guilty only of being young, and innocent of the ways of politics. She was foolish to come to France at this time, yet should she die because of her lack of knowledge of the world?''

''And Monsieur Devlin is willing to pay a great deal to anyone who will help him find his wife,'' Madame de Staël quickly interjected, flashing Gareth a beseeching look and seeing his unmistakable nod of approval. She knew well Georges Danton's penchant toward lining his pockets. He had helped others escape the guillotine for a price.

Danton turned shrewd, assessing eyes upon Gareth. ''Perhaps she is innocent,'' he said at last, a cynical smile tugging at his fat lips.

''Then you will help?'' Madame de Staël asked, her breath held.

Danton, his eyes never leaving Gareth, nodded. ''I should hate to see an innocent woman executed when her only fault is stupidity.''

Gareth reached into his pocket and retrieved a leather purse. He handed it to Danton. ''You will receive further payment when I have Rochella free.''

Danton weighed the purse in his hand and nodded again. ''I shall meet you at the embassy in the morning. From there we shall go to La Force.''

Lying in a fever-induced slumber, Rochella was unaware of the massacre taking place only a short distance from her cell. The insurgents had descended upon the prison at dawn. Armed with rusty pikes, sabers, axes and clubs, they had dragged their victims from their cells, screaming for mercy. Mock trials were set up, and a few brief questions were asked of each prisoner before he or she was judged. Only a few were fortunate enough to be pardoned and released to the cry of *"Vive la nation."* The majority were found guilty and thrust out to the canaille, who slaughtered them in a wild melee of blood lust. Victims' heads graced the pikes of the mob and were paraded through the streets where the mutilated bodies lay piled in heaps. Drying blood stained the cobbles red and ran in streams into the gutters.

As the day warmed and the sun rose higher in the sky, the butchers began to grow weary of their sport. However, the city's mayor soon revived the terror by refreshing their bodies with wine and their minds with his praise for their patriotic duties.

Gareth and Danton arrived at La Force in time to hear the last of the mayor's eloquent speech. Sickened by the scene, Gareth prayed again that they were not too late to save Rochella.

The members of the Commune who recognized Danton as they made their way through the carnage jovially slapped him upon the back. When they reached the gates, they found the warden, drunkenly slouched against the wall, gulping a bottle of wine. He managed a lopsided grin and a feeble salute, answering Danton's questions between hiccups. Before he sagged to the ground in a drunken stupor, he confirmed Rochella's presence in the prison earlier in the morning. However, he could volunteer no further information about her.

White-lipped, Gareth took the warden's keys from the ring on his belt and followed Danton into the dark bowels of La Force. They searched each cell, forcing their way past the sansculottes who were roughly dragging reluctant prisoners through the corridors. With so little time to spare, tension curled Gareth's insides into tight, sickening knots. He knew they had to find Rochella before the mob did, or they would never be able to secure her release.

When they neared the last dark passage, Gareth's shoulders sagged in defeat. Tears of frustration burned his eyes and he wiped at them with the back of his dirty hand. Had he come so close only to find he was too late to save his wife? His throat clogged with emotion.

Danton, sweat beading his scarred face, leaned tiredly against the slime-covered wall and wiped his brow. "*Monsieur,* I fear we are too late. We should leave here before the mob turns on us."

Gareth leveled his angry glare on Danton. "No! I will tear this place apart stone by stone until I know Rochella is not within its rotten bowels." He swung away, renewing his search.

Danton shrugged and followed the angry Englishman.

Only one torch lit the black interior of the passageway. In his rush to reach the last barred door at the end of the corridor, Gareth passed the small door to Rochella's cell, which was obscured by shadows.

He pushed the portal open and peered into the silent, empty room. Bitterness welling within him, he clenched his hands at his sides and fought against the reality that was descending upon him with such brutal force. He had lost Rochella. All hope was now gone.

"Rochella," he cried as a wave of agony knocked him to his knees. He buried his face in his hands and wept his misery.

Danton stood by dispassionately regarding the younger man in his grief. He decided there were far more important matters that needed his attention, and started to turn away when a slight whimper broke through the stillness. Cocking his head to one side, he listened. Again he heard a faint moan.

"*Monsieur,* there is someone within," he called, stepping close to the wall and feeling for the handle of the door.

Gareth was instantly on his feet. He grabbed the torch and rushed to Danton's side. They swiftly unlocked the door. Gareth gave an audible groan at the sight of Rochella lying on the filthy blanket.

"My God, Rochella," Gareth breathed, sinking to his knees at her side and lifting her carefully into his arms. She moaned and her lashes fluttered open. She squinted up at him and raised a trembling hand to gently touch his face before she succumbed once more to unconsciousness.

"She is burning with fever. We must make haste or I fear she will not live," Gareth said.

Danton nodded and quickly led Gareth out of the prison to his waiting coach.

After depositing Rochella inside, Gareth tossed Danton another pouch heavy with gold. The Frenchman smiled. "*Monsieur,* it has been a pleasure to do business with you. The papers I have given the driver should ensure safe passage to Le Havre for you and your lady."

"Thank you, Monsieur Danton. The gold cannot repay you for what you have given back to me," Gareth said, climbing into the conveyance.

Danton nodded and turned his massive frame quickly away, already putting the Englishman from his mind. He now had to think of the rousing speech he would soon make.

Chapter Seventeen

"Gareth, Gareth," Rochella murmured against the satin pillowcase.

Sluggishly Gareth roused from his catnap, uncertain of what had awakened him. He blinked several times to clear his vision and rubbed the sleep from his eyes with forefinger and thumb. Wearily, he stretched in an effort to ease his aching muscles.

"Gareth," Rochella murmured again restlessly.

"I am here," Gareth said tenderly. Getting out of his chair, he bent anxiously over his wife.

"Help me, Gareth. I need you. Please do not let him hurt me again," she whimpered, her fingers digging into the mattress.

Gently Gareth smoothed the hair away from his wife's hot brow. "I am here, love. No one will ever hurt you again, I promise."

The tension eased from her body at the sound of his voice, and her breathing became even as Rochella slipped once more into the void of unconsciousness.

Gareth released a long, weary breath. Since the day he had found her in La Force, she had roused from her fevered slumber only to cry out in fear or pain. She had not been lucid enough to realize she was safe at Devil

Wind where no harm could befall her. Gareth sank back into his chair and braced his elbows on his knees. He covered his face with his hands and for the thousandth time prayed to God to spare his wife's life. Several weeks had passed since he brought Rochella back to Devil Wind, but her fever clung to her like a leech, sapping the strength from her body. Gareth did not know how much longer she could survive if the fever did not break.

"God, let her live," he whispered. He was unaware he was no longer alone in the room until he felt a comforting hand come to rest on his shoulder. He looked up to see the physician from Padstow, Dr. John Connors.

"You need to rest, Lord Devlin. You are not doing your wife any good by wearing yourself out. She will need you when she finally wakes up." Dr. Connors said, setting his bag on the bedside table.

"I cannot leave her," Gareth said, squinting to focus his red-rimmed eyes on the physician.

"Your wife does not know you are here."

Gareth nodded. He knew that, but he could not abide the thought of leaving Rochella. He feared she would slip away from him completely if he did so. In some strange way he sensed his presence kept her alive. It was a foolish belief, but he would not risk the consequences of doing what the doctor asked until he knew Rochella's fever had broken and she was on her way to recovery.

Dr. Connors shook his head. He had been trying to get Lord Devlin to rest since he had returned with his wife from France. He had lived day in and day out in the sickroom, even taking his meals by his wife's bed. Lord Devlin would not even trust his own servants with their mistress. Only the young serving girl named Alice was allowed to enter the chamber. Soon, the doctor predicted, Lord Devlin would collapse from sheer exhaustion if he did not seek out his own bed.

Dr. Connors opened his black bag and took out a vial of laudanum, which he set on the table. He glanced toward the weary-eyed man sitting by the bed and smiled to himself. Lord Devlin might refuse to take his advice but he could always slip the drug into the man's tea. That would make him get the rest he needed whether he wanted it or not.

Pleased with his solution, Dr. Connors turned his attention to his patient in the bed. Leaning over Rochella he listened to her even breathing. A look of relief flickered over his age-lined face when he touched her forehead and found it damp and cool. He glanced at Gareth and smiled. "Lord Devlin, her fever has broken. Your wife is now sleeping soundly for the first time in weeks. I believe she is on her way to recovery."

Unable to believe the doctor's diagnosis, Gareth felt Rochella's brow for himself and then grew weak with relief. "Thank God," he murmured, swallowing against the lump rising in his throat.

"Now, it is time for you to get out of here and get some rest. I do not need another patient on my hands. This one has given me enough worry," Dr. Connors said, his voice stern.

Gareth ran a hand over his beard-stubbled chin, suddenly aware of how truly exhausted he was. He nodded, placed a kiss on Rochella's brow, shook the doctor's hand and left the room. He would sleep for a few hours before returning to his wife's side. She would need him when she awoke.

"The doctor is still with her," Hilda said, nervously fidgeting with the ring of keys at her waist. She had hoped to hear that Lady Devlin had finally succumbed to her fever when she saw Lord Devlin exit the sickroom. However, she soon realized he had only gone to his chamber to rest while the doctor was with his wife.

"So her fever still rages?" Adam asked, his back to the housekeeper, his brow creased with worry.

"As far as I know. Your brother has not allowed anyone near her except himself and Alice. If only she would just die and get it over with," Hilda grumbled.

The housekeeper did not see the annoyed look that flickered over Adam's face. "I disagree, love," he said sweetly. "Our plan would work much more smoothly with her cooperation."

"What do you mean—her cooperation? She is nothing but trouble for us. It would have been far better had Lord Devlin never found her."

Adam's white teeth gleamed in the late-afternoon sunlight streaming in through the window. "Dear Hilda, Rochella is much more valuable to us alive than dead." He chuckled at the housekeeper's scowl and held up a silencing hand. "Who better to confirm the identity of Lord Devlin than his own wife?"

Hilda considered Adam's statement for a long moment before she smiled. "True. No one would ever question the widow. She would know her own husband."

Adam and Hilda's conspiratorial laughter filled the chamber. They would use Rochella's return to their own advantage.

Adam draped an arm around Hilda's thin shoulders and brushed his lips against her brow. "I suggest you do everything in your power to help my brother keep his wife alive. She will be a great asset to us in the near future."

Rising from his long, hot bath, Gareth slipped into a comfortable dressing gown and turned to pour himself a relaxing brandy before succumbing to his need for sleep. When the knock came at the door, he set his half-filled glass aside and cast a longing glance at the bed before he called, "Enter." He had lost so much sleep over the past weeks a few more minutes would not matter.

When the door opened to reveal Dr. Connors, Gareth felt his insides go cold with dread. "Has something happened to Rochella?"

Dr. Connors shook his head and smiled. "My lord, I hate to disturb you, since I see you are finally taking my advice. But I wanted to tell you I have examined your lady and she is fine, as is your babe."

Gareth's mouth fell agape, and the blood slowly receded from his face. "Sir, my wife is not expecting a child."

Dr. Connors's grin widened. "So it is as I thought. She has not told you of the happy event yet. I hope, my lord, you will not tell her I've let her little secret out of the bag. Women like to relate their good tidings to their husbands themselves."

Flabbergasted, Gareth sank abruptly into the chair behind him and croaked, "How can it be? It is not possible."

"Lord Devlin, you are a healthy, virile man. I assure you it is not only possible, it is a fact. After you left your wife's bedchamber, I gave her a thorough examination to confirm my suspicions. In the past weeks I had noted certain bodily signs that are seen in women who are with child, but I hadn't wanted to rouse your hopes until I knew she would survive her ordeal."

Noting the look of pain that passed over Gareth's features, he asked, "Lord Devlin, is something wrong?"

Numbly Gareth shook his head. "No, I am only surprised to learn I am to be a father. It is quite a shock, after all."

"I understand the way you feel. I was thunderstruck the first time Maggie told me I was to be a father."

He had created the life he had sworn never to bring into the world. Struggling for some semblance of decorum, Gareth rose unsteadily to his feet. "Sir, would you join me in a brandy?"

Instantly diagnosing Gareth's faltering speech and movements as signs of the collapse he had already predicted, Dr. Connors held up a hand. "Lord Devlin, please sit. I shall do the honors."

Gratefully, Gareth sank back into the chair. The shock of Rochella's pregnancy had taken its toll on the last of his strength. He leaned his head back against the chair and closed his eyes.

Dr. Connors took the vial of laudanum from his pocket and poured a small amount into Gareth's brandy. A moment later he handed him the glass and raised his own, secure in the knowledge Lord Devlin would get the rest he needed once he swallowed his drink. The man could celebrate his wife's pregnancy after he slept off the drug. He would be in a much better frame of mind. "Congratulations, Lord Devlin. You are to be a father."

Gareth rose unsteadily to his feet and clinked his glass against the physician's. He forced a smile to his lips and drank the fiery liquid, draining the glass in one gulp. He managed to thank Dr. Connors for his assistance during the past weeks and then quickly ushered the man out the door. He needed time to think about the turmoil the doctor's news had created within him.

The fact that Rochella was carrying his child ran repeatedly through his mind, torturing him. Gareth raised his hands to his head and pressed down on his skull. He was responsible for perpetuating the Devlin curse.

An agonized groan escaped him as he raised his eyes to look at the image reflected in the full-length mirror across the room. A muscle twitched in his jaw and he clenched his fists at his sides. The man looking back at him was weak and selfish. He had broken his vows by succumbing to his physical desires, and now the child of his loins would be the one to bear the brunt of his weakness.

Guilt-stricken, Gareth turned to the table that held the crystal brandy decanter. He poured himself another drink and once more drained it in one gulp. The burning sensation had not yet eased before he refilled his glass and downed the contents again. He wanted to forget for just a little while what he had done.

Shaking his head, Gareth downed another glass of the fiery brandy. He had doomed another generation of his family to the scorn and madness that came through their bloodline.

Feeling suddenly dizzy, Gareth lowered himself to the side of the bed and lay back against the pillows. A moment later the glass tumbled from his hand to the floor, shattering as the brandy, the laudanum and the exhaustion finally claimed him.

Leaning back against the fluffy satin pillows Rochella absently brushed the chestnut hair cascading over one shoulder. As she ran the tortoiseshell brush down the length of the shining strands, a warm safe feeling curled in her belly. She was home at last. Her ordeal had left her weak, but she was free of the terror she had experienced since deciding to leave Devil Wind.

A long breath escaped her as she reflected upon her foolishness. Everything had been for naught. She had learned from Alice soon after regaining consciousness that her parents were safe in Austria. Gareth had received word from them only a few days after she had fled. She had been reckless and naive, and it had nearly cost her life. And had Gareth not risked his own to rescue her, she was certain she would now be dead.

Rochella's hand paused in midstroke. A furrow marred her smooth brow. It was a week since her fever had broken and yet Gareth had not been to visit her. She had sent Alice several times to ask him to visit her, and each time the maid had returned with his apology, saying he would see her as soon as his affairs allowed. He had neglected his business while away in France, and until matters were in order he could spare no time.

Rochella suspected Gareth's work was only an excuse to avoid her company.

Her frown deepening, Rochella wondered why Gareth had gone to so much trouble to bring her back to England, when it was obvious his feelings toward her had not changed.

Letting the brush slip from her limp fingers, she leaned back and stared up at the ceiling. "Why did he not just leave me there to die?" she murmured.

"Lady Devlin," Dr. Connors said, surprising Rochella from her reveries. "Did you say something?"

Rochella looked up to see the doctor closing the door behind him. She smiled. She had grown fond of the Padstow physician, whose pale blue eyes reflected the gentle spirit that had made him dedicate his life to helping others. "Nothing of importance. I was only wondering when you were going to allow me out of this bed."

The doctor chuckled as he set down the worn leather bag on the bedside table and seated himself in the chair Gareth had vacated the previous week. He reached out and patted Rochella's hand. "My dear, I think it best for you to remain in bed a while longer. You need to regain your strength."

"But—" Rochella began to argue, but Dr. Connors shook his head to silence her.

"Lady Devlin, I am the physician here and I know what is best. We cannot have you out of bed too soon or you might lose your babe. You have been through a great deal and you are lucky to have your life, much less the child you carry."

Rochella's eyes widened and she regarded the doctor as if he had suddenly grown two heads. "A babe?"

Dr. Connors chuckled and shook his head in dismay. "Both you and Lord Devlin act as if you have never lived together as husband and wife. Lady D-devlin," he then stuttered, "have I m-made a mistake? The babe you carry is your husband's, is it not?" Dr. Connors's face had turned a deep red with mortification. He swallowed uneasily. In all the years he had been in practice he had never insulted one of his patients as he had just done the lovely Lady Devlin.

"Yes, of course," Rochella replied, cringing under his suspicions. "It is just such a shock after everything that has happened. I had been sick before I left Devil Wind, yet I never suspected I carried Gareth's child.''

Dr. Connors seemed to sag with relief. He wiped a hand over his sweaty pate and cleared his throat. "Forgive me, Lady Devlin. I did not mean to imply something illicit, yet in my profession we see many things. A doctor cannot make judgments, but he needs honesty to deal with his patients correctly at all times. Had I not assumed the babe to be your husband's, I should not have told him of your condition.''

Rochella's pale cheeks turned ashen. "Gareth already knows of our child?''

Dr. Connors rolled his eyes heavenward. He had done it again. He had not planned to divulge that bit of information. Resigning himself to his own stupidity, he nodded and gave her a sheepish little smile. "Yes, I told him the night your fever broke. I fear I should have waited and allowed you to relay your good news, but I wanted to let him know you would recover. The news of your babe just slipped out.''

Rochella felt a heavy weight settle about her shoulders. She knew now the reason Gareth had not seen fit to visit her. He knew of the child she carried and wanted nothing to do with it or its mother. She fought to control the hot tears stinging the backs of her lids. Swallowing hard, she drew in a deep breath and forced her voice to remain calm. "I would like to rest now.''

Dr. Connors blustered as he came to his feet, "Rest is exactly what you and the babe need. I only came to see how you were feeling. I want you to remain in bed for the next few days. When I return at the end of the week, if you are still doing well I shall allow you to get out of bed. Should you need me before that time, you only have to send word."

"Thank you, Dr. Connors," Rochella said, striving with every ounce of her willpower to act as if her heart were not shattering into a million tiny pieces.

"Then I shall bid you good-day." Dr. Connors left Rochella alone with her heartbreak.

Chapter Eighteen

Lightning slashed across the sky, sizzling the air and illuminating Rochella's bedchamber as the boom of thunder roused her from her restless sleep. Another jagged streak of light penetrated the night, and she gasped in surprise at the sight of Gareth sitting on the side of her bed.

As she watched, he struck the flint and lit the candle on the bedside table. The soft warm glow surrounded them as they looked at each other without saying a word. Rochella's heart ached to reach out and make sure that he was real and not a wishful dream. Yet she remained still. After months of longing to be in his arms, she knew he did not want her or the child she carried.

Swallowing against the wave of pain, Rochella pushed herself up against the pillows and moistened her dry lips before she managed to ask, "What are you doing here?"

One dark brow arched above his intense dark eyes as he brought up one hand and tenderly caressed the smooth line of her cheek. "I just wanted to be near you for a while. Is that too much to ask of my wife?"

Rochella longed to press her cheek into his hand, to snuggle like a pleased kitten, yet she suppressed the urge and moved away from him. She forced into her voice a calm she did not feel. "I had assumed you did not want anything to do with me since I now carry your child."

His eyes darkening to onyx, her husband's expression hardened to stone. He reached out and grabbed her by the arms, jerking her forward. "What are you saying?"

Rochella eyed him belligerently. In the past she had accepted his mercurial moods but no more. She now had her child to think about. She would not allow Gareth to ride roughshod over her again. She would fight him to her death to protect the tiny little life they had created together.

Rochella raised her chin in the air. "You may not want me, but I shall not allow you to treat our child as a burden that has been thrust upon you against your will. You are his father."

Adam's stony features paled. Rochella's words ended the possibility of any delay of his plans. Her news also made it imperative to rid himself of her as well. He wanted no issue of his brother to inherit Devil Wind. Only heirs from his own loins would hold claim to the title and lands. His children would not be second in line as he had always been.

"You betrayed me," he growled, thrusting Rochella back against the pillows. "I could have given you everything."

"Gareth, you are mad," Rochella cried, scrambling to the other side of the bed.

Adam threw back his head and his evil laughter filled the room. The sound sent shivers down Rochella's spine, and she trembled when he turned his cold, calculating gaze upon her once more. "He has not yet told you of me, has he?"

Rochella swallowed the lump of fear in her throat and shook her head. She glanced toward the door and wondered if she could make her escape before he lost complete control and throttled her.

Again came the diabolical chuckle as he sensed the direction of her thoughts and quickly caged her between his arms, regarding her through narrowed lids. "I am not your precious husband, the one you give yourself to with such passion, the one who put the babe in your belly."

"Gareth, you are frightening me," Rochella said, a cold foreboding chill rippling down her spine.

Adam ran a finger down the smooth line of Rochella's cheek and grinned evilly. "We could have been good together, Rochella. Had you not conceived Gareth's heir, we could have enjoyed each other's passion until I tired of you. Then you also would have had to have a fatal accident."

"Gareth, what has come over you?" Rochella stuttered nervously, still unable to comprehend fully what Adam was telling her.

One dark brow arched and he chuckled again. "You still believe I am Gareth? Dear Rochella, you are a foolish young thing. Surely by now you realize I am your husband's identical twin, Adam."

Realization setting in, Rochella turned a deathly white. As she looked more closely at the face so like Gareth's, she could now see the minuscule traits that made them so different. A mad, angry light flashed in the cold depths of this man's eyes. And his mouth was repulsive with its cynical, snarling tilt. No, this man's face was nothing like her husband's.

Rochella's eyes widened as she recognized the man who had come to her room months ago. Until this moment she had convinced herself she had dreamed his nocturnal visits. Now she realized it was Gareth's brother who had come into her chamber at night and talked to her.

Her cheeks burning at the intimate memories, Rochella voiced her suspicions and cringed when he laughingly admitted his guilt. However, she had no time to say or do more. Adam clasped her about the throat, drawing her near. She could feel the warmth of his breath on her face as she stared up into his mad eyes. "Please let me go," was her whispered plea.

Smugly, Adam shook his head. "I cannot do that love. You see, when Gareth is dead, your child is the only thing to stand between me and the Devlin fortune. Now you will have to suffer the same fate as the one who placed the curse upon my family. She, too, conceived unwanted little bastards, and when they died she placed a curse on the master of Devil Wind for abandoning his own children. My ancestor had the witch punished for the deed, as was her due, yet even from her watery grave her malediction keeps haunting the Devlins. Or so my dear, stupid brother believes."

"Curse?" Rochella said, her words sounding strangled because of the pressure about her throat.

Adam smiled down at her. "Yes, our family curse. That is why your husband keeps me locked away in the north wing. He doesn't want you to know of the legacy left to us by our ancestors. What a shame you will not be here to give him a good set-down for keeping his little secret from you."

"Why do you want to harm me? I have done nothing to you."

"You carry his child and I cannot let you live because of it. Once I rid myself of Gareth, I want no reminders of him about me," Adam said, slowly running his hand down to the base of Rochella's throat. He felt her frantic pulse and smiled at the rush of power her fright sent through him. Soon he would know how it was to be in total command. There would be no more Gareth and no more restrictions to keep him from doing exactly as he wished. He would have it all. His only regret was that lovely Rochella could not live to enjoy it with him.

"You cannot mean to kill your own brother?" Rochella gasped as his fingers tightened about her throat.

"Silly chit. I cannot let him live if I want what I rightly deserve. Once you are gone, Gareth's body will be found at the bottom of the cliffs. Everyone will believe the poor mad Devlin twin killed Lord Devlin's wife and then ended his own wretched existence." Adam chuckled. "And no one will ever know I am not Gareth. There will be much sympathy for a man who has lost his wife and brother in one night. And be assured I shall graciously accept their consolation."

"You are mad. Your scheme will never work. People will know the difference," Rochella said, struggling against his hands.

"Surely you jest. No one will ever suspect I am not Gareth when even you, Gareth's wife, could not see the difference between us. Nor am I mad, my dear. Poor Gareth has always thought me the victim of the curse, but he is a fool. I used his belief to my advantage to create the illusion of madness until the time was right for me to seize what I have wanted all my life. I have planned this for a long while, and now there is nothing to stand in my way of having it all."

A loud boom of thunder rattled the windows as Adam threw back the covers and jerked Rochella from the bed. The crashing roar drowned out her cry for help. Weakened by her illness and unable to stand alone, she stumbled to her knees. Adam lifted her easily into his arms and turned toward the door as another roll of thunder reverberated across the landscape.

Rochella fought him with what strength she possessed, beating futilely at his chest. "You will never get away with this," she panted, straining against the arms encircling her like iron manacles.

"If you hope Gareth will come to your rescue, you hope in vain, dear sister-in-law," Adam said, a cynical little smile curling his shapely lips. "My dear brother is up on the parapet walk, brooding over his cursed life as usual."

"He will hear my screams," Rochella said.

Adam shook his head confidently as he carried her out into the hallway. "Not in this storm. Gareth will not even know you are missing until it is far too late to help you."

Adam strode down the stairs and across the foyer to the main door, where Hilda stood watching their descent. A puzzled frown marred the housekeeper's thin features, yet she didn't question Adam's intentions.

"It is time to put our plan into action," Adam explained, noting her expression. "We can wait no longer. She carries Gareth's babe."

Unable to believe the housekeeper was involved in Adam's devious plans, Rochella watched Hilda calmly open the foyer closet and take out a rain cloak. Without a word she slipped it on and pulled up the hood over her tightly bound hair. When the woman opened the door, Rochella finally found her voice. "Hilda, help me. You cannot let Adam do this mad thing."

The housekeeper eyed Rochella with contempt and stepped aside for Adam and his squirming burden. However, as he stepped out into the rain, she could not resist one barb. "When you are gone, my high and mighty, I shall be mistress here."

She closed the door behind them and followed close on Adam's heels as he strode across the cobbled courtyard and toward the windy cliffs.

When they reached the edge of the cliffs, Rochella realized Adam had been right when he said no would hear her screams. Only the roar of the angry tide beating at the black granite and the howl of the baying wind could be heard for more than a few feet. When he set her on her feet, Rochella looked to the shadowy figure trailing close behind. She had to convince Hilda that Adam would not make her the lady of Devil Wind when he was master. It was her only hope of survival.

The drenching rain making her nightrail cling to her body like a second skin, Rochella turned to the housekeeper and pleaded once more for her help.

Adam laughed at her naïveté. "It is no use pleading with Hilda. She will do as I bid. She wants what I want."

"I shall make a far better Lady Devlin than you. When you and your fancy lord are dead, the expensive gowns and jewels will be my right," Hilda taunted triumphantly. A wave of her hand encompassed the castle in the distance. "This will all belong to my children."

"Do not be a fool," Rochella said, straining to free herself from Adam's hands. "Adam is only using you. He will never make you his wife. He would not taint the

Devlin name by marrying his housekeeper. He will keep
you as his mistress, but he will marry a girl of breeding, one who will have a large dowry. You have nothing to offer him.''

''Shut up, or I shall throw you over the cliff myself,'' Hilda swore, irritated that Rochella had voiced
her own uncertainties.

''Then follow his orders, and when it is too late, you
will know I was right. You can never be Lady Devlin,
Hilda, no matter how many murders you help him
commit.''

''Shut up,'' Adam growled. ''Hilda will not listen to
you. She does as I bid her.''

Rochella looked up into Adam's face, unable to discern his expression in the darkness. ''Are you afraid to
tell her the truth, Adam? Why do you not tell her she
will never have your name or the position of Lady
Devlin?'

''I am afraid of nothing,'' Adam snapped.

''Then tell Hilda she will never have your name or
possess the title of Lady Devlin,'' Rochella said, sensing she had hit a sensitive area between them.

''Adam, is she right?'' Hilda asked, her voice filled
with the doubt washing over her like the waves below
the cliffs.

''What does it matter? Nothing will have changed
between us, except I shall be the master of Devil Wind.
You will remain as my mistress.''

''But you promised you would make me Lady Devlin,'' Hilda said, her voice rising in pitch.

Adam turned on the housekeeper. ''I would promise
I could make the sun not shine in order to get what I
deserve. Now go back to the castle and brew one of

your special teas for Gareth. My brother needs a long, long rest—preferably for eternity."

The hood of Hilda's cloak slipped unnoticed to her shoulders as she shook her head. "For years I have obeyed your every word, but no more, Adam. I shall not take the scraps of your affection, hiding my love from the world as I have had to do since coming to Devil Wind. I have worked to have you and I want all of you."

"How dare you talk to me as if you owned me," Adam said. "You will do as I bid or you will regret it."

"No, Adam," Hilda said, stubbornly folding her arms over her chest. "I shall have what you promised or I shall go and tell Lord Devlin of your plans for him."

"My dear, foolish Hilda," Adam said, suddenly changing tactics and tone. "I have planned far too long to allow you to ruin things for me now. Soon I shall own everything, and then you will have all you have asked. Just be patient, love."

Feeling Adam's fingers slacken on her arm and sensing Hilda's danger, Rochella twisted away from him and cried, "Hilda, he lies."

Her warning came too late. Before Hilda realized Adam's intention, he closed the short space between them. Reaching out, he clasped her by the throat, brutally lifting her off her feet. He shook her like a rag doll before he flung her backward, over the face of the cliff. Hilda clawed at the empty air and her scream ripped through the stormy night. She fell into the turbulent water beating against the rocks below.

Rochella, her wet hair streaming down her face, nearly blinding her, struggled to flee. However, she managed to stumble only a few feet from Adam before she sank to the ground, the muscles in her legs trembling from weakness. She half crawled, half scooted across the ground in her effort to escape, but her night-rail impeded her movements. The wet material wrapped about her legs to trap her like a fly in a silken web.

"Surely, you did not think I would let you escape so easily, my dear," Adam said, towering over her, his legs spread wide, his hands braced on his hips.

Through the rain pouring down her face, Rochella looked up at the black figure of the evil man. She knew death awaited her only a few feet away, yet she was determined that Adam would not find it as easy to murder her as he had the poor housekeeper who had foolishly given him her love.

Calmly Rochella accepted her fate. She would die tonight, but she would do everything within her power to prevent him from fulfilling the rest of his evil scheme. When he threw her over the cliff she would try to take him with her.

The wind and rain beat at the solitary figure standing on the parapet walk overlooking the cliffs. His face raised into the raging elements, Gareth savored the violence surrounding him. As in years past when unable to venture out onto the moors to brood and sort out his feelings, he came to the parapet walk. He was isolated from the world here, high on the castle walls.

Gareth gazed off into the black night. He had spent much of his time here since the previous week when he had learned of Rochella's pregnancy. Tormented by his guilt, he had suffered alone, agonizing over what he must now do. He had desperately needed to go to his wife to ask her forgiveness, yet guilt and remorse had kept him from her side.

She was his life, but he had allowed his lust to doom their relationship. Had he been honest with her from the beginning and told her of the curse that tainted his family, she might have understood why he had vowed to end the Devlin line with himself. Now it was too late. She would suffer the consequences of his deceit, as would their child.

A streak of lightning illuminated Devil Wind's cold, black granite. Glistening with rain, the castle's wet walls seemed to weep with its master as he raised his face toward the stormy sky. A boom of thunder drowned out his cry of despair. His balled fists resting on the time-smoothed stone, he pressed his wet lashes to his cheeks. There was only one decision he could make. He had to tell Rochella about Adam and then suffer her scorn.

A muscle twitched in his cheek as his head fell forward in defeat. It seemed as though he could already feel her hatred seething in the wind's fury. His imagination made her cry of pain and rage so real he thought he actually heard it. There would be no forgiveness when she learned of the secret he had kept from her. And he could not blame her. At the moment he loathed himself for being a coward.

Resigned to his fate, Gareth turned toward the door in the tower wall. A streak of lightning fingered across the sky, illuminating the landscape. The image of three ghostly figures near the cliffs made Gareth pause. Another flash of lightning split the heavens. In the moment before all went black again, he recognized his brother and saw him throw a cloaked figure over the cliff.

Gareth's blood froze in his veins. He turned toward the stairs to the courtyard. His pulse pounding in his temples, his breath coming in short pants, he took the slippery stone steps two at a time. Fear speeding him on, the corded muscles in his long legs stretching to their limits, he ran toward the cliffs, arriving in time to see Adam lift a muddy, squirming figure into his arms.

Adam paused, looked down at the white-foamed, black waters and smiled. "Goodbye, dear Rochella." He released her.

Rochella screamed and clung to Adam's shoulders, her nails digging into his flesh, her fingers tearing at the material of his jacket. Adam staggered and she heard the material of his coat rip as he pried her fingers free. Rochella felt nothing but empty air beneath her as she fell.

Recognizing the scream carried on the wind, Gareth raced toward the cliff. He saw the struggle between his wife and his brother before she disappeared from sight. Blinded by rage, he tackled Adam, with a roar of agony. The brothers struggled on the rocky ground, rolling over and over, battering each other with their fists. Adam clutched a piece of granite, bringing it up toward Gareth's temple. Gareth saw the blow coming yet could not avoid it. It grazed him on the jaw, knocking him backward near the edge of the cliff. Stunned, he rolled onto his hands and knees, his head hanging, mingled rainwater and blood pouring down his face. He tried to collect his wits.

Adam scrambled to his feet and kicked Gareth in the stomach. Gareth groaned and fell to the slippery granite, gasping for breath. Sensing his victory, Adam picked up a large piece of rock. His mad laughter joined the shrieking wind as he raised it above his head, determined to crush the skull of the man who had been his nemesis since the moment of his birth. The weight of the rock and the rain-slick stones made Adam's feet slip. He lost his balance, staggering backward on the wet surface. His heel caught in a crevice worn into the granite by time and the elements, and he tumbled into the roaring darkness beyond the cliffs. His scream ended when he vanished into the wild, rushing surf.

Gareth saw his brother disappear over the cliff's edge without remorse. Hot tears mixed with cool rain on his cheeks as he struggled to the edge of the jagged granite precipice where Rochella had fallen to her death. Overcome by his grief, he felt the urge to follow her into that eternal darkness where he could no longer feel the agony rending his soul.

Rain blurring his vision, he stared down toward the salty waters that had claimed his wife and child. Suddenly his breath left him. His heart constricted until he thought it would burst from the painful pressure that gripped it. Several feet below on a narrow ledge of rock lay the slight form of his wife.

"God," he prayed aloud. "Let her be alive." As if in answer to his plea the furies retreated. The wind died and only a small drizzle of rain continued to mist the night. Gareth closed his eyes for a moment, before he began his treacherous journey down the face of the granite cliff. He had no time to consider alternatives or to seek help. Should Rochella regain consciousness and move a few inches, she would fall into the raging waters below.

Gareth inched his way down the slippery incline to his wife's side. When he reached her he felt her pulse and again thanked God for his mercy when he found it strong. Without further thought, he picked her up and placed her on his shoulder, knowing he could not climb back up the granite surface without the use of both hands to find each tiny crevice.

What seemed an eternity later, Gareth placed his feet firmly on the summit and shifted Rochella gently into his arms. Twice he had come close to losing her, and should God see fit to spare her now, he swore he would never let her out of his sight again. Love, determination and faith leading him on, he strode back toward Devil Wind with his limp burden.

Rochella's eyes fluttered open and widened in horror at the sight of the man staring down at her. She raised her hands to ward him off. Vehemently shaking her head, she cried, "No, Adam, no!"

"Rochella, it is Gareth. You are safe now. Adam is dead."

Rochella threw her arms about Gareth's neck, and he held her close as she wept out her fright against his chest. When no more tears would come, she stuttered between sniffles, "He tried to kill me. He—he said it was because of our babe. He did not want any reminders of you when he was master of Devil Wind." Rochella looked up at Gareth with bright, glassy eyes. "Why did you not tell me?"

Resigned to this moment, Gareth released a long breath and eased Rochella back onto the pillows. He knew he had to tell her the entire story, yet even now it was hard to speak of Adam and the generations of mad Devlins. His shoulders sagged under the burden of the secret he had carried for so long. "I could not," he said at last, unable to look at her.

"You could not tell me you had a brother?" Rochella asked, unable to understand Gareth's continued reluctance to speak of Adam after all that had just taken place.

Gareth shook his head. "Had I told you of Adam, I would have had to tell you of the Devlin curse. You were unhappy about our marriage, and I saw no need to place more dark clouds on our relationship than already existed."

"You could not even tell me when you knew your brother was roaming the halls at night. I thought it was you who came to my bedchamber each night," Rochella said. She could find no excuse for Gareth's actions. He had placed her and their child in jeopardy.

Gareth felt a chill run down his spine at Rochella's words. Stunned to learn Adam had come to her bedchamber, he stared at her as tortured thoughts ran through his mind. He squeezed his eyes closed at the mental image of Rochella giving herself to his brother as passionately as she'd given herself to him. A new fear rose in his heart. The child she now carried could have been sired by Adam.

He turned away from Rochella, a new wave of guilt and heartache making it impossible for him to look at her.

"I am sorry I did not tell you from the first," he said, coming to his feet. "I have sent for Dr. Connors. He should be here soon to make sure you were not harmed in the fall. I shall send Alice to attend you until the doctor arrives."

"Our babe," Rochella said, her hand instantly going to her rounding stomach, her eyes widening with concern. Yet Gareth did not hear her words. He was totally lost in his own agonized thoughts. They were not for his wife or for the death of his brother. They were for the child he had unconsciously rejoiced to bring into the world, a child of his own lions, an heir to Devil

Wind. Now even that dream had been shattered by Adam.

Angered suddenly by the cruel tricks fate kept playing on him, Gareth stormed down the stairs to his study. He poured himself a glass of brandy and slouched into the chair behind his desk. His jaw clenched, he silently cursed the day he had been born.

Gray dawn crept in through the windows as Gareth pushed himself from his chair and stretched his aching limbs. Late in the night, the doctor had come to confirm that Rochella and the child would be fine. Yet Gareth had remained in his study, unable to climb the stairs and face his wife.

Through the lonely night he had sought to come to terms with the new problem his deceit had created. He had sat for hours staring moodily into the jumping flames, going over everything in his mind. He was responsible for what had occurred between Rochella and his brother. He could place no blame on his wife. She had believed Adam to be her husband when she had gone into his arms.

"And now I know not if the child she carries is mine," Gareth said, running a hand through his tousled hair in exasperation. He drew in a deep breath, suddenly making a decision. It was time to put an end to this madness once and for all. Should the child belong to his brother, he would raise it as his own. It was his responsibility now, and he must see to the welfare of the child as well as of the mother. He had to make Rochella understand that he loved her no matter who had sired her babe.

Rochella's eyes were dry and burning. There were no more tears to weep. She was numb, completely devoid of emotion. She felt only a cold despair. Gareth's rejection when she had needed his comfort so desperately had shattered her last hope of ever finding his love. She had lain awake all night trying to sort out what she must do. She knew she could not remain at Devil Wind when he wanted nothing to do with her or their child. Last night when she had mentioned their babe, he had fled the room. His reaction had confirmed her suspicions about his feelings. Now all that was left was to decide where to go.

"I shall go to Austria," Rochella whispered to the silent room. "Mama and Papa will welcome me."

The squeak of a floorboard drew Rochella's attention to the man standing uncertainly in the doorway. He gave her a wary smile. Rochella did not return the gesture. Her voice held no warmth as she said, "Come in, Gareth."

"I had hoped you would be awake," Gareth said, closing the door quietly behind him. Rochella fought to ignore the flutter the sight of him always aroused in her heart.

"Rochella, I am sorry for not having told you about Adam before it nearly cost your life," Gareth said, settling himself on the side of the bed.

"It is over now, Gareth. There is no need for apology," Rochella said, fighting to keep herself numb to the feelings creeping back to life.

"There is much need to ask your forgiveness. I should have told you the truth from the beginning. I can only pledge now to raise Adam's child as my own."

"Adam's child?" Rochella said, dumbfounded at Gareth's assumption.

"No one will ever question the paternity of your babe. It will be mine in every way."

Flushing a deep crimson, Rochella exploded. "How dare you insult me in such a manner? I have not betrayed you with your brother or anyone else."

"I have not accused you of betrayal, Rochella," Gareth said, puzzled by her indignation. "I understand you thought I was the one who came to your bed at night. You have been an innocent victim of the Devlin madness."

Rochella drew back her hand and hit Gareth squarely in the middle of his chest with her balled fist. He grunted, to her satisfaction. "How generous of you not to place blame on an innocent person. But do not feel too superior, dear husband, because I would not accept your gesture had I even slept with your brother!"

Gareth stared at her, cherishing her words deep in his barren soul. He had sired the child Rochella nourished beneath her heart. "The child belongs to me," he breathed at last.

"Yes, you idiot," Rochella snapped, her fury unabated. "But you do not have to concern yourself about my child or me in the future. I intend to leave here as soon as Dr. Connors tells me I am strong enough."

Gareth grabbed Rochella by the arms, holding her still. "You are my wife and you carry my child. I shall not let you leave."

"You have no say in the matter," Rochella said, jerking free of his hands. "We are no longer married. Now you can go to the devil, Lord Devlin."

Stunned, Gareth gaped at his wife. "What do you mean?"

Rochella's emerald eyes flashed green fire. "I divorced you in France."

"It is impossible. Only the pope can end our marriage. There can be no divorce."

Rochella raised her chin in the air and eyed her husband coolly. "The Assembly made divorce legal in France. You are now free of the burden of me."

Gareth could not believe his ears. Rochella intended to leave him. He was losing his wife and child. Something akin to rage blossomed within him. He had endured enough. He had lived under the Devlin curse all his life, and now that he had found happiness, he would not let it go without a fight. When he spoke, his voice mirrored his determination. "I will not let you go."

The light of battle glimmered in Rochella's eyes as she vehemently shook her head. "How dare you threaten to keep me here? I have lived in hell under your roof. You care nothing for me or the babe I carry." Again she shook her head. "No, Gareth, you will not keep me here. You tried once and you failed. You will fail again."

His anger dissolving as suddenly as it had formed, Gareth began to smile. "Will not even my love make you stay with me, Rochella?" he asked softly.

Rochella blinked, feeling new tears spring to her eyes.

"For I do love you, more than you will ever know."

Rochella moistened her dry lips and cleared her throat. "Do not say that, Gareth, not now." She bowed her head in defeat and let her tears flow freely down her cheeks. Gareth had finally said the words she had longed to hear, but only in order to keep her at Devil Wind.

"But I do love you, Rochella."

Rochella raised her haunted eyes to Gareth's face. Her voice quivered from the pain assaulting the heart she had thought dead to emotion. "Please, Gareth. Do not tell me this. I cannot take any more. You do not love me. You want only to keep me here to bear your child."

Gareth wrapped his powerful arms about her and drew her against him. He placed a hand on her swollen abdomen and felt his babe kick for the first time. The pleasure he felt at the movement was exquisite. He brushed his lips against Rochella's brow and tenderly looked down at her. "I do love you, Rochella. I have loved you from the first moment I found you arguing with Hilda. But I denied my emotion because I did not want to be hurt when you learned of Adam. I feared the scorn I would see in your eyes when you found you had married into a family cursed with madness."

Rochella's heart soared on wild winds. She looked up at Gareth and raised a hand to tenderly caress his stubbled cheek. "Gareth, there is no Devlin curse. It is the fear that has kept you a prisoner. Adam's madness lay only in his greed. He was jealous of you and all you possessed, and he used your superstitions to control you. When he knew you had sired an heir, he knew he had to kill us both to complete his evil scheme."

Gareth saw the logic in Rochella's reasoning, yet he was not completely convinced. He had lived with the curse far too long to relinquish his beliefs so easily. He gave her a roguish grin. "Perhaps you are right, but there is only one way to make sure the curse is broken."

Rochella arched one smooth brow and coquettishly draped her arms about his neck. "How so, my Lord?"

"The curse says, 'Till words of love are honestly spoken, then peace will reign as honor is done.'"

Rochella frowned, bemused. "What does it mean?"

"It means, my dear, you must marry me again to assure fate that honor is done. I have already spoken honestly of my love for you. Now there is only one thing left to do."

A devilish, tantalizing grin touched Rochella's sweetly curved lips. "But I have not told you of my love, Lord Devlin."

Gareth's arms tightened about her. "My fiery witch, I shall keep you a prisoner at Devil Wind until you agree to end the curse placed upon the Devlins. I cannot have my children growing up with such a stigma."

Gareth had spoken in jest, yet Rochella sensed he would do exactly that should she refuse him. "Then all that is left for me to do is to say, 'I love you, Gareth Devlin, with all of my heart.'"

Gareth's laughter filled the room as he lifted Rochella into his arms and swung her about. "And will you marry the father of your child?" he questioned.

Giggling, Rochella wholeheartedly agreed.

Epilogue

The sky was gray and overcast on the crisp autumn morn when Rochella walked, as gracefully as her rounding figure allowed, to meet the man she loved down the aisle of the Devlin family chapel. They knelt in front of the priest to receive his blessing upon a union that had already been forged with much suffering and love. At the precious moment when they made their vows to love and honor each other for eternity, the sun came from behind the clouds and streamed through the stained glass windows, surrounding them in warmth, banishing any shadows that might have remained to darken their future together.

Glowing with happiness, Rochella looked up at the man who held her heart. The sun was an omen of the future they would share. Their lives would be bright with joy. Had the Devlin curse ever existed, Rochella knew that at that moment their love had finally brought it to an end.

As the priest pronounced them man and wife, she raised her lips to Gareth's.

* * * * *

This October, Harlequin offers you a second
two-in-one collection of romances

A SPECIAL
SOMETHING

THE FOREVER
INSTINCT

by the award-winning author,

Now, two of Barbara Delinsky's most loved books are
available together in this special edition that new and
longtime fans will want to add to their bookshelves.

Let Barbara Delinsky double your reading pleasure with
her memorable love stories, A SPECIAL SOMETHING and
THE FOREVER INSTINCT.

Available wherever Harlequin books are sold.   TWO-D

HARLEQUIN
Romance

**This September, travel to England
with Harlequin Romance
FIRST CLASS title #3149,
ROSES HAVE THORNS
by Betty Neels**

It was Radolf Nauta's fault that Sarah lost her job at the hospital and was forced to look elsewhere for a living. So she wasn't particulary pleased to meet him again in a totally different environment. Not that he seemed disposed to be gracious to her: arrogant, opinionated and entirely too sure of himself, Radolf was just the sort of man Sarah disliked most. And yet, the more she saw of him, the more she found herself wondering what he really thought about her—which was stupid, because he was the last man on earth she could ever love....

Harlequin Superromance®

Available in Superromance this month
#462—STARLIT PROMISE

STARLIT PROMISE is a deeply moving story of a
woman coming to terms with her grief and gradually
opening her heart to life and love.

Author Petra Holland sets the scene beautifully, never
allowing her heroine to become mired in self-pity. It
is a story that will touch your heart and leave you
celebrating the strength of the human spirit.

Available wherever Harlequin books
are sold.